Thought Seeker

Eclipsing Trilogy

Book Two

Nia Dragin

Nia Dragin Books | 2015

Florida

Copyright © 2014 by Cynthia Ayala

Published in the United States by Nia Dragin Books

NiaDraginBooks.com

Summary: Two thousand nine hundred and sixty-two years have passed since the day Selene and Eris Sintas were turned into Vampyres. The world has evolved and changed. Eris is the Coven Master of the Telos Coven and his sister is the Huntress, leader of the Hunters force of that coven where they hunt those Vampyres that break rules of the Vampyre Doctrine. Selene's life has not been without it's hardships. She lost the man she loved…until she met Jason. Jason is an ordinary Witch who looks like Pietro in every way but couldn't be more different. And Eris, after seeing him vows to find him and if need be destroy him. He will do everything in his power to protect his sisters heart and life, even if it means losing her himself. As Selene falls more into the light Eris falls to the darkness and Selene must make a choice. Sacrifice one to the Dark and save the other. Her brother or her love?

ISBN # 978-0-9906284-3-9 (Kindle Edition)

ISBN # 978-0-9906284-4-6 (Nook Edition)

ISBN # 978-0-9906284-5-3 (tr. pbk)

[1. Supernatural—Fiction. 2. Reincarnation—Fiction 3. Love—Fiction. 4. Vampires—Fiction 5. Mythology—Fiction]

Cover design by

Printed in the United States of America

In order for the light to shine so brightly, the darkness must be present.
— *Francis Bacon*

S elene tore off the head of the Vampyre on trial. Her brother
had given her orders to hunt down the renegade and bring him
to justice. Jeanette and Blake, her seconds in command, took
the body away for burial. At least now, the lives he had taken had
been avenged. Two witches and a Reborn, dead, taken so young. This
death though, would not be mourned. Looking over at her brother,
she took her seat on his right side. She really needed this meeting
to be done and over with; there was somewhere else she needed to
be, someone she needed to see. Selene looked around the Covenant,
catching the looks of fear that fell on her. Others were older than
she was of course, from the previous regime that slaughtered her
people, but she was the fastest and strongest of them all. Her runes
glowed as she made the lights flicker. Amusement tickled her spin
as she toyed with the electricity in the hall. She heard Nivette, her
brothers' consort, giggle. Her brother merely smiled.

"I do hope you all know by now that taking a life is prohibited.

Do so and your life is forfeit. You're all dismissed." Selene stood up only to find her brothers hand clasp around her wrist.

"Where are you going?"

"Hunting, maybe a walk."

"Why?"

"Because I've been hunting that Vampyre for the past two week's brother." She smiled and gently uncoiled his hand form around her wrist. "I need a little me time."

"Be back by dawn all right?"

"Don't worry," she said, bidding him farewell as she took off. Briefly stopping in the hallway, she looked at her watch and swore. Selene hated to be late.

Selene entered the simple one bedroom apartment through the window. She had lied to her brother, but she knew what his reaction would be if he knew. Eris would not approve, and given the past, his anger might get the better of him. Locking the window behind her, she crept inside.

Flicking a switch, turning on the light, she made her way to the kitchen. She hadn't truly fed in two weeks but regular food would have to suffice for the time being. She could (and most likely would) grab a snack in the Dark Alley, also known as the Darkling District beneath the city, created and lived in by the scum of Witches, centuries past. If there was anything she hated more than a renegade Vampyre, it was a Darkling, a Dark Witch.

Selene grabbed a suitable snack, a bowl of fruit, and headed to the living room, kicking the fridge door shut. As she sat down on the sofa, she waved the television on with her magic. Amazingly, word had already reached the news that the Vampyre she had executed had been found dead, his body burned to a crisp. A pity she would not get full credit. Many people preferred to ignore the existence of Vampyres, even those that were good.

The door lock clicked open and she was at the door. The person swore as he entered his hand flying over his heart that was beating faster.

"Dammit Selene, don't do that."

Selene almost laughed. "Forgive me Jason, I forget how easily you Witches scare."

Jason rolled his teal-colored eyes as he entered the apartment, bolting the door shut behind him. "You used to be a mere Witch too Selene."

"That was a very, very, long time ago." Selene had moved out of his way in the small hallway connecting the living room to the entrance. Jason dumped his backpack onto the ground and tossed his keys onto the small desk, large enough for only a bowl to sit atop it, in the hallway.

"You keep saying that." He looked at her. "How have you been?"

Selene smiled. "Sometimes I forget you are not like Pietro, he would have gone digging through my thoughts."

"I respect privacy. However, if you don't tell me, I will go against those wishes." His grin betrayed the lie.

"No need. I was hunting that Vampyre, the one who had those three murders on his hands."

"You found him?"

"Yes. He stood trial by brothers' council and was found guilty. I executed him."

"You took his life and don't even care?"

How callous he made it sound, forcing her to look away. "I care more about those innocent lives. Their blood is on our hands as much as on his."

"Why do you say that? Because you turned him?"

"Yes. He sought us out, dying from that lung disease; we gave him a second chance. We traded three lives for one. Three innocent lives for one. Our background check was not thorough enough. We let sympathy blind us." Inside she seethed, covering it up with a nonchalant shrug as she walked back to the living room. Maybe seeing him was a bad idea. He wasn't Pietro. He may look like him, have his abilities, but he wasn't him.

"Selene, your Coven did a good deed. You are not responsible for what he did with his second chance." He was closer, his hand wrapped around her wrist, sending a shiver over her skin. Selene stared at his fingers before looking at him and smiling.

"Maybe not, but mistakes like that cannot be afforded."

"That...is true." He released her, crossing her arms. "You haven't truly fed have you?"

Selene shrugged, acting like it was less of a big deal than it was. "I was thinking of getting a little snack in the Darkling District when I headed home."

"No need. I work part-time at a Hospital remember."

"It's better when it was fresh."

"Perhaps, but this'll do won't it?" His brow creased as he picked up his bag. Inadvertently, she licked her lips. Jason laughed, reaching into his bag. He pulled out a blood bag and tossed it to her. Her hand caught the bag easily in mid-air and her mouth quickly found the opening, suckling on it like it was a juice bag. Jason smiled at her, charmingly and sweetly, unlike Pietro had in his arrogant fashion.

"Thank you," she said taking a break to wipe a drip down her lip.

"Think of it as a welcome back and job well done present."

"Don't humor me."

Jason laughed and headed to the sofa. "But that's half the fun."

Selene growled and followed him back onto the sofa. Then there were those moment when he was exactly like Pietro.

E ris stalked the night for food. He peeked into the Shadow
Realm, hoping a certain Shadowling was not stalking him
tonight. Her presence, of late, was beginning to be a nuisance.
The smell of jasmine distracted his and he looked away from the
shadows. The girl was closing up a coffee shop. She thought she
was safe now that the Vampyre had been disposed of. No one was
ever truly safe. Least of all from him. Eris used his magic to make
the lights among the street flicker. On his back, his rune throbbed.
He watched the girl look around startled a she fished around her
purse, probably for her car keys. Traveling through the shadows, he
slid up behind her as he continued to make the street lights flicker.
Eris stepped forth, looking more like a Shadowling than a Vampyre.
Cutting the girls scream short, hand clamped tightly over her mouth
as he dug his fangs into her collarbone, the sound of her keys hitting
the floor briefly noticeable. Through the blood, he sought out her
juicy memories. Eris jumped back, involuntarily letting the girl drop

to the ground. A face in her mind stirred up long forgotten feelings of hate within. There was someone in her life who was all too familiar. Pietro. Eris had hated him two thousand years ago, why was he here now? How could he be here now? Picking up the unconscious girl, dug through her mind, taking away the last few moments of her memory, and then sought out the name of the man who looked like Pietro. His name was Jason. Eris almost snapped her neck in his rage. Cradling the girl in his arms, he unlocked the car door with a wave of his fingers. Gingerly, to make up for initially dropping her, he sat her in her car seat. Once she was settled and strapped in he picked up her keys, put them in key with the electrical rune etched on it, into the ignition and locked the door.

"Jason you teal eyed fool, who are you really?"

Eris stood on the clock tower. The city was large and vast. This was what had become of his small village, expanded into a vast and brilliant city. He wondered if this was Naavah's doing, as a way to make amends and repair the damage done so long ago.

"Why are you up here?" came a voice. Eris growled and stared at Shira across the landing.

"What do you want now?"

"You cut your meal short, why?"

"Because I saw something I did not like."

Her black eyes glistened in the dark with mischief. "What?"

"Why do you care?"

"I don't, but you look furious and I would love to know what had done this to you Eris Sintas." The hatred in her voice and eyes were clear to see, especially behind her malicious smile.

Eris still watched her carefully, deciding on what to do. He could use her, manipulate her, get the thorn in his side to become more like splinter on his finger. If the girl was going to be around, she might as well make herself useful.

"How long would it take you to find someone?"

"I am not a hound. It could take weeks to months. There are hundreds upon hundreds of people in this city alone."

"Can you find someone or not?"

The muscles in her jaw tightened. "Yes."

"His name is Jason."

"That's very helpful," she muttered, the sarcasm dripping from her sour disposition.

"He has blond hair and teal colored eyes."

"That's very—oh, so that what it is. This Jason is that fool Pietro. How amusing!" Her cold detached laughter filled the air. Eris cut it off quickly, wrapping his hands on her throat. The hatred in her black eyes shot daggers through him.

"I don't care how long it takes you. Take all the damn time in the world if you want, just find him!" Letting go, he took a step back, watching her as she tentatively massaged her throat.

"Are you sure Selene has not stumbled across the face her long lost beloved?"

"Selene would have said something," he muttered, looking away from her and into the night sky.

"Are you sure?" Eris growled at her as she slunk into the shadows of the clock tower cast by the moon. Rolling his eyes, he walked to the edge of the clock tower and leaned against the building, arms crossed, as he stared up at the moons. What are you Gods playing at, he asked himself, thinking of the last time the Gods had turned his life into a chessboard.

J ason hadn't been expecting to see Selene. Half of him was thrilled while the other half of him had been hoping never to see here again. Vampyres were never wholly accepted into society and if his family ever found out, they would not be happy. His father might understand, but his mother, not too much.

Watching her sleep, he thought about waking her. Looking over at the clock, he noted the time. Dawn was in five hours, she could sleep a little longer.

Jason didn't know what to think of her, didn't know exactly how he felt or what exactly it was that he was feeling. When she had first tried to feed on him, she said two things had caught her off guard. The fact that she could see his thoughts but not taste and take them, and the fact that he looked like someone she had known a very long time ago. Jason had been prepared to kill her but like her, when faced with what she looked like he hadn't been able to move. She was beautiful.

Slinking away to his light blue bathroom, he splashed his face with cold refreshing water.

"What have you gotten yourself into Jason?" he asked his reflection

"I wouldn't worry about it." Jason spun around, slamming his hands on the porcelain sink counter behind him. His heart was going a hundred miles a second.

"Will you please stop doing that!"

"My apologies," she said with a slight smile. Calming down, he watched her look over her shoulder, back towards the living room. 'Jason, I caught sight of your assignment. It's incorrect." Jason walked past her and picked up his paper from the coffee table.

"Not according to my books."

"Politics," she scoffed. "They didn't bring down the barriers in peace. In fact, the Council had nothing to do with it whatsoever." Selene grabbed the top book on the stack on top of the coffee table and flipped through the pages mindlessly. "Oh what a waste of paper. This is all—"

"My father is part of the council Selene."

"Congrats to you," she said dropping the book back onto the table with a loud thump, "this is all still lies."

"Fine then, you tell me what happened then?"

Jason watched her purple eyes sparkled as her face lit up with a radiant smile. "I brought down the barrier. I had the power and the blessing of She of the Light. Report that and see what kind of a grade you get." Jason grabbed a notebook and dug through the coffee table drawers for a pen. Once settled he met her even look with another.

"All right then, talk."

Jason sat in class staring blankly at the board. He didn't mind school, not at all, and it as his final year at the University, which he was grateful for. But as he saw the time click by, he found himself thinking of the night and of Selene. The latter was the problem. He was spending more time with Selene than with his own girlfriend. Jason could see the fury in her light brown eyes of late. He felt bad, but ever since he met Selene, things had become complicated. Woe onto him, he thought to himself, quoting his favorite poem.

The bell chimed and he was eager to rush out. That was until his Professor called him to a halt. He adjusted his bag on his shoulder and walked back to her vast oak desk, past his fellow classmates who rushed by him.

"Yes Professor?"

"Here's your paper," she said handing it back to him. "I gave you an A+. I must know though, how did you know this?"

Jason took his paper, almost bursting into laughter. Selene had not lied. "My, uh, father he discussed it with me."

"Hmm, he shouldn't have." She looked at him thoughtfully. "I must ask you to no discuss this with anyone. I hope you understand."

"Oh, uh, yes I guess I do."

"Good." She smiled and looked at the paper in his hand. "I'm glad he was able to recount everything about Selene. She was a good woman."

"You knew her?"

His professor laughed. "Oh my dear boy, indeed I did. She left an impression on all of us. She was strong, willful, and quite brilliant in terms of magic. Not to mention she was exceptionally beautiful, thoughtful and quite wise for one so young.

I often wonder if she is still alive." She looked past him, love in her eyes. "I wonder about her brother as well."

"She has—had a brother?"

"Oh yes. His name was Eris." Her eyes glazed over. "He was a good man." She shook her head and smiled at her relived memories. "Tell your father I said hello Jason." He turned her back to him, her honey gold wings fluttered as she began to tidy up her desk. Jason left the room, looking back only a few times to see if she was all right. It was obvious she was distracted he noted as she reorganized the same pile of papers two to three times.

Jason was only a step out of the door when he heard someone call his name. He looked down the bustling hallway. Heading towards him was Miranda, his girlfriend. Her brown eyes glared into his. Jason leaned against the wall and waited for her to get closer. Like him, she was a Touched Born. She was not, however, one of the Noble Bloods, like himself. She was strikingly beautiful, with her brown hair that fell like waves down her shoulders, shimmering in the sunlight. However, her beauty was currently marred by her obvious fury.

"You're hiding something."

"Hello Miranda. You look beautiful today." He leaned forward to kiss the top of her head only to have her shove him back into the wall.

"I'm surprised. I've hardly seen you in the last two months. Now what are you hiding? I can see it all over your aura. What are you hiding?"

Jason sighed. "I am entitled to my secrets."

"Not in a relationship you're not."

"I'm not having this argument again." Jason moved his hand through his blond hair and let out a sigh.

"Then tell me what you're hiding. You're keeping a secret. You're not allowed to keep secrets. It's not fair!"

Rubbing his temples, he looked down at her. "Miranda, I will not have this stupid pointless argument again. I love you, why isn't that enough for you? Does it mean anything to you?"

"No...I mean, yes. Look, it's hard okay. I see you and I see your aura and it bothers me to know that there is something you can't or won't tell me." She wiped away at her cheeks, at the imaginary tears that had not fallen.

"Miranda this is nothing against you. I just don't want to talk about it. Besides, talking about it doesn't guarantee that it'll go away." Jason took her face in his hands. "Miranda, I love you and I love that you care but please, if or when I want to talk about it I will." Jason bent down to kiss her. She tasted like cherries.

"Very well." She laced her arm through his and pulled him along. "So have you heard?"

"Heard what?" he asked, letting her pull him along.

"One of our classmates got attacked by a Vampyre a few days ago."

"Really?"

"Yeah. I'm guessing it was one of those Vampyres that live on the outskirts of town."

"Why?" he asked trying to control his emotions.

"Because it's part of their so called 'code'. They attack and feed and take away the thoughts and memories of the attack."

"So how do you know she was attacked if she doesn't remember?"

"Her neck silly. She woke up in her car, her neck was sore so she checked it out and low and behold, two puncture wounds."

"I wonder why the Vampyres do that."

"Who knows? Something really should do something about

those Vampyres though. They're a menace."

Jason stiffened. "I don't think so."

"Why not? All Vampyres are a menace. We are food to them for the love of all that it bright."

"I don't think so," he said softly.

"Why?"

"Didn't you see the news the other night?"

"Yeah so," she began with an eye roll, "what does that have to do with anything?"

"You know how the Vampyres work. That was the Vampyre who had killed those people. He was reported to be dead. Murdered, burned and beheaded. No Witch could have done that. Shadowlings couldn't care less. A Vampyre did that. We're not just food to them. They respect us. They respect life. They respect the fact that we are all living beings with souls and lives Miranda. We're more than food to them." Jason stood there and stared at her. He noted the look in her eyes. She was reading into his aura. Jason dug into her mind. She suspected that he knew more than he was telling her. Jason calmed himself.

"What aren't you telling me?"

"Something that doesn't concern you." Jason pulled away from her. "Stop reading my aura. I don't read your thoughts whenever the hell I want, so just stop. Why can't you just trust me?" Jason saw the hurt in her eyes but for some reason, for once, he just didn't care.

Selene lay in bed, the covers drawn up to her chin, tossing and turning, her hand clutching her marble of light tightly and of its volition. She was dreaming of Pietro. One of the last moments, she had seen him, on the day he had announced his reluctant engagement to her. An engagement arranged by his overbearing family.

"Turn me," he had said grabbing her shoulders fervently.

"I-I can't. I won't."

"Why not! Futuo Selene! I love you, want to be with you! I don't want to marry that woman. She may be beautiful on the outside but she's like Kyra. Her thoughts are vile. She's vile. I do not want to marry her. I want to be with you."

"This is not a life I would wish upon you. Being this," she said addressing herself with a wave of her arms, "it changes you. I'm a killer. First Larkin and then Kyra. I almost killed a child a few nights ago! Would you like that?"

"Selene, I love you," he said, blind to what she had said. "All I want is to be with you, no matter the cost."

Selene had shaken her head sadly. "I will not risk your humanity Pietro. I love you too much. I'm sorry." Selene kissed him then left, hoping never to see him again. Later she had found out that he had a twin boy and girl. He had named his daughter Selene, in her honor. Even that could not sway her to visit him.

She wished she had though.

His wife, Katherine, had killed him in his sleep, one night in a "fit of madness" the courts said. In her rage, Selene had hunted her down and killed her, ripping out her heart and tearing her to pieces. Selene had more than mourned his loss, she had wished for death. A wish denied her.

Jerking awake, her body shooting upright in bed, beads of sweat dripping down her forehead, she whimpered, holding herself tighter and tighter. She should have taken him away with her. He had not deserved the fate he had been given.

Pulling herself together, wiping away the runaway tears that had slipped past her guard, she slunk out of bed, headed to her freezer pressed deep into the farthest corner of her room—the electrical humming incessant—and grabbed a bottle of blood.

Slowly she made her way back to her bed and sat on the edge, drinking the blood methodically. Once again, she wiped the sweat from her face. Placing her arm on her leg for balance, she leaned forward and stared into the dark and still embers of her fireplace. Snapping her fingers, drawing power from her Fire Rune, she lit up the emptiness. Entranced, she continued to stare at the flames as they danced before the darkness. She could never tell if the darkness was tormenting the light or if the light was taunting the trapped darkness. Maybe it was neither, maybe it was just fire reacting to the wood. But she could never convince herself of that.

Something in the back flickered, and she narrowed her eyes.

"Eris, please get out of here." Eris swam from the shadows, his body leaning against the wall he sprung from. A look of concern covered his face.

"You don't look well."

"I'm not."

"Why?"

"The past." Her violet eyes searched his knowingly.

"It still haunts you?"

"Doesn't it haunt you?" She saw him stiffen and his face-harden. Eris's jaw set was firm like stone and his eyes looked dead.

"Many things haunt me; I just don't let them rule me."

"You also have not taken as many lives as I have."

"Why does that effect anything?"

"Because Eris," she says sighing, "taking a life kills a piece of your soul and mine is beginning to wane."

"I don't believe that."

"Try killing a few people brother," she said eying him. "I do all the killing. I'm fine with it, don't get me wrong, but I have nothing else. You have Azelia—"

"Whom I haven't found." He looked away, his face almost obscured by shadow. "You should go out. You need to feed on fresh blood."

"No need."

"Oh, there is a need. Now go." Something was different about her brother. She saw it in his eyes before he left. The chime of her clock drew her attention, drawing her out from her inner hollow and allowing the semblance of a smile to creep onto her face. Suddenly instead of thinking of the past she was thinking about the present; she was thinking about Jason. Her smile broadened but only just. Selene smiled when she thought about his assignment.

* * *

Tapping her fingernails against his living room window, she saw him jump and swear. She smiled to him as he opened the window.

"Did I frighten you?" she asked, crawling into the apartment like a spider.

"Yeah, ya did. Can't you knock on the door like a normal person?"

"Where would the fun be in that?" She looked around finally finding his bag on the floor near the hallway. In a flash she was at it, eager to see his grade, eager to find out if her existence was the shame of the Reborns or not. "How did your classes go," she asked, shuffling through his bag and pulled out the paper that was all about her.

"You never told me you had a brother."

"Didn't think it was important," she said, marveling at the 'A' and let the bag fall from her hand. "Marvelous grade."

"Don't change the subject."

Selene eyed him, ambivalent. "Very well. How did you find out that I had a brother?"

"My professor, she's a Reborn. She knew you, as did my father apparently. Selene, who is your brother?"

"Who is your father?"

"My fathers' name is Michael."

"I knew no Michael." She walked past him to the kitchen and scavenged the fridge.

"Michael isn't his true name. Reborns never go by their true name anymore."

With a roll of her eyes, she muttered, "how the times have changed," with sarcasm thick. Grabbing a bottle of Sweet Water and poured herself a glass.

"Selene?"

"Jason?" she mimicked.

"Why didn't you tell me about Eris?"

"So that you wouldn't go looking for him."

"Why not?" The confusion almost made him look adorable, the way it scrunched up his brow.

"Because you look like Pietro and he hated Pietro." She finally faced him, aware of how close he was to her.

"How many Reborns did you know?"

"Enough. I even trained a few."

"Well you certainly lived quite a life."

Selene shrugged. "I guess so." They stood there staring at each other. Her feelings stirred, making her mind spin.

"Why does your kind regard life so highly?"

"Because we miss it. So many have suffered from Vampyre attacks and we, my brother and I in particular, see to live above that. We seek to rectify it. Why the sudden curiosity?"

"My, uh, friend brought up the discussion of Vampyres. Apparently one of our classmates was attacked—"

"When?" Selene's heart quickened. "Where?"'

"Near the center of the city at the old coffee shop next to the clock tower. It was a few days ago. Why?"

Selene's thought were racing. That was where Eris hunted. "Did you know the victim?"

"Not personally. We just attended the same University, had a few of the same classes. What's wrong?"

"My brother hunts there." Selene looked away, her mind

elsewhere. "I should go." She turned to go but Jason grabbed her arm, keeping her there.

"Why? Selene what's going on?"

The words came of their own volition. "My brother can never find out you exist Jason."

"Why not?"

Selene looked at his hand before she locked her eyes onto his. For an instant, she saw the same passion she saw in Pietro's eyes. For a moment, she saw Pietro, and her heart felt like it was breaking again. "Pietro got married," she began more to herself than to him. "His wife killed him in his sleep. Years before that happened though, he asked me to turn him so that he wouldn't have to marry her. I refused. His death, and hers, are on my hands."

"Why is her death on your hands?"

"Because I killed her Jason." Her voice was cold her level gaze unflinching. "I hunted her down and I killed her with my own hands." She watched his eyes widen and felt his hand loosen, heard it fall back to his side. He stared at her with such pity and sadness. Her heart shattered.

"It's not your fault."

"In part it is. Eris is very protective and I was about to let myself drown in my grief. A great betrayal to him, even I cannot deny that. He would do anything to protect me...even from myself."

"Even kill me?"

"Yes." Selene turned her back to him and headed to the window. This time he let her go.

Five

Jason's mind was racing. Who had Pietro been? Why did he look like him? A while back, just after Jason had first met Selene, he had written to his father, asking for a genealogy tree. He wanted—no, he needed to know if he was his descendant. If he was, that would explain why he looked so much like him. In fact, it would explain a great many things. Not only why he looked like him but why he also had the same power. It would also explain why he was so attracted to Selene, despite himself.

A week passed since he last saw Selene, and he began to wonder he would ever see her again. He thought about seeking her out but other Vampyres, including her brother, could find him first. That wouldn't be the best thing to happen considering she left to keep him safe and spitting on that would insight her wrath. And that was something he wanted to avoid.

Another week passed, finally bringing word from his father. Looking at the size, no wonder it took so long, the package was enormous and heavy, filled with centuries worth of information. He hoped that it went back two thousand years. Next time he was home, he was going to have a long discussion with his father about why Selene's place in history was hidden. Politics probably, like Selene had said, but it was the truth and she deserved the recognition.

Someone knocked at the door and he raced to it, scattering the mound of papers that had accumulated around him. Hoping it was Selene, Jason even peeked into the thoughts on the other side of the door. Skidding to a stop shell-shocked, narrowly avoiding his tall coffee table, he stared at the door letting those on the other side knock again. Taking a deep breath, counting back from five, he regained his composure and padded his way to the door, his bare feet moving slowly on the wood floor. Standing just on the other side of the threshold were Miranda and his two friends, Cecilia and Nicholas, bags of food in hand.

"Hey guys," he said, welcoming them in. Taking Miranda's coat, he kissed her lightly on her warm and rosy cheek.

"We haven't seen you around much," said Nicholas nudging his arm.

"Perhaps we should have called first," said Cecilia looking around. "This place is a mess."

"She's right. What's with all these papers?" asked Miranda, one arm wrapped around her waist while her other addressed the mess before them, brows arched high on her forehead.

"Oh, um, just some family records. There's an ancestor of mine I'm curious about."

"Oh! Well we can help!" chirped Cecilia picking up a sheet of paper. "How far back are you going?"

"About two thousand years." Through his peripherals, he caught Miranda eying him suspiciously. Nicholas punched him in the shoulder again, causing Jason to wince. Sometimes Nicholas didn't know his own strength.

"Good thing we came along then man. How you ever get along without us is beyond me." The big brute slumped down on his sofa, grabbing a wad of paper. He shifted through them, in his own way, tossing page after page to the ground, studying the pictures of women in his way, making the mess even larger. "I forgot how many hot Reborn chicks you have in your bloodline."

"The person I'm looking for was Touched Born named Pietro," he said snatching the paper from Nicholas. The last thing he needed was Nicholas's perverted thoughts filling the air.

"Very well." Nicholas shrugged picking up another stack of papers. Jason left to grab some plates so that they could eat, wishing he wasn't aware of Miranda following.

"What's wrong?" The tone of her voice gave away her annoyance, but what did she have to be annoyed about? Nothing he was doing had anything to do with her.

Pressing down on the bridge of his nose, he leaned against his counter top. "Not now please."

"No, tell me now, what's wrong?" The insistence in her voice was fueled by her anger.

"I just need to know about him. I just want to learn about him. Ever since that assignment in Professor Gildian's class about the 'Barrier's Fall' things haven't been adding up. The council is hiding parts of history, parts the Professor has forbidden me from sharing. And she told me that I reminded her of someone who had been exactly like me, right down to my gift. These are questions I need answered Miranda, is that good enough for you?"

Miranda nodded, gently touching his cheek. His whole body lit up at her touch and he wrapped her in his arms tightly, taking in her sweet perfume. Despite everything about her that pushed others away, he loved her.

"Hey Jason! I think I found him!" called Cecilia from the other room. Letting Miranda go, grabbing the plates Jason returned to the living room, coming face to face with a grinning Cecilia.

"You're phenomenal," he said trading the plates for the papers.

With a wink, she said, "I'm aware."

"So what's so special?" asked Miranda sitting on the floor next to him.

"His name was Pietro Amedrade," began Jason. "He was a Touched Born—"

"Here's a portrait of him," interrupted Cecilia, handing him the old portrait. Of course, you wouldn't be able to tell. Magic held the portrait together, making it look unravished by time. Jason grabbed the portrait that was obviously protected by magic. The strength of the magic hadn't been what caught his breath though. Wrapped in the loving embrace of his arms was Selene. She had on a bright smile on her face and her hair was done up in an elegant braid with lavender stems entwined within. A twinge of jealously hit him.

"You look exactly like him," commented Miranda full of awe.

"Uncanny," muttered Nicholas, mouth full of food.

Cecilia took the delicate portrait from him and studied the faces. "I wonder who the girl is. She's beautiful."

Jason looked at the back of the portrait. "Her name was Selene Sintas. It says on the back right there."

"What else does it say about Pietro?" asked Miranda, her voice soft like wind.

"Oh, um, he married four years upon the 'death'," he began, adding air quotes as he spoke, "of Selene. Selene was turned into a Vampyre after an attack on her home village, currently known as the expanded city of Telos."

"Shame man. That Selene was one beautiful lady."

"How tragic," muttered Cecilia, covering her mouth with her

hands.

"Continue love."

"Pietro married Katherine Venatia. They had three children before she killed Pietro in his sleep, stabbing him repeatedly."

"Oh dear heavens!" exclaimed Cecilia. Nicholas laughed at her exclamation. Jason ignored them both, reading on.

"She was—"

"She was killed by a Vampyre, as was her sister, her brother and her brothers' son," finished Miranda.

Jason looked at her concerned. "Miranda how do you know that?"

"Katherine Venatia was my great plus aunt. I am the descendant of her niece on her sisters' side, and hearing this now, I know which Vampyre slaughtered my family. It was Selene Sintas." Miranda snatched her jacket from the back of the sofa and stalked from the apartment in her thick clunky heels banging against the wood floors. Each step she took tore Jason in half. He didn't know who he should worry about more. Miranda or Selene? Jason looked back at the portrait, at the beautiful smile that made her face glow. So in love...

S talking the hall, Eris made his presence known to all, dragging the shadows along the wall after him. Most were in the dining hall eating whatever concoction of raw bloody Jeanette had prepared. He was a personal fan of her rare steak and potatoes with a side of green beans. Sometimes he wondered how Nivette made the deal with the food companies. However, considering her attentiveness and her ability to be both kind and frightful, it didn't surprise him how she manage to procure the amount of food they needed.

Next, on his little stroll through the halls, he passed the library. Designed by Selene, the room had bookcases filled to the rim, tables here and there with chairs strewn all around. Someone was always in the room, and today, one of the few situated in the little room was Blake, leg crossed over the other, book in hand. Unfortunately, his little sister was not in her not-so-little sanctuary. Thankfully, though, her scent was strong in the air. Following it, he found himself on the threshold of the Training Room. Hardly anyone ever went in there anymore. Only Selene and her Hunters. Opening the door ever so slightly, he peeked inside to watch Selene, studying her moves. She was fighting hard, pumping her muscles as far (perhaps farther) than they could go. It was obvious that something was bothering her. She hadn't been this vicious and forceful in months.

"What are you fighting," he asked, leaning against the threshold, tossing the door open.

"It'll be you shortly if you don't leave me alone." She stabbed at the concrete floor, easily pulling her blade back out, sending pieces of concrete scattering on the floor.

"Hostile today aren't we?"

"Very much so."

"Why? Upset that you haven't gone hunting lately? I would think that would be a good thing."

"It probably is, but I'm a Hunter. I need something other than deer to hunt brother dear." Leaping onto the wall, she launched herself at another, arching her back and easily landing back on the ground, her eyes closed, her mind focused on chopping off the head of an imaginary foe in the process.

"I should search the news then shouldn't I?"

"Don't bother," she said flying through the air. "I already have."

"Are you no longer content here Selene?" he mocked. Selene shot him a look through her long bangs as she landed on the ground, fist clenched.

"I enjoy seeing the world Eris; I do not like being kept in a single place for so long."

"So then go off. Visit Naavah."

A shrill sound filled the air. It could have been laughter. "You must be kidding. I'm not welcomed there. Not anymore." Sadness swept over her purple pupils. When had she become so sad in spirit? Eris clenched his hands at the reason that permeated his mind.

"You probably shouldn't have done what you did."

Selene licked her lips, her pupils turning red with rage and thirst. "They deserved no less. The lot of them. Besides, I was pardoned." *How could she be so flippant about it*, he thought. How could she disregard her actions as though they had been nothing? Did she not know how she had broken his heart? Did she not know, or did she just not care? All these thoughts spun through his mind, setting his emotions ablaze, heightening his darker urges.

"By luck," he said, containing his urge to shake and scream at her. "There are still rumors that his Queen bestowed favor upon you."

"It's absurd. I don't even know her. I never met her nor her husband. It was just good luck." Selene waved him away. "Now please, leave me be." Her runes glowed and the door slammed shut in his face quickly, barely giving him time to move out of the way. A low growl escaped his throat before he walked off.

It only took moments before he sensed her and smiled. He stopped walking and looked in her direction.

"Hello Negal, long time." He watched Negal seep from the shadows clad in a dark black gown, a silver crown on her head, small and delicate. Even after all this time the anger and heartbreak had not left her eyes. "Really? It's been over two thousand years."

"Why have you enlisted Shira's help to find someone? Who is this Jason?"

"A Witch, with sandy blond hair and teal colored eyes. See my problem?"

"You are an overprotective controlling fool."

"You saw what happened the last time. She went on a killing spree! She slaughtered her and most of her family." It took all of his strength to keep his voice level.

"They deserved to die."

"She incited his wrath purposely. She was seeking death!" His voice rose higher than he liked, and with a clenched jaw and a deep breath, he continued, "I will not have history repeat itself."

"Who says it will Eris? She might never find this Jason. She might never take notice of him in her nightly walks. And should they cross each other's path, why wouldn't you want her to be happy? She could get a second chance at love. This could be fate."

"But of which side of the pendulum Negal? Already our fates, according to Selene, were stripped from Those of Light. Now, I never liked Pietro. I could sense that something was not right with him. Something about him felt unnatural. Who wrote out his fate? Light or Darkness?"

Negal regarded him coldly while he waited for an answer. "If I find you that answer, will you let him be?"

"That depends. If Light has weaved his fate I will let him be. Should it be Darkness, I will kill him."

"What if it's both?"

He let the thought sink in. Would that even be possible? After a moment, he shook his head. "If that's the case, I would need to think about my actions."

"Think quickly." She vanished and Eris looked back down the hall. Wondering if maybe this truly was Selene's second chance at happiness, to be with the man she loved to much she spilt blood.

Stalking the cave, he had hunted down Shira, only to have her vanish. And right when he needed her most. Lucky enough for him, he was able to corner Jeanette. Her icy blue eyes glowed against her skin as they regarded his hatefully. He smiled at her charmingly.

"Jeanette I need you to do something for me."

Jeanette snorted. "I am not at your beck and call like a dog." His name came out like a hiss through her lips and sharpened fangs.

"I follow Selene's orders, not yours. And that is due to rank, not choice."

"Bitterness makes you less and less appealing."

"I don't care." Her tone was slow, deliberate. "You have Nivette and that lost Reborn. As they say nowadays, four's a crowd." Jeanette made a move to walk on past him, but he stopped her. Jeanette growled, barring her fangs that shined like the moon, illuminated more so by the dim light of the cave.

"Tsk, tsk. I could kill you if I chose, but I won't, considering our past. So please, stay and listen." Eris said in a patronizing tone, throwing her against the wall. Her body hit the stone wall hard. Cracking her neck, he watched her try to hold her composure while she embedded her nails into the wall.

"What do you want?" she growled.

"I need you to try to find someone tonight."

Confusion washed over her, turning her red eyes blue again. "Why not ask Selene? She's bett—"

"You'll find out if you find him," Eris said, cutting her off. There was a method to his madness. "A Touched Born named Jason. Check the blocks by the clock tower."

"A name? That's it? How in the world am I supposed to do that? A description would be nice Eris."

Eris's eyes twinkled. "Don't worry you'll know him when you see him." Walking off, leaving her boiling. "One more thing," he said, spinning on his heel back to face her, "keep this from Selene."

Jeanette growled. "Very well, but let me make this clear. I am only doing this tonight and tonight alone. I will not waste my time with a needle in a haystack." Eris waved off her agitation and headed back to his bedchamber where, sure enough, Nivette was waiting.

"Hello beloved."

S elene sat in her bedroom, practicing her alchemy. Most Witches never got past the basics, but then again, she never had been like most, not then and certainly not now. What made her even better than most the fact that she had over a thousand years of perfect the art. She grabbed a ruby, turned it into a sapphire. It was perfect in both color and shape and would certainly get her a vast amount of Fairy Dust in the Under City, also known as the Darkling District. Selene would be dealing with all those Dark Witches, which she detested, but she did enjoy the company of Witchlings. He picked up a diamond and crushed it into a bowl with her hands before she added Lavender oil. She lit the bowl easily with the use of her Fire Rune. She muttered some words under her mouth and watched the diamond dust solidify and turn into a round ball of pure platinum. Selene blew out the fire and took out the cooling piece of metal. She flipped it over her fingers, watching her knuckles redden, but she felt no pain. Sometimes she wished she could still feel what burns felt like, but her very immortality denied her that. No pleasure, no pain, nothing that could remind of her humanity was left to her.

So lost in her thoughts, Selene forgot about the metal ball rotating in her hand that she let it drop, barely catching it as it bounced on the floor. Selene shook away all her dismal thoughts and shoved the metal and jewels in her bag before she shoved the bag under her bowl, in a hollowed out piece of the rock that she had created so long ago. This was her personal stash of jewels and steel and Fairy Dust. She sat there staring at the bag before replacing the thin sheet of rock she used as a cover and wondered why she had it. She knew exactly why.

Eris. Jason.

A part of her wanted to escape from them both and find Ranita, Urit, Uriel and Naavah. They would comfort her and care for her, even hide her from Eris. Hide? That was a funny thought. Eris was her brother, he understood her...didn't he? No, not completely, that was why she was keeping Jason's existence secret. Eris cared, a little too much, always had. Selene was his little sister. What he failed to realize was that she was more than capable of protecting herself.

The door swung opened and Selene's body jerked in that direction. Jeanette smiled at her and kicked the door shut, using magic to silence the room.

"Are you finally going to kill me?"

"No, but I should. Would save you a lot of heart ache."

"What are you talking about?"

"Why is it you get a second chance at love hmm?"

Selene's heart quickened. "What are you talking about?"

"Oh Selene, do not be so coy. You're pet Jason."

"Do not call him a pet," she said heatedly, quickly regretting it.

Jeanette laughed. "How cute."

"You know, bitterness kill your beauty Jeanette." Jeanette barred her teeth and growled like a feral dog.

"I wouldn't be so cruel to me."

"How did you find him?"

"Funny thing about that, he actually came for me. He's just lucky I was out on the tow, and no one else. Everyone else would have begun to buzz about the teal eyed Touched Born looking for Selene."

"So why not tell anyone?"

"Because I know Eris, as should you. You do realize you're putting his life in danger don't you?"

"His appearance does that, and besides, I haven't seen him in weeks anyway. I do not want to put his life in further danger."

"A bit late for that isn't it? He said he needed to speak to you, urgently."

Selene thought it over, lifting herself from the hard ground and perching herself on the edge of her bed. Jason...you are not Pietro... why do I ache to see you?

"I can't see him."

"Ugh, yes you will! You have a second chance Selene!" she said grabbing her arm firmly. "You have a second chance to be with the one you love and to do what you should have done the first time. Do not forgo it out of fear. That is not the way to live Selene."

"Eris will kill him."

"If he finds out. I will not let that happen—that I promise you."

Selene laughed. "Whatever happened to you despising me?"

"I despise your father far more."

"Thank the Goddess for that." She looked at her old friend and hugged her. "Thank you."

"You're welcome Selene." They hugged each other for a moment longer before Jeanette pulled away. In the briefest moment Selene saw a bit of her old childhood friend return as she fixed her hair and posture.

"Jeanette, how do you suppose I see him? Night is to big of a risk."

"Then go during the daylight. I know you have Fairy Dust, you might as well use it." Jeanette's hair flew behind her as she headed out of the room. Selene stared at the closing door and looked at her watch.

***

It was hard for Selene to find something to wear. Everything she owned was "retro" and black, mostly because that was mostly because that way she didn't have to worry about blood stains. So she took the thoughts and memories of a shop keeper, enabling her to snatch a white spring dress with butterfly depictions all over it and a pair of high heeled strappy sandals. She felt uncomfortable, naked.

Selene stashed a bag with the clothes, into the hollow of a tree. In the bag were also all her supplies for the days venture. No rest for the wicked.

Selene sought refuge in her room, getting some sleep, despite the fact that she needed none. It was there, in her room that she waited for the waking of the dawn before she snuck out.

Selene hastily changed making sure her marble was secure in her bra. She chose that place because that way it was close to her heart, where it should always be, where it would never get lost.

Selene buckled up her leather garter, hooking it up high so that her dagger would not show beneath the dress. Then she grabbed a hand full of Fairy Dust and with her toe, she traced a binding rune onto the ground. Her runes glowed, warming up her skin and her soul. The wind blew around her and she blew the Fairy Dust from her hand, letting the wind whip it around her, allowing the magic to bind it to her skin. She grabbed a little mirror and examined herself. Every inch of her skin shimmered in the dim rays of the moonlight. She almost looked human again. Her eyes reminded her of the illusion, rimming the purple irises red. It was a good thing she had remembered to snatch a pair of sunglasses.

Selene got dressed, slipped on her shoes and shoved the rest of her stuff back into the tree. Her nerves rattled and she just stood there, alone in the sunlight that should be burning her skin. Selene took a deep breath, and then another before she ran off to the edge of the city, her shoes pounding lightly against the ground.

Selene made her way down the cobblestone streets. The University was in the middle of the city, and considering the time of day, she paced her way, knowing that when the cities bells rang and echoes through the air, he would be there. Selene looked up at the sun as it rose high into the sky. She had until Twilight, and then her brother would find out she was mingling and grow suspicious. Selene walked as quickly as she could, keeping in mind the pace so as not to draw suspicious glances from those that were out and about.

As Selene neared the University, she saw the clock tower glow in the sun. My, my, what a wonder, she thought as she made her way through the throng of students in search for Jason. It took her only minutes to catch sight of him, and quick as she could, she made her way to his side and grabbed his arm tightly, resisting the urge to break it.

"Do you have any idea how reckless that was," she said shoving him into the side of a building. She watched him scrunch up his eyes in confusion and stare at her blankly.

"Selene?"

"Yes you dolt."

"You—you look human."

"Fairy Dust, available on the Black Market in the Darkling District. Vampyres use it to live their old lives."

"You—you look beautiful."

Selene almost blushed. "Yes well, do you have any idea how lucky you are? Jeanette thinks about killing me in my sleep. You're lucky she detests my brother more." She released her hand on his arm and smoothed out the material. "You said this was urgent."

"It is." Jason's eyes turned cold as he reached into his bag to pull out a portrait. Selene's heart contrasted and it was willpower alone that kept her standing. "I thought you might like to have this." He held it out to her and she took it gently in her hands. Her fingers graved upon the preserved art and the memories of that day returned to her. She and Pietro had stood there for hours, although it hadn't seemed like it. Holding the smile and being in his arms was a moment she had cherished even then. Pietro though had made joke after joke. They got scolded for laughing time after time.

"Where did you get this?"

"I asked my father to send me my entire genealogy and to involve photographs if possible. I thought you would appreciate this."

"I do. Thank you."

"Don't thank me yet. You killed his wife's whole family, why didn't you tell me?"

Selene stiffened. "They didn't matter."

"They didn't matter? Do you hear yourself?"

"They were all murders!" she hissed. "Abusers and degenerates. They did not matter and deserved their deaths." She looked won at the portrait. "Thank you for this, but I think I should go now." Selene was about to leave when Jason pulled her back. His teal eyes looked down at her pleadingly.

"Don't leave. Please. I—I enjoy your company."

"I should leave. I've put—"

"Jason!" interrupted a shrill voice that sent a familiar tendril of hatred through he veins. Selene's eyes widened behind her thick round sunglasses as she stared onto the face of the girl who wrapped herself around Jason. Katherine.

Eight

J ason watched Selene's entire body stiffen. He knew the reason why too; Miranda looked like Katherine, Pietro's wife, his murderer. The fact of which was making him a bit reluctant to be around her. What if history repeated itself, he thought shivering.

"Hello, I'm Miranda. Who are you? I don't think I've ever seen you before. And here I thought I knew all of Jason's friends."

"My name is Anita," answered Selene in a disjointed and stiff tone. It was almost as if she wasn't there,only her body.

"Nice to meet you. Are you just starting?"

As her smile turned up on the corner, Jason sensed her humor return. "I graduated long ago."

"When?"

"A very long time ago." Her smile widened, lighting up her face. Knowing the truth, Jason smiled.

"Then what are you doing here?" Miranda's humor was gone, replaced with a sternness, both harsh and cold.

"Visiting Jason."

Wide eyed, Miranda shot a stare at him. "Jason?"

"What? Oh yeah, um, Anita here is visiting on behalf of my father. She's a friend of the Council."

Miranda's eyes seethed and pulsed with animosity. "I find that hard to believe."

"I wouldn't," echoed Selene's chilling voice.

Jason, sensing the tension, asked "how's my father?"

"Michael's fine. He wanted to know why the sudden interest in your family tree. I'm wondering the same thing. Shouldn't you be focusing on your studies?"

"My studies are going very well. Thank you for your concern."

"You're confusing concern with curiosity."

"Well you are cold aren't you," hissed Miranda.

Jason watched Selene's lip curl into a cruel, vindictive smile. "Oh, you have no idea." His eyes widened when her hand reached up to pull off her glasses. His breath caught when he saw the lack of red in her violet eyes. She looked like she had centuries ago. Except now, instead of looking happy and full of life, she looked tired, sad, pained.

"You look familiar," said Miranda. This time, Jason stiffened. Quickly pulling away from Miranda, he stepped up to Selene's side.

"Miranda, we've got to go. I'll see you later." Not waiting for a goodbye, he pulled Selene through the throng of students. Selene replaced her sunglasses back onto her face and pulled her arm out of his stiff grip easily. Underneath the glasses, Jason could tell that she was scowling.

"Oh don't give me that look Selene."

She crossed her arms over her chest. "The question is do you know why I'm giving you this look?"

"Because I look like Pietro and I'm dating Miranda who looks like Katherine. Yes, I know."

"Impressive. I should kill her."

"No. My god, do you have a bit of the humanity you once had left?" Selene shrugged carelessly. Jason resisted the urge to shake some sense into her. What have the centuries done to her, to make her so cold, to make the girl in the portrait obsolete? "What happened to you?"

"I died."

"That can't be all Selene. What happened to you?"

"I killed."

"Dammit Selene—"

"Oh shut up. I am a killer, a hunter. That's what Vampyres are. We are predators!"

"No you're not! You're more than that!"

Selene snorted. "Enlighten me. You don't know me. You know nothing about me!"

"Wrong. You're name is Selene Sintas. You have an older brother named Eris Sintas. You were being hunted by the Vampyre King while your brother was being hunted by the Shadowlings. The Queen and her court came to get two bright minds and protect them. To protect you and your brother. You fell in love with Pietro. He came to the Palace to see you. It was there that you fell in love—"

"Stop—"

"Then the Night of Darkness came! Shadowlings attacked, killed your friend Urit, took Azelia from your brother—"

"Enough—"

"So then you and your brother went away, back home, to a trap, breaking the barrier of your home! The center of this city! Many died! You were turned! You killed Vampyres! Killed Kyra and Larkin! Took down the—"

"Shut up!" Jason stopped talking and stared at her dumbfounded.

Fist clenched, body shaking with rage, Selene was glowing. That's when he saw them. The runes on her body lit up through her dress like beacons. Eight. There were eight of them. But that wasn't all. Something in the center of her chest was beating with a light of its own. But there was something else. Strapped to her thigh was something that pulsed with darkness.

"Selene—"

"You know nothing about me Jason," she said before she collapsed onto the ground.

Nine

A sudden surge of power jolted Eris awake. It was searing his heart, and blinding his minds eyes with a powerful white light. Something that made the shadows quiver. Nuri's Shadow especially. Alarms rang out in his head; this power was a threat. Suddenly he saw himself forging a sword alongside Azelia. He shook the vision with a curse from his mind. Whatever this power was, whatever this light, it was a threat to him. Climbing out of bed, careful not to wake Nivette, he sought out the source of the power with his minds eye. But just as quickly as it appeared, it vanished, inciting another curse. He sought out Negal in the Shadow Realm of Seraphim. She sat there reading in the obscurely lit library.

"I was expecting you Eris," she said keeping her eyes on the page.

"What was that surge of power?"

"So you felt it too. Interesting." She flipped the page absentmindedly.

"It can kill us can't it?" Negal finally looked up, eying him suspiciously. Gently, she shut the book, studying him while she twirled her black wedding band around her finger thoughtfully.

"Shadowlings yes. But you're a Vampyre Eris, it can't harm you anymore than you can harm it. Whatever this is, it is your equal. Darkness and light."

"Why do I fell like it can kill me then?"

Negal stood up, tossing the book onto her seat. Her eyes searched his face for something, he didn't know. "Because of your gift Eris and much, much more. If only you weren't cut off."

"Cut off from what?"

Negal, with a look akin to sadness and anger, looked into his eyes. "Yourself and Nuri." Negal vanished, leaving Eris snarling. Nuri. That name mean nothing to him, the visions meant nothing to him. Nothing meant anything to him. Nothing except...

S elene woke near mid-afternoon. The last thing she remembered was yelling at Jason, holding her portrait and, strangely, glowing. Her head was pounding, and she focused on her surroundings. She was in Jason's bed, in his apartment. Sitting up, she studied her skin, which was back to normal, thankfully. But how had that happened? In over two thousand years, something like that had never happened. Her body had filled up with such power, escaping through her skin. Looking back at her hand, she tried to summon it again, to no avail. What was it? Looking up, she watched the door creak open and Jason step in.

"You're awake."

"Just woke up."

"I see." Jason just stood there for a moment. Once again she found herself thinking about Pietro. Pietro wouldn't have just stood there with that look of gentle endearment on his face. No, he would have walked right in with that frustratingly arrogant and charming look on his face.

"You can come in," she said smiling a bit. "I won't bite."

Jason smiled back at her. "You sure?"

"Well, not unless you ask."

"That might not happen. Not today anyway." Grinning, he walked in and took a seat on the bed next to her. "Selene I, uh, wanted to apologize—"

"Don't," she began, placing a hand on his shoulder, "thank you but you don't have to. I lost my temper but you don't understand. I took lives that weren't worth anything. I still do. What I do, what I've done, it's not easy to understand, not something anyone human should understand. And I haven't felt human for so long, haven't felt—" Selene stopped, speechless. She didn't know how to explain how she felt. "Jason read my—"

"Selene, have time?" came a cold chill voice that Selene recognized. She watched as the shadows converged and pull together, her heart racing. The shadows curved around the farthest corner of the room, hug low there before whipped at the air. Soon enough there stood Negal, her form elegant and deadly. She wore a long black trench coat over her tight black clothes. A part of Selene was happy to see her, the other part of her saw the visit as an ill omen.

"What the—"

"Calm down Jason," she said standing, a firm hand on his shoulder. "Hello Negal."

Negal gave her a sad yet happy smile. "I see you found him."

Selene ignored the comment. "It's been centuries Negal, what's wrong now?"

"You as a matter of fact. That power you hold."

Selene bristled, her arm muscles tensing with calming restraint. "What power?"

"The power you exerted a few hours ago. You shook up the

Shadow Realm."

"So?"

"That power is seen as a threat Selene."

"I don't care. It's about time Shadowlings had something to fear."

"It wasn't just the Shadowlings." Negal took a seat on the chair in the far corner of the room, lacing one leg onto another. She took a second to look at Jason, her eyes flashing red quickly returning to black as they fell upon Selene again. "Your brother came to me."

"Eris?" Fear gripped her heart. Negal nodded, solemnly, sensing her fear.

"He sensed that power Selene, *he* sees it at a threat."

"He won't hurt me."

"Can you be so certain?" Selene just stared at her, stiff as stone, watching the sadness on Negal's face grow. "I thought so. It was nice to meet you Jason and, as always, it was a pleasure to see you Selene, despite the circumstances." Negal vanished into the darkness and Selene sat back down. What could she ever be certain about? Eris had changed, she found herself reconnecting to herself, to her humanity, to her love and thought of the reason why.

"Selene, are you okay?" Selene looked into his teal eyes and smiled weakly. He was the reason.

Selene sat in her bath, her new clothes hidden under her bed along with all her Fairy Dust and jewels. She thought about Jason who was completely different from Pietro. It made her feel...what? She didn't know how she felt. It was confusing. Everything was so confusing.

Grabbing her silk robe, she unplugged the drain. Indoor plumbing, pure magic, she thought, slipping out. It was one of the few things she allowed herself to enjoyed about these past few centuries.

Making her way to her bedroom, her feet leaving wet footprints on the smooth hard floor, she stopped in her tracks. Standing across from her, sitting on her bed smiling, was Jeanette.

"Did you have fun on your little rendezvous?"

"That depends on your definition of fun." Selene leaned on the stone wall, crossing her arm.

"What did he want so urgently?"

"He wanted to give me something."

"And that would be?" Jeanette's eyes sparkled like they used to. Selene went over to her bedside table and unlocked the top dresser. Gingerly, she pulled out the portrait and handed it over to Jeanette. "This."

Jeanette took it, her face softening. "You look so happy here. You haven't looked this way in such a long."

"What should that matter?"

"Because for the longest time you lost yourself, you lost your humanity, you closed off your heart. You became your brothers second in command. His hunter."

"How does that make me any different than you?"

"I never stopped feeling," she yelled standing up and throwing the portrait onto the bed. "You are the hunter! The Selene I knew died when our home was slaughtered. But now, I see the light in your heart and soul slowly returning. You're no longer this unfeeling obedient hunter. Your heart is opening."

"No it's not."

Throwing her arms up in frustration, Jeanette gripped Selene's shoulders. "Oh shut up! Selene, you have a second to love, a chance to repair your beaten and shattered soul. I see it in your eyes! You aren't beaten, you're not mindless. Selene you have a second chance to be with him."

Selene pulled her away, shaking her head sadly, knowing what Jeanette meant. "Except he's not Pietro and I don't know what I feel."

"Selene, whatever you feel, Jason is the cause, you can't forsake that which is good for you." Jeanette picked up the portrait. "You're right, Jason isn't Pietro. I like him more and prefer this Selene to the one that took her place." Jeanette smiled at her, the way she used to and walked let her alone.

Eleven

Eris stalked the night, searching for his prey. All he wanted was blood, to succumb to the Blood Hunger. Destroy. Maybe his sister was right. He didn't know what killing did to the soul. Licking his lips, he thought about the sweet tangy taste. Just once, that's all he wanted.

No, he told himself, he was the Coven Master, he was suppose to uphold the Vampyre Laws. Eris punched a tree. Why did he have these dark urges? All he wanted was Azelia, to live and love. Except, lately, different urges drove him. He felt like letting that little voice in the back of his head take over. Selene would never approve, she might even lead the hunting party after him. Hell, she might do it alone. Selene was a hunter, and despite the fact that she had been pardoned for the lives she had taken; it was something to live with, the path she chose, to separate herself from her emotions and live with the weight on her shoulders. He saw the dead look in her eyes when she would kill any Vampyre who broke the rules. It was her punishment, her fate.

Sitting down, he thought about his sister. Something was bit different about her. His thoughts swam to the Witch Jason. She could never find out about him, she could never find him.

Eris thought of a plan. He licked his lips, while his thoughts swam in desire as he caught the sight of his prey. She was fumbling with her keys, trying to get into her apartment building. Most Witches wanted to be indoors by twilight, but it looked as though she had put in a late shift at work. Her white collar shirt was crinkled, her perfume strong, mixed with the sweet smell of the diner just down the street, the onion, fries and spiced beef, her hair was fall.ng out of her once delicate bun. He looked around, shut his eyes and listened for anyone around. Silence. Eris licked his lips and lunged. Her scream died in her throat. Eris pinned her against the wall, engulfing them in shadows and sucked on her blood, loving the way it tasted. Her struggle was futile and it didn't take long for her body to go numb. He knew that he should stop but he couldn't. Soon enough, there wasn't a single drop left. Eris dropped her to the ground, carelessly. Some blood still lingered on his lips and he felt both thrilled and disgusted with himself. He began to walk away, then stopped briefly, catching the sight of something that glinted in the dim street life. There was a diamond ring on her finger. The poor girl, he thought before running away, would never get to see her wedding day.

***

In the deep darkness, above the buildings, Ettore and Vega watched the scene unfold. Vega tucked her hair behind her ear while her husband wrapped his arms around her nimble shoulders.

"So what does this mean?" asked Ettore.

Vega shook her head. "It's not good Ettore, he killed someone."

"Do we tell Blaine?"

"No, but we should report this to Negal." Vega stopped walking and looked up at her beloved. "He's falling to the darkness Ettore, I saw it in his eyes. I saw Nuri's darkness thrive."

Ettore kissed her forehead. "Nuri was never a murderer."

"Because he fell in love with Azelia. He needs to find her before he loses his soul."

"It's not our place to decide."

Vega's shoulders slumped, defeated. "What of Selene?"

"She hasn't exhibited another surge of power."

"Is that good or bad?"

Ettore shrugged. "She has the power, but I think it's locked after what Negal told us."

Vega nodded, passing her hand through her short and curly black hair. The wind flapped at her long and heavy black trench coat. "Do you think he'll kill her?"

Ettore shrugged. "If he thinks he's protecting or saving her, he might just slit her throat and watch her bleed." Vega acknowledged the somber conclusion. What had the centuries done to him?

Twelve

Jason sat with Cecilia in the coffee shop around the corner from the school, waiting for Nicholas and Miranda. Looking up across the table, he smiled at Cecilia who was giving him one of her 'I-know-you're-hiding-something' looks. He smiled. Cecilia never probed, unlike Miranda, she always let things come as they pleased.

"Cecilia?"

"I'm listening," she said smiling, her eyes twinkling, taking a small sip from her coffee.

"I can confide in you right?"

"Of course."

"All right." He let out a breath. "Let's say I met someone who at first thought I was someone else turned out to be someone completely different. Let's also say—"

"That you have a crush on her, however teeny weeny," she winked. It always astonished him how perceptive she was. "Is this the girl Miranda has been complaining about? She said she looked a bit young."

"Her name is Anita."

"Uh huh, what an evasive answer. Now, given that lack of an answer, why are you still with Miranda? She knows that you're hiding something and personally, it's getting annoying. And I'm past being exhausted by it."

"Sorry, it's just things with Anita are complicated. She has this overbearingly protective brother and this very large family that just makes it even more complicated."

She eyed his suspiciously over the rim of her ceramic coffee mug. "You're not telling me something."

"Not my secret to tell Cecilia, I'm—"

"Jason don't worry about it," she said laughing. "I totally understand. Unlike someone else we know."

"I wish Miranda would."

"Miranda is Miranda," she began shaking her head, "it's just part of her personality and—oh hell, we'll finish this later." Brushing her bangs out of her face, she forced a smile, standing up to wave over Nicholas and Miranda. Nicholas punched Jason's arm lightly, as always, before taking a chair and flipping it around and sitting down backwards, leaning his beefy body over it. He grabbed a piece of Cecilia's blueberry muffin, inciting her to slap his hand away. Jason snickered, distracting himself from Miranda's nimble body inching its way close to his body while she kissed him on the cheek.

"So what were you guys talking about," she asked, leaning on Jason. He tried to relax his body.

"I was asking him about Anita. You said so much with so little that I grew curious. I wanted to know more about her."

"You know, I was thinking the same thing. I would like to know more about her too." Something in Miranda's eyes sparked with something unfamiliar. "Jason, how does she know the whole council?"

"Her mother wa—is a Reborn on the Council," he lied.

"Oh. Jason, do you think you could invite her to dinner tonight? I would like to get to know her better." Jason saw the look in Miranda's eyes grow, turn bitter, into a manipulating and dangerously dark look. It upset him to know that she could be so petty. Jason scooted away from her, just an inch so as not to make it noticeable.

"She might be busy."

"But I thought she was here solely to see you?"

"She has other responsibilities than keeping track of me," he said heatedly.

"Like what?"

"Miranda stop probing," complained Cecilia. "You're interrogating him like he's a criminal."

"Whatever." Crossing her arms, Miranda pulled away from Jason, settling into her own chair.

"Don't talk to her like that," defended Nicholas.

"For heavens sake, all of you shut up! She's a Vampyre liaison. She came here to also talk with the coven on the outskirts of town. Can we not argue about this?" He looked back and forth between Cecilia then at Miranda. "Look, I'll invite her to dinner, happy?"

"I'm not disappointed." Miranda smiled smugly and laid her head into his chest. He stiffened, uncomfortable and gave Cecilia a pleading look. She looked at him empathetically. What had he just stepped in?

***

Jason threw his bag on the floor and waved on his ResoScreen to catch the last bits of the news. He listened for anything interesting to come on while he poured himself a can of Beunerry Juice, a thick blue syrupy from the Beunerry twig. What he heard almost made him drop his glass. A young woman had been found dead, her throat gashed open, her blood gone. There was no doubt in his mind that this was a Vampyre attack. Biting down on his lip, he hoped that this attack was just a simple Blood Hunger attack, and only the first of one, not many. No more people needed to die.

Sitting down, Jason propped his feet on the coffee table and thought about dinner, stifling a curse. How the hell was he suppose to get in touch with her before nightfall? As he stared up at his ceiling, he saw the shadows shift and change from the turning fan inspiring him. It was probably a foolish idea but he not other alternatives came to mind. Taking a deep breath, wiping his sweaty palms on his jeans, he sat up.

"Um, hello," he called out to the empty room, feeling incredibly stupid. "I really hope you're there or else this is one of the stupidest, embarrassing moments in my life." Silence greeted him before a male laughter filled the room. Jason jumped up and watched a man, clad in black with a big heavy trench coat step forward. He sat across from him.

"That was one of the most hilarious things I have seen in centuries," laughed the dangerous being. Grinning, he crossed his legs and leaned back into the chair comfortably. "I'm Ettore. Negal is busy at the moment but I can take a message."

Jason swallowed down his fear. "I need you to give a message to Selene."

Ettore's black eyes widened with his mouth twitching into a small sly smile. "Oh? Do tell."

"My friends would like to meet her and, well, I was wondering if she would like to, um, you know, join us for dinner."

"Are you insane?" Ettore's face turned serious and dark, his eyes turning to a dark red, bright against his pale flesh and black hair. "You do know that you're life is in danger right? I mean, so is hers but she can handle herself. Trust me," he continued with a wink,

"I've seen her in action."

Jason stood straight. "I can take care of myself too."

Ettore laughed. "Yeah, sure you can, but not against Eris." Scratching his chin he looked at Jason up and down. "You do know we Shadowlings can't be killed right? Good," he said not letting Jason answer with his mouth agape. "Well Eris can kill us. He already has. There's a lot about himself that he doesn't know about, Selene as well. It's complicated."

"I can take care of myself," said Jason assuredly. Ettore gave him a scrutinizing look, his eyes fading back into black.

"You may look like him but you sure as hell aren't him." He chuckled under his breath. "Very well, I will pass on your message to Selene. You know, I like you more than I liked Pietro. He was way too arrogant—even for my taste." Ettore dispersed into shadows, his laughter echoing in the air.

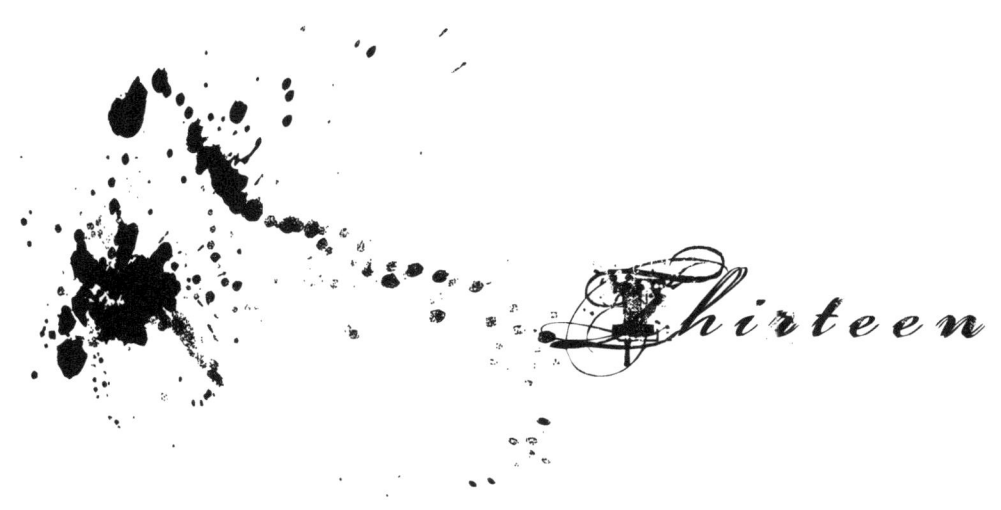

S elene bit down into her tarty apple as she strode through the hallway, an open book guiding her way. She had read and re-read this book many times over the centuries. Its yellowed pages, torn along the edges, corned crinkled and folded from years of page turning. The leather cover was just as worn, the gold lettering on the cover so faded, the title illegible. Selene turned the corner, barely thinking. After over two thousand years, she knew her way around without having to think about it. What she hadn't counted on was Eris blocking her path, a dazed look in his glossing over her eyes. The sudden shock of his appearance made her jump.

"Hello brother," she said, catching her breath.

"Have you seen the news?" He stared past her, as if mesmerized.

"The Vampyre killing? Yes, what of it?"

His gaze shot down to her, dilating to a deep red. "Why

haven't you organized a search party?"

"It was one killing Eris. Probably just a Newborn. We ever go after first offenders."

"So you're not leaving?"

"No, I'm not, but if it will make you feel better I'll grab Jeanette and Blake and patrol tonight." Selene stared at her brother, watching the red in his eyes darken to a near black shade of red. A shiver went down her spine.

"Fine. I want a full report at dawn."

"Very well," Selene gave him a slight bow. "I'll fetch Jeanette and Blake." Eris gave her a scathing look that forced her eyes to the ground as Eris walked past her. Once past, she followed him down the hall. Something wasn't right. Selene finishing off her apple, tossed the core to the ground and tucking her book under her arm before she ran off to find Jeanette and Blake. Sniffing the air, she followed their scents to the library. Blake, as always was situated on a chair near the fireplace reading while Jeanette sat in an hollowed out hole in the wall, that let Jeanette stare out at the sky through a high pitched window. Blake turned and looked at her. Jeanette's eyebrows arched.

"Yeah?" asked Jeanette.

"We need to go on patrol tonight."

"Why?" asked Blake setting his own book down.

Selene shrugged, tossing her old tattered book onto a chair near her. "Eris is worked up about that Vampyre attack. He wants us on patrol."

"The whole squad or just us?" asked Jeanette coldly.

"Just us. I suspect that it's just a Newborn. There haven't been any reports in any of the other cities and the authorities have not sought us out."

"Hopefully," repeated Blake. "When do we leave?"

"Dusk."

"Maybe them but certainly not you," came a chilly voice. Selene rolled her eyes and looked at Ettore and his dramatic entrance of coalescing shadows. Arrogantly, he flashed his white teeth in a big grin. Despite herself, she hugged him, glad to see him. Even Blake and Jeanette appeared happy to see him.

"What was all that gibberish you muttered Ettore," questioned Jeanette, jumping down from her perch to step next to Selene's side.

"She might have dinner plans."

"What dinner plans?" asked Selene. "I have no—"

"I bring a message from your dear Jason darling."

"Who's Jason," asked Blake. Jeanette punched Ettore as Selene covered her face, more embarrassed than anything. Ettore smiled and feigned surprise.

"Oh! Did I speak out of turn? So sorry."

"No you're not," muttered Selene.

"Who is Jason?" asked Blake again, his voice more stern. Selene and Jeanette exchanged looks of concern.

"You explain to him while I try to make sense of this mad man here."

"I'm hardly mad," he laughed while Jeanette pulled Blake to the other side of the room.

"Speak."

"Jason's friends have become deeply curious with Anita. They, particularly Miranda, want to meet you for dinner tonight."

"Is he insane? Does he not know the danger he is in?"

"I said that! Apparently he says he can take care of himself. Very humble about that too. I like him." He winked at her, leaning against the wall. Selene tried to suppress her smile.

"It's too risky."

"Hardly," chimed a voice. Selene looked over Ettore's shoulder at Jeanette's warm smile and bright eyes. Even Blake looked happy.

"*We'll* go on patrol and keep an eye out for Eris," said Blake.

"I love going behind his back," commented Jeanette, eyes wide with mischief.

"You see! You have the perfect cover. Besides, I'll have Vega keep an on eye Eris from the shadows." Selene smiled at her friends. Guilt smothered her soul however. She was supposed to be Eris's protector. Yet here she was, going behind his back. Looking out the window at the horizon, she remembered the days when she and Eris would tell each other everything.

***

Selene blew the Fairy Dust onto her skin and put on the gown Jeanette had stolen for her, a simple short deep blue dress that went all the way to her collar bone. Jeanette really did have good taste, especially in this century. Wrapping her hair up loosely, she exited the darkness of the forest. In the moonlight, Jeanette and Blake stared at her in awe.

"Oh my—" stammered Jeanette.

"You look beautiful," finished off Blake.

"Doesn't she," mocked Ettore playfully. Selene looked at him, as he wore the nicest dress suit he could steal. Blake and Jeanette had bound Fairy Dust to his skin. She had agreed to go on the condition that she go with him, posing as her brother. He lowered his sunglasses and sized her up.

"Well, don't you look human," she muttered in a low breath, stepping up to his side.

"I could say the same for you. Now let's go. We have a dinner to attend." He slowly shrank back into shadows and

Selene slipped in after him, giving Jeanette and Blake one last look.

***

Ettore deposited himself and Selene in an alleyway near the restaurant. Selene looked back at the wall where the shadowy portal swirled then vanished. Selene scowled at him as she stepped on something wet and squishy. So much for her new kitten heels.

"Couldn't you have at least picked a clean alleyway?"

"Picky today aren't we my dear," he laughed while her frown deepened, causing him to laugh more. "My dear, there is no such thing as a clean alley. Well, only on trash day." He laughed some more while she huffed, exiting the alleyway, arms crossed. Patting herself down, fixing herself up, she looked in both directions.

"Well don't just stand there I don't want to be late." She walked off and he caught up easily.

"My, my, aren't we anxious."

"Nervous actually. I can't believe I actually agreed to this. This is insane."

"But so very fun!" he said gripped her shoulder. Selene could not suppress her smile and stopped in front of the restaurant.

"You've got me there." Ettore smiled at her and opened the door in an unlikely chivalrous manner.

"Let the fun begin." Selene rolled her eyes and waved a finger over her eyes to conceal any shade of red. Ettore left his sunglasses on. This was going to be interesting, she mused.

Selene took a tentative step and entered a gold band over her left wrist while three silver bracelets banged together on her right. She drew stares from all over the room with her grace and beauty. Living within the Palace had given her etiquette and poise. The concierge stumbled over his words upon her approach. Selene smiled, amused and embarrassed.

"We're here to meet a Jason Elfinos?"

"Oh yes, this way, follow me." He grabbed a pair of menus and directed them to follow him. He led them down a row of tables. People continued to stare at Selene annoyingly. She resisted the urge to show off her fangs. Soon enough, (thankfully enough in her opinion) she approached Jason's table. She blushed when she saw the relieved look on his face. He stood up and hugged her quickly. She was taken aback and shot Ettore a deadly glance when he snickered. Someone coughed, causing the two to separate quickly. A girl with soft brown hair and brown eyes approached her with a warm smile.

"Hello, I'm Cecilia. We've heard a lot about you."

"Have you now?" she said shaking Cecilia's hand. Cecilia nodded and laughed.

"Well, mostly about your job and I must say, you look a little young. You're very beautiful though."

"Nice! Isn't she a nice one," snickered Ettore as he took a seat next to a broad shouldered guy with gray eyes and jet black hair. Selene glared at her "brother".

"This is my brother Ettore."

"I am also a Vampyre liaison, in a matter of speaking."

"He's also an obnoxious ass." Selene took her seat between Jason and Ettore and noticed that Miranda was staring at Ettore, frightened, her eyes wide and bulging. Selene's eyes flared.

"Is there something wrong?" she asked more heatedly than she had intended.

"H—his aura, it's pitch black!" Selene swore under her

breath. She was a Touched Born with the gift all too familiar to her. Quickly, Selene traced her fingers over Ettore's leg, crossing rune after rune until Miranda's expression changed into one of confusion.

"Miranda are you okay?" asked Cecilia gently touching her shoulder. Miranda muttered under her breath, shaking her head. Jason looked at Selene worried. She brushed it away with a smile.

"I'm Nicholas," said the handsome brute extending his hand to Selene.

"It's a pleasure to meet all of you."

"Hmph," said Miranda placing a napkin on her lap. "While we wait for the waiter tell us about your job."

"I work for the Reborns and High Witch Councils to talk with Vampyres. I usually help in the murder investigations that are caused by rogue Vampyres. I'm here mainly to confirm that the death of the Vampyre who was responsible for those three deaths was properly executed by the Hunters."

"What are the Hunters?" asked Cecilia taking a sip of water. "I mean, my brother works with them from time to time, but he's ever explained to me what they do exactly or what their purpose is."

"Hunters are a small party of very powerful Vampyres. Here in Telos, the Hunters are a party of six led by the Coven Masters sister."

"What's her name?" asked Nicholas with a spark in his gray eyes.

"Her name is Selene Sintas," continued Ettore. "And she is truly an efficient Hunter. Even puts the King's Garrison to shame." He snickered while Selene simply smiled.

"Excuse me?" said Miranda in a demanding tone. Selene

eyed her angrily.

"He said her name is Selene Sintas, why?" Selene studied her, tried to see if Katherine was there in her in more than just appearance.

"Selene Sintas should be dead by the laws of her kind."

"Why is that?" asked Ettore.

"Because she's a murderer!"

Selene clenched her fists under the table, her nails digging into her hard porcelain skin. That rage, that fury, it was too familiar. "Selene Sintas is not a murderer."

"Oh no? How many lives has that dead Witch taken?"

Trying had not to lose her composure, Selene breathed in and out as humanly as possible. "She was exonerated for those deaths, by both the Reborn Council and the Vampyre Court."

"I don't believe that."

"Kyra and Larkin, Witches in the Reborn Council, suppressed the barriers of the Capital City of Seraphim which resulted in the deaths of countless Reborns and Witches alike by Shadowling hands. Katherine—"

"My ancestor."

"Your ancestor murdered her husband in his sleep. Her sister abused her children and her brother and nephew were perverse men who mistreated women, held them captive, and tortured her to death. Their lives meant nothing to o one."

"How dare you," she seethed. "That is *my* blood you speak of!"

"Yes, which begs the question of your 'goodness'?" Selene took a sip of her water and snapped for the waiter who basically abandoned his table to serve he.

"Yes madam?"

THOUGHT SEEKER | 75

"I believe we're ready to order." She knew this dinner was a bad idea.

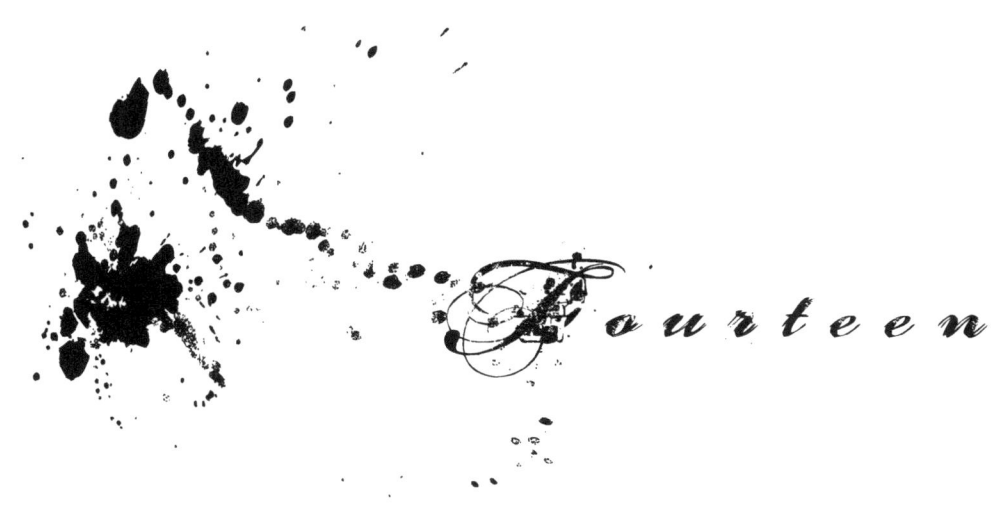

Fourteen

E ris sat in his room, staring. It was upsetting that Selene had taken the mater of the dead victim so lightly. The most she would do was go on patrol. He felt insulted; he was the Coven Master, his word was law. Or was supposed to be. A growl rose within him, tightening his vocal cords. The Blood Hunger rose and threatened to take over. He shook it away, but still thought of succumbing to it. If he went out now, Selene would surely catch onto his scent and discover that he was the one who had killed the Witch. However, she was in the east part of the city while Jeanette and Blake scoured the west. But thankfully, they were not as skilled as her. The dark temptation bubbled higher and higher, urging him to feed his dark urges. He would be able to sneak a victim and drain them dry. Maybe a man for dinner tonight, their blood was more fluid, salty, tasty. He licked his lips. Men also fought harder for their lives. His own blood warmed at the thought. He loved it when they fought. Selene thought the only lives he had taken were those of the former Coven Master and Senid. She was wrong. He had killed twice more.

The first had been a young man, near the City of Nephilium. He remembered his blue eyes and sandy brown hair. His appearance had been similar to Pietro, which may have had something to do with why he had chosen him for prey. Remembered how he ran. It had been exhilarating, the chase. He initially intended to take a pint or two of blood. Next thing he knew, the body was drained to nearly the last drop. Eris had felt a little remorse as he buried the body deep into the ground. It had been an accident hadn't it? Thinking back now, he wasn't so sure.

The second victim was more than just a face. Her name was Rebecca, a Witch with a sweet and gentle smile that reminded him of the way Selene used to smile. Alive. All he had wanted then were her memories, to see what made her smile. But she wouldn't stop screaming and Eris had snapped, as did her neck. He left her body, near the bottom of the staircase, making it look like an accident. One that worked. Everyone had concluded that she had fallen and thus broke her neck. Did he truly feel remorse for it? Or was he truly dead inside as Selene made herself to be?

Everyone had different ways to cope. Nivette became arrogant, Blake read, Jeanette cooked and Selene detached herself from humanity itself, more so than others. It's why she was the most skilled fighter, hunter and killer. No one dared trifle with her or him for fear of inciting her wrath. All Vampyres forgot their humanity, but there was a difference between forgetting and forcefully detaching oneself from it.

That was exactly why Eris needed her out of the city. He

could not risk her falling deeper into the dark hole she had created for herself. Furthermore, he knew that if she found that man named Jason, she would spiral further down her dark creation and be damned. The only thing that had saved her life, after her murderous rampage, was the lack of morality within her victims. Selene hadn't counted on that when she had sought death. Eris feared for his little sister, he did not want her to wish for death again. With that conclusion set in his mind, he made up his mind. Diving into the Shadowrealm, traveled to the west side of town he stepped out onto a deserted alleyway, near a ritzy restaurant and whistled, just as a man passed by. The man stopped, adjusting his messenger bag on his shoulder. Peering into the dark alley, he took a tentative step into the darkness. Eris hid in the shadows as the man took steps deeper and deeper into the alleyway.

"Hello? Is someone here?" Eris waited for the man to take another step. He did. Eris launched himself from the shadows and found his fangs around the throat. His victim flayed his arms, punched and tried to pry Eris' fangs from his neck. His grip only tightened. His victim fell to the ground, gurgling something incoherent as his heart beat slowed. Eris pulled away when his felt the last drop land on his tongue. He turned the body over and looked at it pitifully. Maybe now Selene would take him seriously. Maybe now she would gather her hunting party and set forth.

Eris sent out a shrill whistle, in hopes of attracting a lot of attention. Laughter greeted him instead. Eris spun around and glared at Shira behind him.

"Oh my, what a killer you are." Eris ignored her and ventured to the Shadowrealm. She appeared at his side.

Gritting his teeth, he said, "I do what I do to protect my

sister."

"Whatever helps you sleep at night!"

"I don't sleep at night."

"During the day then. Now do you want to know what I think?"

"No."

Ignoring him, she spoke up, flipping her hair over her shoulder. "I simply think that you are finally letting your darker—truer—self take over." Eris turned to snap at her, but she was already gone. Eris fought against the thought that maybe she was right.

Fifteen

Jason knew that this dinner had been a bad idea. He peeked over at Selene who was eating her meal in silence, lips pursed. She wasn't the only one, they were all silent. Looking over at Cecilia, he hopes that she would break the silence. She gave him a questionable look, eyebrows slanted, as if to say "well what do you want me to say?". Jason rolled his eyes and pointed to Selene then at his wrist making a little inscription. Cecilia's eyes widened.

"So Anita," began Cecilia, "I see that you have a rune on your wrist, can I ask which one that is, I can't tell from here."

"Stealth."

"Body or spell?"

"Both."

"Whoa! That's one powerful rune," exclaimed Nicholas. Jason watched Selene smirk and relief flowed out of him.

"Why that one," asked Cecilia.

"It seemed prudent at the time." Jason glanced at Ettore who laughed.

"What's so funny?" asked Miranda.

"Oh," began Ettore, dabbing it the corners of his mouth with his napkin, "Was I laughing? Pardon me."

"Don't mind him," said Selene, smacking his arm with her napkin. "Ettore is just an idiot."

"Oh Anita dear! I take that to heart." He laughed. "Anyway why don't you show then your other runes?" Jason caught her flinch, biceps flexing.

"You have more than one rune?" asked Cecilia.

"That's insane," remarked Miranda suspiciously, her voice low. There was something in her eyes that seemed to zero in on Selene, studying her.

"But wicked," said Nicholas. Ettore raised his glass to him and they clinked, clearly getting along. Jason smiled despite himself.

"And against the rules!" scolded Miranda. "I should report you."

Selene's eyes darkened and for a second Jason saw the vampyre behind the mask. "Go ahead, all eight were sanctioned by the Queen herself."

"That's a lie."

"Hardly." Selene smirked maliciously.

"Oh Anita! Brilliant idea! Show them the other runes!"

"Ettore—"

"No, I want to see," demanded Miranda. Jason saw the slightest hint of fear in Selene's purple eyes as she unclasped her gold wrist band. What he saw made his eyes widen.

"Oh my heavens!" exclaimed Cecilia.

"S—Anita," began Jason fearful, "why is it moving?"

"It's not moving," began Selene replacing the gold band over it.

"The power is," finished Ettore. "Anita used a Shadowling blade and shadows are like poison to us normal beings, but we were able to temper it with the help of the goddess so it wouldn't poison her. The dark power, as you saw still moves and shadows are always flickering." Jason looked back and forth between them, willing Selene to look at him. When she finally did, she smiled. His face warmed as did his blood. Suddenly, an earth shattering scream pulled their gazes apart.

"Vampyre!" Jason watched Selene jump up soon followed by Ettore, both ran out for the restaurant. Jason quickly placed a bunch of Felucian coins and bills on the table and followed them out of the restaurant towards the gathering crowd. He didn't have to look back to see his friends follow. He shoved his way through the crowd and stopped next to Selene.

"Selene?" Jason studied her appearance, watched her subtly sniff the air, eyes dilate.

"I need to leave."

"Why do you look scared?"

Selene turned to him and in hushed tones said, "There is no scent, as though whoever was here, wasn't. We all have scents." Her worried expression grew cold and her muscles tensed. Her back became straighter, her head held higher. To Jason, she looked almost regal.

"You'll have to excuse us. Considering the recent tragedy, there are important matters that I must discuss with the Coven. It was a pleasure to meet you Cecilia, Nicholas. Goodbye Miranda, and Jason, I'll see you soon. I still have matters to discuss with you regarding your father." Jason watched her walk away, her head held high, her black hair flowing behind her gracefully.

"Let's do this again sometime," grinned Ettore, tipping his head in a playful salute.

"Ettore!" Ettore smiled and ran off after Selene. Jason followed them both with his eyes until they were out of sight, swallowed up by darkness.

"I like her," said Cecilia as they made their way out of the crowd. "She looks familiar though."

"I like her too," said Nicholas. "She's hot and knows how to show you up Miranda. No offense."

"Oh shut up," said Miranda, shoving people out of the way. "I don't like her, nor her brother, nor those pet Vampyres she calls comrades. The whole lot of them should be exterminated. Besides there's something off about her and her brother, too much darkness in their auras. Black means death."

"Oh blah, blah, blah," said Nicholas waving his fingers in front of his car, unlocking it. "All you ever pay attention to is auras. Where's Anita to shut you up?"

"You are such a jerk," screeched Miranda childishly, fist clenched.

"Nicholas shut up. Miranda lets go," he said gently touching her shoulder. Miranda shoved him away.

"Don't touch me," she practically screamed, yanking her body away from him, looking at him disgusted, wagging her finger at him. "I saw your aura too. I'm walking home. Alone!" Miranda took off her shows and ran off down the cobblestone street.

"Miranda, be reasonable," called out Cecilia. Nicholas got into the drivers' side of his car and stuck his electric runed key into the ignition, instantly starting it up. Jason felt the electricity in the air as he stared off after his girlfriend in her burgundy dress running down the side walk. A part of him wanted to run after her, but another part...

"Oh let her go. If she wants to pout let her. She always reads too much into things. In any case, I like Anita more; you should try getting with her." Nicholas winked at Jason and drove off the moment Cecilia got in. Jason just stared at his car before looking up at the moons exhausted,

"Why," he asked out loud, "why me?" Jason made his way to his silver car, exhausted and unaware of the two women hidden by darkness watching him. One stood in a white robe with glistening silver like hair and gray eyes while the other leaning against a building, a sneer on her too pale skin made paler by her black hair and coal like eyes. Her robe cast a shadow over her face.

"He damned her once," said the woman in black.

"He was yours then and I won him over before the end," countered the woman in white. The woman in black let out a cold harsh laugh.

"Oh dear, sweet, naive sister, this is a whole new battle. He'll be mine again and foul up whatever fate you have for them."

The woman in white stared at her sadly. "I will protect them."

"Well you're doing a lousy job." She vanished in a swirl of smoke, leaving the woman in white alone to look at Jason once more. Selene had suffered enough for no fault of her own, and as her righteous mother, the Goddess of Light *would* win over his soul again.

Sixteen

Selene sat in the council room stoic as her brother yelled at her, Jeanette and Blake. However, most of his anger was directed at her.

"You said you were on patrol!"

"I was," she lied, studying the ethereal silver swirls in the granite table.

"Really? Then explain to me why there was another murder last night? Well? Answer me Selene!"

"There was no scent!" she screamed, banging her palms against the table, cracking it. Selene did not need him screaming at her, she felt guilty enough.

"That's not possible!"

"Eris there was no scent!" shouted Blake. "The Vampyre must have Fairy Dust. It's the only way."

"I will not stand here and listen to excuses! I don't care if there was a scent or not! You are the Hunters, you should have been doing your job! Or is one of you the killer?"

"Oh you insensitive bastard!" exclaimed Jeanette. "I will not sit here and be insulted! We were on patrol, we caught no scent which means either magic or Fairy Dust! That makes it harder to track them! Of course you wouldn't know, you get to stand around and sit on your ass all day."

"I am Coven Master Jeanette and you would do well to watch your tongue."

"I will not let you accuse us of crimes we did not commit. If you want my head, take it. I will gladly pay the price for disobedience."

"Okay enough," yelled Selene. "Eris we will find the killer, it just might take longer than we'd like."

"You do it soon, if the murders hit four, the King's Garrison will arrive. Do you want them here Selene?" Selene flinched at her brothers' cold and uncaring tone. She was not on good terms with the King's Garrison. Not after the things she had done.

"No."

"I thought so. Find the Vampyre, bring him in for his hearing. Meeting dismissed." Eris left the council room, followed by the other members of the council. Nivette and herself were the only two left in the room.

"I wouldn't mind him Selene."

"You weren't the one he was screaming at."

"True, that was...unsettling. You're usually the only thing he ever cares about."

Selene took her seat, slouching back, leaving her fingers on the table to trace over the new cracks. "Usually. Something has been bothering him, can't you tell? He's not himself."

"Oh, I've noticed," she said staring at the door. "But there is little we can do about it Selene."

"Please try to figure out what is wrong with him. I've no desire to be scolded again."

"I will talk to him, but I make no promises." Nivette left, leaving Selene alone with her thoughts. She should not have attended that mistake of a dinner. She should have listened to her brother, maybe then she would have caught the Vampyre who's longing for blood had suddenly grew strong.

Selene don't fret, came a familiar voice in her thoughts. Selene felt comforted by the voice of the Goddess. *I assure you, all will be well.* The tender voice vanished, leaving Selene feeling cold again.

***

"How could there be no scent," asked Eno, sitting across from Blake in the Hunter's Room.

"They could be using magic or Fairy Dust," said Dimitri.

"If it's magic we should be able to trace the spell, hopefully witches don't use that alley way," said Cinio.

"In any case, I don't want the Garrison to come," stated Selene. "I'm on thin ice as it is." Selene rubbed her temples. "We need to find whoever this is. It doesn't look like these two murders are their first. Investigate other cities and suburbs. If there are any similar cases I want to know. Blake, Jeanette, stay, I want to discuss something with you two. The rest of you are dismissed." Selene watched the rest leave. Once the door was shut she put up a silencing spell. Jeanette and Blake looked at her concerned.

"Selene?" Selene looked up at Blake, letting out a heavy sigh.

"Whoever this is knew where to go."

He scrunched up his eyes confused. "What?"

"You think it might be someone in the coven?" asked Jeanette.

"I think so. We were on patrol in the east because killers feel more comfortable in one spot. Whoever this is, was or is, in the coven. They knew how we work and how the system works. The Vampyre went from East to West, over night."

"But it couldn't be someone in our coven," stated Blake agitated.

"It could if they're ingesting Fairy Dust like Witches. That stuff is like poison, makes them delusional."

"If it's Fairy Dust and that's only if their ingesting it. If not, then whoever this is, is a cold blooded killer."

"What happens if we don't find whoever this is after four. We haven't seen the Garrison for centuries."

Selene eyed them both fearfully as well as angrily. "They'll have their own suspicions and I'll be number one on their damn to kill list."

***

Selene packed up her stuff from under her floor, shoving everything into a bag and waiting for Jeanette to give her the go ahead. She wasn't going to get rid of the stuff, she was just going to hide it before she went back to meet with the Enforcers to further examine the crime scene.

"Selene, he's entering the Grand Hall, come on." Selene swung the bag over her shoulder.

"I'll meet you at the crime scene. I have to drop this stuff off."

"Cautious aren't we."

"I've killed six people in my life time. Technically, I should not be alive. So yeah, I'm cautious. See you guys in a few." Selene ran off, out of the cave, threw the woods and headed to Jason's house. As always, he was alone doing his homework. Selene tapped on the window and for once, Jason didn't seem startled to see her.

"Hey," he said opening the window."

"I can't stay, I have to meet some Enforcers back at the alley. I came to ask if you would hold onto some things for me."

"What is it?" he asked taking the bag.

"Jewels, money and Fairy Dust."

"Fairy Dust? What are you doing with that stuff?"

Selene stared at him incredulous as she made her way in, taking her bag back as she lifted the a few floorboards of his apartment up. "How do you think I get my pale skin to look like yours Jason," she asked as she dumped her stuff into the whole, sealing it up with magic. "I'm a Vampyre Jason, I'm dead and the dead have no Light."

"Oh."

"Just leave it alone. I'll see you around." Selene bid him farewell then climbed back out the window.

Seventeen

E ris arrived at the crime scene where his sister and comrades were already situated. Selene was trying to weave a Spider Cell. It was an ethereal like box that floated in the air, consisting of spell tracers with timings attached. If there had been magic it would show up and show at what time. Eris was thankful for his Shadowling abilities. Still, he wondered why he had left no scent, not that he wasn't thankful for that too. Nonetheless, it still unnerved him though.

The web of magic was finally complete and he watched his dissect every strand. Obviously there would be nothing left behind from him. He watched her face harden as she waved her arm through the Spider Cell, dissipating it.

"Well?" he asked her. Selene gave him an annoyed look, the red in her eyes, obscuring the violet.

"They didn't use a Marking Spell. That only leaves Fairy

Dust. They are either using it as a cover or ingesting it. Either way, whoever they are, they're dangerous."

"So investigate Selene," he scolded.

"What does it look like I'm doing," she seethed

"Let's not argue here," said Blake stepping up between them. "We'll go to the Darkling District and investigate the sellers and buyers of Fairy Dust."

"We'll go as well," said the leader of the districts Enforcers, Conner.

"You sure about that," asked Jeanette. "These Witches delve in the dark arts, they're not likely to cooperate with you breathing down their necks."

"We have the right to arrest whoever is making that Dust."

"That you do," answered Selene. "We'll go, get a name and then we'll turn it over to you."

Eris stared at his sister shocked. "Selene!"

"Shut it," hissed Blake, glaring at him. Eris snarled. Blake was always defiant, always harbored a small seed of hatred for him, no matter how small the situation may be. Eris had never really liked hi, even as children.

"How dare you!"

"How dare I?" Blake turned and glared at him. "You have the nerve to say that to me? You, who cares for nothing. Who never has! You have not done one thing to help this investigation! All you do is chastise and you know what Eris, never have you been too quick to send us out. It was almost like you knew."

"What are you insinuating," he growled flexing his muscles.

"Figure it out." Blake turned to walk away and Eris, in his fury, yanked his arm back and punched him, sending him sprawling into the side of the building, quickly regretting it when Blake lunged at him, not holding back. Slammed down into the ground, Eris's fury only grew with every kick and punch. When he finally knocked Blake off himself, he soon found himself slammed against the side of a building, a thin lean arm pressed against his chest.

"Enough!" echoed Selene's voice in the alley. Eris looked down at her strong purple eyes. He quickly relaxed and looked over her shoulder at Blake who was being held by Jeanette, both were furious.

"You can let go of me now."

Eyebrow raised, Selene studied him with a set face, devoid of any lightness. "Are you sure?"

"Selene, I'm fine."

Purple eyes slanted, she took a step away, watching him. "At least act disgusted brother. Jeanette, Blake, let's go." Eris watched his sister walk away, not looking back at him. For the first time, he felt very distant from her. He tried to fight the feeling.

"Selene!"

"Go home Eris," she called. "You're Coven Master, we're the Hunters, we can do our job without you." She stopped walking and looked back at him. "Go home Eris, all this bickering will get us nowhere." Eris was stung. As she walked away, he knew it had not been the words that had stung her, but rather the look in her eyes. *You're not wanted.* Eris punched the wall.

* * *

Eris lay in bed, his hands behind his head. What the hell was he doing? Killing and picking fights with Blake. The killings were justified right? Yeah, he answered himself, he needed to keep Selene preoccupied, just until Shira or Negal told him more about Jason. He'd rather commit unspeakable acts before he let Selene fall deeper into her own darkness.

"Oh my, my, having regrets?" Eris didn't have to turn to look to know that it was Shira.

"Hmm, I was just thinking about you."

"Oh! How delightful." Shira's hand slithered up his chest. His heart beat fluttered and suddenly, he remembered a time that did not exist. A time when she looked happy and in love. A time where he, Negal, Senid and Shira were together, all smiles. He shook the image away.

"Don't be flattered."

"Oh, how hurtful." He felt her legs wrap around him. Eris shut his eyes. Another vision flashed. He was holding her, feeling nothing but love, kissing her. Eris opened his eyes and noticed her hovering above him, her body close to his, her black leather bodice pushing her cleavage higher than possible and tight black leather pants,that highlighted her slender legs. Her eyes, like black pools seemingly glowing against her skin.

"What do you want Shira?"

Her eyes flared, briefly turning bright red before returning to black pools. "What is rightfully been mine."

"And that would be?"

Shira's voluptuous lips were at his ears, her cold breath sending warm shivers over his body. "You." Eris shut his eyes tightly when her lips touched his neck. He felt them move up his chin and knew soon enough that they would be on his lips.

Eris could push her off, he had the power to, but Eris was tired of fighting off his darker inhibitions that he knew existed. So he stopped. Eris kissed her back, fiercely, tightening one hand around her neck while he ripped off her bodice with the other. He was tired of ignoring his darker urges.

Eighteen

Blake watched Selene walk down the dark alley stairs ahead of him to the Darkling District. Practitioners of the Dark Arts lived here, ignoring the rules of their kind, unfortunately smart enough to never get caught. It didn't matter that everyone knew who and what they were, without evidence, there was little that even the Enforcers could do.

As he followed Selene, who was walking with her head held high, her long black hair flowing behind her. He looked around and caught the looks that she attracted. Fear. She was Selene Sintas, who had killed more than her share of Dark Witches. They all knew better than to take her on or lie to her. She had gotten away with six deaths, what was one more to add to the list.

Selene led them to a house and knocked on the door. Blake shared a confused look with Jeanette. His eyes widened when he saw a Witchling answer the door. Witchlings were feline-like people, once they were cats, simple familiars who were then turned into Witches, partially, with the use of Dark Magic. Witchlings still had their feline like grace, fur, eyes and ears, but they also had beautiful long legs and slender bodies. This one crossed her arms and leaned against her door frame, tapped her fingers against her arm, a sly and secretive smile on her face.

"Hello Selene." Selene hugged her and the Witchling laughed, hugging her in return. Once the embrace ended, the Witchling welcomed them into her home. She locked the door once they were all in.

"Blake, Jeanette, this is Zoë."

"Hello," greeted Blake. Jeanette, as was her newest custom, didn't say a word.

"So, what can I do you for you today," asked Zoë, sliding onto her divan, stretching out like the cat she originally was.

"I need to know if there have been any Vampyres who have bought Fairy Dust?"

Zoë laughed, her golden eyes glittering. "Other than you? Only a few, why?"

"Have you heard about the two recent murders?" asked Blake. Zoë looked at him, her gold eyes dilating in the dim light.

"Yes," she purred.

"Then that's why," said Jeanette.

"Talkative isn't she," joked Zoë. "Quite honestly, I don't know how many exactly, but for you, I could find out."

"We need those names as soon as possible," said Selene.

"All right, don't worry. I know the maker, I'll inquire delicately and have the names for you tomorrow. Sound fair?"

Blake watched Selene nod and hold out an uncut diamond to Zoë. Blake watched Zoë in amusement. He wondered which life she was in. Witchlings were almost like Reborns. They were reincarnated nine times and regained the memories of their past lives. Zoë reminded him off someone he knew. She must have caught him staring because she looked up from her divan and smiled at him warmly.

"Thank you for the diamond Selene. It was nice to meet you both." Zoë smiled again, at Blake more than anyone else and snapped her fingers, unlocking the door. As they left, Selene stayed behind and exchanged hushed words with Zoë.

"Do you think Selene is okay," he heard Jeanette ask him. "I've never seen Eris show such lack of care towards her. He's never been so harsh with her, not since Katherine's death."

"Eris is a horse's ass. Something is bothering him and he's taking it out on her." He looked at her. "I implicated him."

Jeanette smiled. "I know. It was brilliant. Stupid, but brilliant."

"Thank you?"

"I think you might be onto something though," said Jeanette, ignoring his question.

Blake nodded. "So you feel it to huh?"

"Something isn't right. Do you think he knows? About Jason?"

"I hope not. But if he did, why hasn't he done anything to confront Selene?"

"Maybe he doesn't know she knows."

"Eris doesn't know." Blake and Jeanette jumped at the sudden reappearance of Selene at their sides. "Jason would be dead if he knew."

"We were having a private conversation," scowled Jeanette.

Selene merely smiled that mocking and arrogant smile of hers.

"Then you should have gone down street. I barely had to heighten my hearing to eavesdrop on you two."

"Selene you have to—"

"Yes Blake, I feel it to. I even sense the change in him. But if he knew, either Jason or I would be dead and we aren't. Something else is going on. Something within him. It's a change I've only noticed in him once before, a change in his eyes. He's tired."

"Of what?" asked Jeanette hotly.

"Of waiting for Azelia. He's tired of living." Blake watched the sadness in her eyes grow. It only served to make her dark beauty more alluring. "Head back to the cave. I need to find my human dealer."

"Why?" asked Blake.

"Just a precautionary measure. I need to do a Memory Wipe."

"Don't you think we'll stop whoever this is before four?"

Selene shook her head. "I don't know, but I can't risk it." Selene took off down the street. Blake looked at Jeanette, who shook her head in answer to his silent question. He had to agree, his hope just as fleeting.

Nineteen

J ason sat on his bed waiting for Cecilia to arrive. She had called him up, a little while after Selene's visit. She sounded like she was out on her ConEx. What struck him the most about the call was how annoyed she sounded. That only made matters worse. He expected this type of attitude from Miranda, who wasn't returning his calls or messages. She had left him one though, certainly telling him off leaving him unsure if they were still together or not. Thinking back on it, he couldn't say he was upset. He had loved her, was sure he wanted to be with her always, but lately, he was seeing her in a different light. Miranda didn't have many friends. At first he hadn't understood, she was pretty, sweet and smart. Soon though he figured out the problem. Not only was she Touched Born, which made people prejudge her and those who gave her a chance, quickly regretted it. She was an Aura Seer. People had secrets and they liked their secrets. Some people had personal problems and didn't want to discuss them. But Miranda was Miranda and was forever persistent. He understood her need, it made sense. To see ones aura and those colors swirl and reveal oneself, it was such an insight. But a lie or something bothering you, bothered her. She alienated herself but she had never alienated herself from him. Not until lately, when he began hiding something from her. It made him feel both a little guilty and confused.

A knock sounded at his door and he knew that it was Cecilia. He was shocked to see how angry she looked as she stormed into his apartment.

"You idiotic fool!"

"Nice to see you too," he said closing the door before following her to the living room.

"Oh no! Do not take that stupid tone with me. You know when I saw 'Anita'," she began making air quotes as she spoke, "I thought she looked familiar, too familiar." Cecilia bent down and picked up the stack of papers. "And then when she told me she had not one, but eight runes, well that certainly rang a bell." Cecilia threw the papers at is face. "That girls name is not Anita, she is Selene Sintas; and I saw her today with the Hunters when I visited my brother at the crime scene. Oh, and that guy Ettore, that was no her brother. He wasn't a Witch and I'm willing to bet he isn't a Vampyre either. I also saw her there with her brother, her real brother. He has a temper. So sit down and tell me what the hell is going on!"

Jason stared at his friend. Was it worth even trying to lie to her? Cecilia always knew too much. Jason sighed and took a seat.

"Yes, Selene Sintas is Anita. Four months ago Selene

attacked me, planned on feeding on me, on my thoughts, not my blood. But when she attacked, my gift prevented her from taking my thoughts, taking her by surprise, she couldn't steal them and thought I was Pietro. After that, we just sort of kept in touch."

"And Ettore?" Her foot began to tap against his wood floors impatiently.

"A Shadowling, a companion of hers."

"You're insane."

"Oh really? Cause I though hanging out with a Shadowling and a Vampire may want to kill me was the best decision in my life."

"Don't be sarcastic." Cecilia looked at him as thought he was a child playing with fire. "I like her and I can see why you like her too."

"Actually," he interrupted, "I'm not sure how I feel."

"Awesome, well you better figure out soon along with where you stand with Miranda." Cecilia sat down next to him. "Jason, Selene is a Vampyre, this, you being involved with her is dangerous, even if it's innocent. I don't need to be an Aura Seer to know that you care about her deeply. In the name of the Gods, even Nicholas noticed, and he's oblivious to anything that doesn't have breasts or a pretty face." Jason laughed and watched her face break into a smile. "Yes, yes, but all humor aside, you do know it's against the Vampyre Doctrine, for her to even talk with you right?"

Jason furrowed his brow and stared at her confused. "No."

"Obviously, you aren't taking the same courses as me. Look it's one of their rules that they are supposed to live separately from us, they are not allowed to form relationships of any sort. It creates complications. Only a select few and only with the authorities."

"What happens if the coven master finds out?"

"After a first offense? Nothing. After a second offense, they are reported to the Vampyre King. He decides their fate. If they survive to make the mistake a third time, they are sentenced to death."

"Death?" Cecilia nodded. Selene was putting her life at risk, further into jeopardy. Her brother, Eris, would probably kill her without sending word to the Vampyre King.

"She really didn't tell?"

"She told me other things."

"Like what?"

"When Pietro died, Selene said she went mad with grief. We know what she did. She said her brother would kill me, to save her from that grief again. I see the look in her eyes, I think she believes he would kill her too. I see the look in the eyes of her Shadowling friend as well. Eris has gone mad, and even Selene fears it."

"So you've put your life in danger huh? My lord, you love her!"

Jason shook his head. "No, I don't."

"Oh but you do, you idiot. You just don't see it."

Jason glared at her. "Have you heard from Miranda," he asked changing the subject.

"She called. She hates you but she is still in love with you and wants to know what is going on with you, wants to know if this relationship is even worth repairing. Is it Jason?"

Jason looked away from her strong penetrating gaze. "I care about her, I truly do, but...she doesn't let anything go. She doesn't just separate herself from her gift. She doesn't even try."

"How do you know if that's even possible? How do you know she hasn't tried?"

Jason arched his brow and gave her a knowing look. "One, she's Miranda and two, all Touched Born's can control their gift, they can shut them off. I can read thoughts but I'm not always digging through people's heads. She could choose not to see auras."

Cecilia shrugged. "Well I'm not a Touched Born so I don't know how it all works."

"I'll talk to her. This can be repaired but she needs to give a little, not just me."

"Miranda's always been a bit selfish."

"Only girl who turns Nicholas off," joked Jason. Cecilia slapped his arm before she burst out into laughter. Jason was glad that the dark mood was lifted.

Twenty

S elene sat alone in the fading autumn sunlight. She soon saw the moon, named Aurora, rising far in the horizon. It would be another four hours until the second moon, Cynthos, would rise above the horizon. Selene closed her eyes and found her mind two thousand years in the past. Her home was in shambles and all she wanted was to see her mother again, but why torture her. She was already a wreak with two husbands dead and her only children presumed dead. Selene left her alone but always left a tulip on her father's grave hoping to giver her mother a sign that she was alive. Then one day she found a book laid out on her fathers grave. It was her mothers book about Vampyres. The very book Selene had perused so many months ago. Inside the leather cover bad been a message:

To my children,
I will love you for as long as you live.

Selene opened her eyes and stared up flickering stars in the darkening sky. She missed her mother, angry with herself for denying that one memory. For denying her anything other than thoughts of hunger and death. She snorted at her stupidity. What a pitiful life to live, forcing herself to feel nothing, had allowing death and hunger to be her motivation to continue living. She had, as Jeanette had put it, severed herself from her humanity. Jason was bringing it back though, repairing her without even knowing it. Something about Jason was making her feel...what? Love? Pain? Anger?

Confused, she didn't know how she felt about him, about anything concerning him. She knew she cared for him, but did she care about him for the right reason? Was she attracted to him because he looked like Pietro? No. Pietro wasn't a factor anymore. She knew that she would always love Pietro but Jason, his persona was that of a completely different person. He was humble where Pietro had been arrogant, respectful where Pietro had been intrusive. When she looked at Jason, she no longer thought about Pietro, no longer saw him in Jason's teal eyes. All she saw was Jason, a very different person.

Selene didn't know if her own personal changes bothered her. She had been content with her life. What truly bothered her though was the sudden changes in her brother. Never in his life had he been so cold to her, so cruel and distant. Once upon a time, Selene had been the center of his world, he cared, or had cared, about her more than anything and yet, he would always stand by her side and respect her wishes, even when it was something had did not approve of. This sudden change troubled her.

Selene sat up, only to find Vega leaning against a tree staring down at her with great sympathy.

"Really? Can you not sneak up on me?"

Cocking her head to the side, Vega offered her a gentle smile. "You're a Vampyre, you're not using your senses."

"All you Shadowlings, you all just love to sneak up on us beings of Earth and Heaven."

"It makes us good killers," she muttered sadly.

"You could choose not to kill."

"If only it were that simple. Besides I'm content with my fate, unlike you."

Selene looked away. "Do you know what's wrong with Eris?"

"What makes you think there's anything wrong with him?"

"You're avoiding the question Vega."

"Have you seen Nuri's Shadow? Have you felt how cold it's gotten?" She nodded towards Selene's thigh where there was a dagger sheathed. Looking down at the dagger herself, Selene took a breath, lacing her fingers around it. With a gasp she felt the cold on the silver handle. It was too cold, even for a Vampyre. Selene used her fire rune to warm her fingers as she pulled the dagger out of it's sheath. It was darker, the shadows were growing, licking the blade from the inside, as though a black fire were burning from inside. She dropped it to the ground and stared at Vega angrily.

"What does that mean? Vega, what is going on?"

"You're brother and that are connected. He's beginning to succumb to the darkness."

"What does that mean?"

"That your life is in danger." Vega vanished, her body fading back into the shadows, licking the ground. Selene snatched up the blade, sheathing it quickly before her fingers froze again.

***

Selene stood at the clock tower, her eyes scanned the ground beneath her, trying to catch anything that was off. She saw Witches, smelling of fear, stroll by alone. Most traveled in packs of three or more. Nothing would be different this night, even for an exceptional Vampyre Hunter like the one she was hunting.

Something isn't right...

The thought kept tearing through her mind, leaving her distracted while her encounter with Vega had left her anxious. She touched the blade's hilt that was buckled to her. It still felt colder than death, an she was the undead. She was a creature of the Gray, a Vampyre.

What bothered her the most was that Vampyres were dead, the cold couldn't and shouldn't affect them. Even tricking the mind into thinking it was still alive, while it weakened them, still couldn't allow something as simple as the cold affect them.

Then there was the Vampyre she was hunting and suddenly Selene was thinking about his diet. Vampyres who fed strictly on blood could not digest "regular" food. While Vampyres that fed only on thoughts and memories were left weakened. Tricking the body too much made everything impossible to digest. The body knew it was dead and would force the host to face it too. You needed the diet of all three to feel even remotely human. One or the other destroyed the mind and body. The body made a person succumb to the Blood Hunger while the mind just drove them plain mad. And there was no question about it, something was very wrong with the Vampyre she was hunting.

Taking a life was punishable by death. Using Fairy Dust recklessly was too. It made a Vampyre delusional and hid their scent. There would be no trial, only capture, then he would die. Most likely by her hand.

Selene found it a bit hypocritical. She had taken six lives and yet, here she stood, centuries later. Who was she to pass judgment? She was the Executioner. Sometimes she wondered if living with her crimes was a worse punishment than death.

"Selene?"

Selene jerked, lost in the mass of thoughts that threatened to drown her. Turning her head, she stared up at a concerned Blake. "Did you find anything?"

"Nothing out of the ordinary. No Vampyre in my district, other than myself that is."

Selene sighed. "Whoever it is, I don't think they will attack tonight."

"Why?"

"Whoever they are, they're too smart."

"Selene, I'm worried about you."

"Don't be."

"Selene whoever this Vampyre is, they are smart and clever and I...I don't think we'll be able to stop the call to the King's Garrison."

Selene let out a bitter laugh. She had been thinking the same thing. "That certainly wouldn't be good."

"Only if they think that you've got something to hide, which you do. Did you successfully Mind Sweep your dealer?"

Selene nodded. "That stuff should be banned, or at the very least monitored. Too many people abuse that vile stuff."

"They can't though, it has too many magical uses and for those that suffer Demde, they need it, it's the only thing that keeps them sane."

"I know Blake, I still think they should regulate it."

She heard Blake sigh. "Maybe, not in this century, but soon." They stood there a moment in silence and Selene looked at him, fearful.

"Blake, can I ask you a question?"

"Of course."

"Do you think Eris would kill me?" It was a question that had been bothering her since the night she saw Negal. Blake didn't answer her, instead he took her up in his arms and hugged her and kissed her tenderly, gently on the forehead. Her heart constricted while the tears welled up in her eyes.

"I'm sorry Selene," he mumbled holding her close.

Twenty One

Eris lay in Shira's bed in the Shadowrealm. She was sleeping soundly, her back to him. He noted how small her back was and how different she looked when she wasn't dressed like a killer. She could almost pass for a Vampyre. The difference may be subtle, but no one missed them. Eris moved over to her, taking her in his arms to kiss her on the neck. She woke up instantly, turning to him to kiss him full on the lips. Eris hugged her tighter as her legs wrapped around him. Shira sat up, slipping out of his arms easily. Straddling him, she traced one long black fingernail across his chest.

"You seem happy Eris."

"I'm content."

"Really?" Her finger moved down his chest. "Will you ever be happy?"

His thoughts immediately turned towards Azelia and he suddenly grew very sick with himself. Why had he succumbed to her? He shut his eyes, not wanting to look at her. But he still felt her as she moved on him. He grabbed the sheets, tightly, hating h_mself. Her hips moved slowly in a circle.

"Well? Happy yet?"

Eris tightened the hold on his eyes. Against his will, his eyes opened wide as she began moving her body in intoxicatedly sensual ways. He stared at her, hungry and jerked up, digging his fangs into her neck. Her blood, black as night, dripped down his chin and down her neck. He loved how it tasted, better than any type of human blood, making him feel even more powerful. His excitement rose as her nails dug into his skin He did not know how long they been going when he finally collapsed back onto the bed.

"Happy now?"

"I need to go." Eris collected himself and left through the shadows of the shadow realm.

Back in his room, he sat on the edge of his own bed and rubbed the bridge of his nose, conflicted. He didn't know what he was. Was he happy? Was he even sane? He didn't know either way anymore. All he knew was that Selene maintained her sanity, her life. If Jason turned out to be a creation of the Dark Ones, then he would hunt him down and kill him before she had a chance to encounter him. If he turned out to be a creation of beings of Light then he would turn him. Before, she found him of course. If she found him and fell in love with him history might repeat and she...she might get her wish this time around. Her grief would see to that.

His bedroom door swung open, sending vibrations through the air. He did not need to look up to know it was Nivette. When her feet, bare and gleaming in the dim light, were next to his feet, he looked up and met her eyes that stared back blankly at her.

"I've been looking for you."

Fear seized him. "Why? What happened?"

"We need to hold a meeting, according to Selene. And with some urgency."

"Why?"

"Oh would you just come already. You're Coven Master, it's your job. So be at the meeting. Besides, it involves the hunting." Nivette left the room, coldly, slamming the door behind her. He stared at the door cautiously, wondering if she suspected where he had been. Pulling himself together, and brushing the thought away, he stood up, looking briefly at the shadows as they flickered in the candle light before he left. He knew by now to suspect that he was always being watched.

Eris walked down the hall to the Spelled Council Chamber. No sound ever left the room so when he entered he was surprised to see that they were all arguing.

"No one in this Coven would even take a life, no matter how insignificant," shouted Miagra, and older Vampyre from the previous regime. Miagra had not mourned the death of the previous Coven Master and knew well enough to fear him and Selene, a fact that had kept her on the council.

"We have three names," shouted Selene, sounding exasperated. "Not one, not two, but three! Whatever they are doing with it, they have it in their possession. Unless they use it for magic, their lives are forfeit."

"Who do the names belong too?" Eris saw his sister stiffen while she looked at him coldly. "And how many others are on the list?"

"There are seven names total. The three belonging to this coven are Calpurnia, Amelia, and Aero."

"Do you know the others?"

"No," she said shaking her head. "They are either from another Coven or Roamers."

"Find the Roamers."

"Eris I think—"

"Find the Roamers!" Eris watched her stiffen, saw Nivette stare at him shocked, the hatred in Jeanette's eyes flame and the distrust in Blake's eyes grow.

"Very well Eris. I will not rest until I find them." Eris watched his sister bow stiffly and leave the council room. Her garrison quickly followed, each sparing one glance at him in different shades of concern and distaste. He waved the door closed and turned around to face the only person left. His head snapped to the side and he lost his stable foot, stumbling back a few paces. The cuts from Nivette's slap healed up before a single drop of blood could truly escape.

"What the hell has gotten into you!"

"Don't hit me," he said regaining his balance.

"Oh, I will do whatever I damn well please Eris. That is your sister and you just brushed her off as though she meant nothing! Did you not see her stiffen when you simply entered the room? Did you not see her flinch? You didn't even listen to what she had to say!" Her voice kept rising and rising and with his heightened hearing, he could hear her pulse quicken.

"There was no need."

"No need? Three of our own are on that list! It's likely one of them is the killer!"

"It's also just as likely that the killer is one of the Roamers."

"It's a possibility, but it would have made her job easier if she cleared those names first instead of always having the lurking thought that it could still be one of our own. Thoughts hinder investigations! And what if it is one of them? Hmm? She could nip it in the bud just like that," she finished snapping her fingers for emphasis.

"I will handle them," he exclaimed losing his temper and shoving her away from him. After a few deep breaths, he stared at her blankly. "Happy?"

Nivette stared at him disgusted. "No. What happened to you? You are practically giving your sister to the dogs! You know the Kings Garrison does not like her. They will find any little excuse to kill her. I thought you cared about her?"

Eris glared at her, baring his teeth. "Never question my love for her."

"Then don't put it into question." Nivette stalked from the room. Eris slammed the door behind her. He leaned forward on them, breathing heavily. He muttered a few words, sealing the doors with magic.

"Shira, I need you to do something?"

Shira materialized, leaning against the wall. "I thought I was supposed to find Jason?"

"I'll do that. No, what I want is for you to find one of these Roamers. Just one, preferably a male."

"Why? Oh my, you're going to frame him aren't you?"

"In time, just watch him when you find him and learn his routine."

"That will take some time Eris. Can you hold out that long?"

"I don't intend to Shira."

Shira studied him for a second. "Very well." She turned away, her body already slinking back into the shadows. "One more time Eris. Are you finally happy?"

Despite himself, his lips curled into a sliver of a smile.

"Ecstatic."

Twenty Two

J ason woke to the tapping at his window. Groggily, he stumbled from his bed and with a yawn, let int he cold air alongside a slender, lithe beauty of the dark. Selene crept in and closed the window behind her, shutting out the cold.

"Do you have any idea of what time it is?" he yawned.

"Near dawn."

"Exactly," he said yawning again. "I'm a Touched Born, not a Reborn or Vampyre. I need to sleep during the night."

"And I need a place to stay during the day."

"I haven't seen you for days Selene and why can't you just go back to the cave?"

"Because my brother has ordered me to go on full alert and find some Roamers."

"What are Roamers?"

"Vampyres with no home, no jurisdiction. It's a new thing for the better part of this century, particularly since the invention of Fairy Dust."

"Why since then?"

"Well, you see what it does to Witches, you don't want to see what it does to Vampyres. It has been a subject of disagreement among our kind. Outlawed to some degree for a reason."

"You use it."

"Properly, and for magical purposes only. The Roamers, they tend to use it the same way to blend back into society. Technically speaking, it is against the law but The King allows it for the time being. Fairy Dust is a complicated matter, the Kings Council is still trying to find ways to properly dealing with it."

Jason yawned again and made his way back to his bed, catching the time on his clock. As he collapsed on his bed he heard Selene open the floor she had hid her bag under. His body sat forward, against his will.

"What are you doing?"

"Getting my Fairy Dust."

"Why?"

"I'm going to bind it to your windows."

"Again," he said yawning, "why?"

"You're leaving in the morning," she said, not answering his question.

"Not before the sun rises. Now, again why do you need that?"

"The sunlight. When it shines in, if this is not bound to it, I will have to tip toe around your house. I don't have that much resilience to the sun."

"You're going to snoop through my stuff aren't you."

"If I get bored."

"Ugh." Jason slumped back onto his bed. "Wake me up in

six hours."

"Will do."

Jason smiled and closed his eyes, fading back into a deep slumber.

***

Someone was poking his chest, he swatted at the nails that seemed to pierce his skin. They didn't hurt him, they were just annoying. Jason swatted at them again, until the hand caught his wrist.

"Wake up already Jason, you have class." His eyes jerked open and kneeling beside him on his bed, holding his wrist, firmly, wearing nothing but her undergarments. Jason jumped out of bed, trying to avert his gaze.

"Selene! Wh—why aren't you dressed?"

"Because I just got out of the shower." He peeked at her, from the corner of his eye and saw her pink lips curl into a smile. It was beautiful, the way it curved on her face, fitting in perfectly, the little dimples on her cheek, highlighting her delicate cheekbones. It was just like the smile she had in the portrait. Still standing there, speechless, he watched her shake her head, let out a small laugh while she quickly snatched up one of his shirts from off his oak wood floors, and slipped it on. It was his favorite blue plaid flannel. "Better?"

"Yes, much better." Jason rubbed his forehead and sniffed the air. "Did you cook?"

"Yes. Sausage, eggs and a cup of Burberry Juice. My mother always told me breakfast was important, no matter how late I wake up. I was scolded if I didn't eat something." Jason watched her tuck a stray stand of black hair behind her hair. Her pale long nail grazed her upper cheek, as she smiled slightly.

"Different times Selene," he said taking in her appearance.

Her long black hair was still shiny with sheen from her bath and her legs tucked beneath her.

"Breakfast is still important." She gave him that mesmerizing smile once again as she hopped of his bed and headed to the kitchen. Her emotions left him with whiplash. Still, following her with his gaze, he smiled and followed her. There were two plates, from his plain white set, set on his mocha colored dining table, and filled with his favorite foods. Selene poured him a glass of his favorite drink. His stomach growled at the sight of the food. As he stuffed his face, he was very much aware that she was staring at him as she ate.

"What's going on? With the hunt I mean," he said wiping his chin as some juice dripped down it. Selene swallowed her food and crossed her legs. The bottom of his shirt slipped up her leg showing off her firm thighs. Looking back at her face, he noticed her change. Another whiplash. Her posture had stiffened and her face had grown somber.

"No where. There haven't been any more murders but there are seven Vampyres, known in the Darkling District, that buy Fairy Dust." She took another bite of her food. "Three happen to be in my coven, but my brother would rather I waste my time searching for the Roamers."

"Why won't he let you investigate your coven members?"

Selene shrugged. "I don't know. As of late, he's changed. I don't know what it is but, it's like he's finally snapped."

Jason took another bite from his food and looked into her eyes. "Are you scared?"

"My brother can kill Shadowlings...so yes, I'm very scared."

"I thought Shadowlings couldn't die."

Her smile returned and her posture loosened. "Eris is a very special Touched Born."

"What can he do," he said with his mouth full.

"Ha can manipulate shadows."

"Whoa."

"I know it's pretty cool. Back when we were kids he would make the shadows in my room dance. I always loved it." Her tome was warm, she looked alive, her eyes stared down but she was somewhere else.

"He always watched over you didn't he."

"Actually it was the other way around. I would look after him, keep an eye and make sure that he didn't get into too much trouble. Eris never quite found the balance between being protective and being controlling."

"Which is he now," he asked cautiously, already knowing the answer.

"Controlling. He doesn't even care if the Kings Garrison comes here."

"Why do you?"

Selene scoffed at him. "We're not on the best of terms to say the least." She finished off the rest of her food and set her dished in his stainless steel sink. Jason was about to say something when his ConEx rang, a flute melody filled the air. He knew it could only be one person.

"Hey Miranda."

"Hi...Jason, you aren't busy are you?"

"No, I just finished breakfast, why?"

"Because we need to talk...about us Jason."

Jason got up and left the room, settling in his bedroom. "Miranda I care about. Hell, I might even love you, but you abuse your gift. I am entitled to my privacy, to my own thoughts. You need to learn to shut up your damn gift and stop invading people's privacy. You're driving a wedge between everyone, including me."

It was quite a while until she finally answered him. "You're right, I know that, but—"

"No, no buts, you need to at least try. For us, and I will try to be more open, but on my own terms Miranda, not yours." Silence greeted him from the other end of the ConEx.

"Yeah, okay. First period was canceled by the way, so you can stay home a little longer. Love you, see you later."

"Love you too," he mumbled, hanging up. He hung his head down confused. Miranda was exhausting. He looked up as the door opened. Jason looked up at Selene who was leaning on the door frame, her arms crossed. Jason blushed again; he hadn't noticed how long her legs were. Not in those black pants and boots she always wore. He swallowed.

"Is everything okay?"'

"It's nothing. Miranda and I are just having problems."

"I don't like her, she thinks to highly of her bloodline."

"She doesn't believe they were that bad."

"They were. The four of them should have been killed long before I did the deed."

Jason stood up and leaned against the wall. She turned her head towards him. He noticed her eyes, so purple, so wide and full of pain. They made her look even more beautiful.

"Shouldn't you be going to bed?"

Selene shrugged. "Maybe but I'm not tired."

"Well I've got a free hour."

"I heard."

Jason smiled. "There's a thing called privacy you know."

"I'm well aware," she said smiling. They stood here for awhile. Jason wanted to kiss her. "Selene I—" Jason was interrupted by a knock at the door. He scrunched up his eyes in confusion until his eyes fell on his calendar on the circled date.

"Jason?"

"My dad!" Jason fumbled though his stuff, throwing on a shirt with a blue stain and a pair of pants that also needed to be desperately washed. When he looked back at Selene she was in the butterfly dress she had worn the day she passed out.

"Your dad was in the Council correct?" Jason read her thoughts, his eyes widened.

"Oh no, no, no, no. My dad will freak!"

He watched her smiled and take a step into the hallway. "Not if he was one of ones who enjoyed my company." She vanished and Jason ran, forgetting to buckle his pants. She winked at him before swinging the door open.

"Selene?"

"Uriel?"

Jason was confused. His dad, whom he knew as Michael, was hugging Selene. His dad knew Selene.

"Um, Selene, can you close the door." Both separated, forgetting their surroundings and he watched his father enter the apartment. Jason watched as his father leaned in to kiss Selene on the cheek. She plucked a feather from his wings.

"Your wings have changed color."

"It happens Selene."

"They're teal."

"I know." Jason saw them exchange a look. All the joy in their reunion vanished, replaced by sadness.

"Hi dad." Jason made his way to his Reborn father, embracing him.

"Jason...buckle your pants son." Jason blushed, buckling his pants while Selene laughed. It was a beautifully soft yet loud sound. He saw his dad give him a scowling look.

"Dad, what is it?"

"Why didn't you tell me you ended things with Miranda?"

"Because we haven't, why would you think I did?"

"Selene?" His dad's voice was commanding and angry. Jason read his dad's thoughts.

"Dad! I'm not having an affair with Selene. We're friends, just friends. She—"

"I was out hunting," interrupted Selene, stepping up to his side. "Thought seeking actually. And think of my surprise when I can't steal my prey's thoughts. Then I looked at him."

Uriel sighed and sat down on the kitchen table. "Yes, I noticed. Oh how I hoped history would not repeat."

"You and I both," said Selene and Jason in unison. Jason smiled at her, and took a seat next to his father. Selene did the same sitting across from him, on his fathers' right.

"Oh dear." Jason heard his dad sigh. "Selene what are you doing here?"

"I needed a place to stay during the day. At night I'm hunting down four Roamers."

"You're breaking your laws by being here. A law created because of Katherine."

Her eyes flared, briefly turning read. "I don't regret what I did," she growled.

"Nor should you, but should anyone find out—"

"I know Uriel. Trust me, I know. Speaking of Katherine, Jason's dear Miranda looks just like her. Identical in fact." Jason didn't know if he should be pleased that she was jealous. It felt...well maybe wrong wasn't the right word because it made him feel great. He wished she hadn't said that to his father though, no matter how true.

"Jason! Is that true?" Jason winced at the fear in his fathers' voice and fear.

"Uh, yeah, I guess."

"This isn't good."

"Why?" asked Jason.

Uriel sighed. "I'll talk to you about it later but forgive me when I say I wished you had broken up with her."

"Dad, not now okay." A part of him was already thinking the same thing. A part of him had wanted to kiss Selene.

"New topic!" chirped Selene, clapping her hands. "Uriel, why are you in town?" Jason smiled at her once again. Her posture, her smiled, both different from months before. She was like a different person.

"I'm in town per Council orders, to see about the latest graduating class of the Enforcers and Guard Academy."

"Such a militant."

"Dads the best fighter around."

"Not the best son."

"But even the Queen says there is no one to beat you yet, since the beginning."

"Well I'm highly offended! Has Naavah truly forgotten about me?"

Jason stared at Selene, mouth agape, while his father laughed aloud, wholeheartedly. "You beat my dad?"

"As a Witch too," she winked. "Best fighter around."

"She really is," continued his father. "Son, never get on her bad side."

"Kind of already figured that out dad."

"Oh boy, Selene, what did you do?"

"Uriel! I'm hurt, how could you think I did anything." Jason laughed at her pained acting. His dad accompanied him. Selene smiled at them, rolling her eyes all the same. Jason grabbed his ConEx home line and sent out an order to be delivered, all the while watched the change in Selene continue. It was as though she had been a flower that had wilted in the darkness, but now, something has shined a light on her and she was blooming. Blooming beautifully.

Twenty Three

Selene laughed, glad to know that Uriel was okay, glad to hear his voice. Her own happiness began to vanish when white light covered her vision, and the lightheadedness came, bringing the dark urge with it. Rubbing her temples, she focused on her breathing as she tried to suppress it.

"Selene," she heard Jason say, the confusion mixed with concern.

"It's the Blood Hunger," said Uriel.

"Selene, when was the last time you had any blood?"

"It's been a while," she said, fear constricting her lungs.

"Jason," began Uriel, "do you have any bags from the medical center in house?"

"N—no."

"You need to run down there and snatch a bag now. I'll stay here and help." Selene's eyes widened. She didn't have to be a mind reader to know what he was thinking.

"Dad—"

"Go!" Uriel's voice bombarded against the light blue walls of the kitchen. She saw Jason shoot her a concerned look as he grabbed his keys and ran out the door.

"Uriel, you don't have to—"

"Oh shut up Selene. You know, you don't have to carry the weight of the world on your shoulders and you don't always know what's best, especially for yourself." Uriel handed over his bare wrist. "Take enough until Jason returns." Selene tried to pout or laugh at his stern face, but could not. That left her with no other choice other than to bite down into his wrist. The sweet and salty warm blood filled her mouth. Immediately the dizziness began to recede. When it was nothing more than a tickle in the back of her head she stopped. Licking her lips, she wiped up the blood that painted them red before grabbing the washcloth that hung on the cupboard door behind them. Selene placed it on his wrist, tying it up tight enough to cause pressure. She offered him a thankful smile.

"Why are you here Selene?"

"I needed a place to stay."

"You could have stayed with some Dark Witches."

"I despise Darklings, they sicken me."

"He is not Pietro."

"I know that Uriel. He's Jason, a completely, different and better person."

"Why didn't you visit us against after Pietro passed?"

"How could I face you after what I had done?"

"We understood Selene, we are the reason you are still alive, the entire council vouched for you! All of them. We understood."

"Fine then. I was angry at you." She bit the inside of her

mouth, angry for admitting the truth.

"Why?"

"Because I wanted to die."

"You don't mean that."

"You didn't see his body." Turning away from his gaze, she inspected his wound, trying to focus her thoughts on something else just so that she didn't need to remember the horrific image. "You're bleeding out. I bit too hard. Apply pressure while I get something to help." Selene handed him his wrist, running off to grab her duffel bag, pulling out one of her smaller versions of Fairy Dust. She ran back to the kitchen, grabbed a small diamond and crushed it on the table with ease. Sprinkling some Fairy Dust over the crushed diamond, she bit her wrist to mix in some of her own blood. She twirled her finger in the mess she had made, mixing it together then traced a healing rune on his wrist. Uriel's wound healed up instantly.

"Selene?" muttered Uriel, pulling his wrist back.

"Yes?"

"Did you really mean that?"

Selene looked at him calmly, corking up her vial. "Yes."

"How did Eris feel about that?"

"He wasn't pleased. But you already know that Uriel." Selene averted her gaze while she twirled the little vial in her hand.

"How is Eris anyway? Still carefree?"

Steadily, Selene tried to look at him, but she could not force her eyes to face him. "No. He's different."

"How," he asked, pausing to study her face. "Selene, what's wrong?"

"He's different Uriel," she said, in a firmer tone. "And it's so sudden. He yells and demands everything. It's his word and nothing else. He's become controlling, vindictive, cruel. I flinch I try not to. I'm scared and I don't want to be. I fear for my life." Her voice dropped down to a whisper.

"Does he know about Jason or are you putting my sons' life in danger?"

"Uriel, Jason's life was put into danger the day he was born."

"What are you going to do?"

Selene shrugged, sitting down to lean her head on the table. "Not much I can do except hide and keep him secret. I've tried to end whatever this is but your son doesn't handle rejection well apparently."

"It's obvious why Selene, the real question is do you feel the same?"

"I—I don't know. I'm so confused. After Pietro died I dedicated so many centuries to not feeling anything and then I met him and slowly, it's been coming back. At first, I thought I had Pietro back, but I did not because Jason, he's as different as he can be! He's not obnoxious or arrogant or invasive. Jason," Selene paused to sigh, "he's just Jason. All I know is that I want to be a part of his life."

"I pray you figure it out soon. You deserve another chance."

"Maybe. You know Miranda wants to kill me, for what I did centuries ago. She reminds me too much of Katherine. Selfish and vile."

"Let's hope history does not repeat then."

"Yes," she began more to herself than to him, sitting up in her chair. "Let's pray."

The front door opened and Selene watched Jason run into the kitchen.

"Sorry, traffic was a pain." He sat down and handed her two bags filled with blood. Selene smiled at him graciously.

"Thank you Jason." Selene watched him return her smile.

Uriel coughed and stood up.

"I need to get to the Academy. Selene, please visit sometime. We all miss you. Urit included."

"Tell her I said hello and that I'll try to visit soon."

"Very well. Jason shouldn't you be headed to school?"

"Right, um, let me grab my bag. Selene you'll be all right on your own right?"

"I'm a Vampyre, being on my own is sort of the lifestyle." Smiling at him, she let him go easily. Uriel looked at her briefly before closing the door behind them, a discernible look across his heavenly face.

The lock clicked and Selene was left alone to her own dark thoughts. She stood there a moment, her hand on her chest, thinking of Jason. Falling to the floor in exhaustion, she merely wished she wasn't so confused about him.

Twenty Four

Cecilia stood with Nicholas, hiding away from Miranda. Cecilia looked at Nicholas, half wishing he would grow up and stop checking out the girls who passed by. Then again, it was one of the reasons she was unfathomably attracted to him.

"Would you stop for one minute."

"Oh what's wrong Cecilia," he said smiling at her charmingly. "Jealous?"

"In your dreams."

"Don't mind if I do. One question though, does that include envisioning you naked?"

"You're such a pig." Cecilia smiled despite herself.

"Eh," he began shrugging, "I don't care. So, what's up, why are we hiding all the way over here?"

"I'm hiding because Jason asked me to, he said he needed to speak to me privately, away from Miranda. You followed."

Nicholas snorted. "You know how much I hate her, she's so fr—"

"Intrusive?" suggested Cecilia.

"Well aren't you nice, but no, that is not what I was thinking."

"Be nice."

"I'd rather not. I don't like her, she's just, I don't know, something is just off about her ya know. I can't believe Jason doesn't see it."

"He's is beginning to."

"Only because he's fallen in love with Anita."

Cecilia let out a bitter laugh. "Try telling him that."

"I will, even if I need to beat it into him." Cecilia wished he was joking but he wasn't. Nicholas tended to resort to violence far too often. "Hey, by any chance, since we're on the topic of Anita, did she, I don't know, look familiar to you?"

Cecilia's smile faltered and she tried to look confused. "No, why?"

"I don't know. Remember that portrait, the one of that Selene chick with that ancestor of Jason, Pietro? Well at dinner, she looked exactly like her. Like exactly the same. And they, Selene and her brother, they were the last of their line."

"What are you getting at?"

"You tell me Cecilia." Nicholas leaned over her, placing his hand on the brick wall above, his shadow blocking out the sun. "I know you know something."

"I haven't the faintest idea of hat you're talking about."

"Selene, Cecilia, I know you know that Anita is Selene. I'm not that thick headed."

"Yes you are."

"But I'm right aren't I." It wasn't a question. Of all the

moments to not be oblivious, why did it have to be this one.

"I can't say."

"Can't, or won't?"

"It's not my secret to tell Nicholas and I probably wouldn't bring it up with Jason, not while he's trying to figure stuff out."

"He loves her."

"Yes well let's hope he figures it out soon before things with Miranda get complicated."

"They're already complicated," came a voice. Cecilia turned and saw Jason. Exhaustion covered his face.

"Jason, hey."

"My man, break up with Miranda." Cecilia elbowed Nicholas in his stomach. She watched Jason make a pathetic attempt to smile.

"What's wrong Jason?"

He shrugged. "Same old. She called while I was with Anita. We talked and—I don't know anymore."

"Oh Jason."

"What she means is you're an idiot and that's it's not that complicated, all you need to do is break up with Miranda."

"You act like it's that simple."

Nicholas opened his mouth but Cecilia answered first. "What he's going to say is that it is simple. Besides you should end things soon, before she gets hurts."

"Don't you think I know that! But I can't, not yet anyway. My dad came by to visit and just told me some disturbing news."

"What news?"

"My mother called Miranda's mother and invited her entire family for the Silmarine Solstice."

"The entire family?" squeaked Cecilia. Jason nodded. "I'm

so sorry Jason."

"This is just not your day man."

"What's that suppose to mean?" Cecilia shook her head when she saw Jason glare at her. Nicholas burst out laughing.

"I knew it!"

"Cecilia?" growled Jason.

"I said nothing. He remembered the portrait. She's a girl, he remembers what girls look like."

Jason groaned. "Great."

"Oh this is awesome. You've fallen for the same girl your ancestor did. The same girl! And to make matters worse you're dating the descendant of the girl who murdered him!"

"Nicholas, shut up!" chastised Cecilia. She saw Jason turn pale. "Jason? Are you all right?"

"I—I gotta go." Jason ran off, dumping his bag into the ground. Cecilia called after him, ignoring the stares of his fellow classmates. She went over and grabbed his bag. It was slightly open. Cecilia opened the bag and saw a letter from his mother.

"Cecilia, are you doing what I think you're doing?"

"Oh hush." She pulled out the letter and zipped up the bag, tossing it at Nicholas. She began to read. "It's a letter from his mother and—" Cecilia clasped her hand over her mouth. "Oh my heavens."

"Cecilia, what's wrong?"

"His mother says 'Jason dear, it's been four years, why haven't you proposed to that darling girl you talk so highly of. I invited her family over for the Solstice. You have until then to propose to her. I know I sound like a pain, I understand that, but you talk so highly of her in your letters and her parents say she loves you so much. But they are concerned that you are just stringing her along. I love you my son and I can't wait to meet the darling girl. Lots of love, your mother." Cecilia looked up at Nicholas frightened.

"I really should think huh?"

"That suggests you actually can think." Cecilia walked off, followed closely by Nicholas.

"Where are we going?"

"To find Ettore and do some research."

"Oh yay." Cecilia rolled her eyes; she couldn't care less about how he was feeling at the moment. She just needed to figure out a way to help her friend before things took a horrible turn.

Twenty Five

Negal called for a meeting with the First Born's. The table had two empty seats that made her heart ache. Her brother and her husband. Both were gone and they weren't coming back. She looked around at her companions. Vega, as always was calm and resolute, filled with so much sadness for the life she lived. Her brother Void, was as stoic looking as ever. Sometimes Negal worried about him. Evida and Ettore sat together, back to back, always at odds.

And then she came, Shira, taking the seat opposite of herself. Her long black hair was loosely braided, exposing her bruised neck. Her eyes glowed a bright red and were coupled with a curled smile that betrayed the thoughts circling within her mind. Negal knew. She saw the victorious malevolence in her eyes, she knew they were tied to those bite marks on her neck. Negal's fears were beginning to pass.

"I called this meeting to swear a pact. What we discuss

today does not leave this room. Not now, not ever." Negal placed one of her shadow blades on the table, everyone followed suit, even Shira. "Repeat. By those of darkness, our mother and father, by the shadows of my being, I bind myself to this pact to never divulge what goes on today for the punishment is death by Their holy fire." The shadows of her blade flickered and sought out the others. As everyone else repeated the pact, their shadows attached to hers. Even Shira repeated the oath without hesitation.

"By our shadows I bind us." The shadows attached to one another, growing, glowing with a dark purple light, weaving together into an intricate web. The web, as if alive, imprinted onto each of the blades before winking out of existence.

"A Touched Born has been Reborn but he does not know it," she said sheathing her blade, crossing her arms.

"Like him?" asked Evida.

"Yes, but different. He is an abnormality. His birth in the beginning was brought upon by those of Darkness, now it is one of Light."

"Why?" asked Shira hotly.

"For love Shira. This one is named Jason, we knew him as Pietro, the beloved of Selene Sintas, Eris's sister."

"What concern is this?" asked Evida. "He is Reborn, so what?" Evida's eyes were blank as usual, there was no emotion within her.

"Eris cannot find out." Negal eyes Shira who stared back at her defiantly. "Nor can he be allowed to find him. Those of the Dark are trying to repeat history. I cannot allow it."

"Why not?" demanded Shira.

"Because Selene is more deserving of love than you."

"He belongs here, with us! We are his blood, his kin!"

Negal slammed her hand against the table, rattling the room, shutting up the defiant Shira. "And innocent lives have been caught in the crossfire. I will not allow it to happen again."

"You sicken me."

"And you sicken me. I want Jason protected and Eris watched. I do not want him falling back into darkness anymore than he already has. This meeting is over."

Shira watched Negal vanish. She saw Vega and Ettore share a look before vanishing together. Only Evida and Void were left.

"Leave me out of whatever you are planning Shira," Void stood up, looking at her steadily.

"Whatever do you mean?"

"I mean I won't choose sides. I want to be left out of it. So say nothing to me. I'd rather not know whatever you're planning." He left without another word, turning his back on them. Shira looked at Evida who looked unsettled and confused as she stood. This was the most emotion she had shown in centuries.

"What are you planning and why? It's over and done with Shira. There is no getting Nuri back."

"You don't know that for sure. Besides, he's slowly slipping towards the darkness already, this meeting confirms it. Her fears, Negal's fears, they are coming into play." Her voice was wild, frantic, captured within a whisper.

"She'll never trust you."

"No, but she might trust you."

Like a bird with a blank stare, she cocked her head. "Explain."

"I'm going to divulge everything to you and you are going to tell Negal all of it. Then you are going to 'spy' on me and we are going to help Eris with everything."

What if she doesn't believe me?"

"She will. She's too desperate not to. The darling girl is still broken from my brothers' death."

"Why aren't you?"

"Because that was Eris' first step to darkness and my brothers only chance at peace. Now go!" Evida dissolved into her surroundings leaving Shira alone with her thoughts.

Her memories began to swarm her thoughts and suddenly she was back in her room with her brother. They were fighting, or at least she was fighting him. Eris had just been turned.

"Senid! Will you listen to reason? You don't have to fight him!"

"He's coming for me, so yes, I do."

"He can kill you! Besides, he's a Vampyre, he's already partly in the dark—"

"His soul is not Shira." His voice had been calm, resolute. Senid turned his back to her and began to leave. But no, she wouldn't let him go, not like this, in such a calm fashion.

"No!" she exclaimed, grabbing onto his arm. "Senid don't! You might kill him! He might kill you. Please! You're my brother, I can't risk you too!"

"Shira," he began cupping her face. "I won't kill him. I wanted to, I've thought about it so many times over the centuries. When I killed his father, I wanted to kill him. I've hated him for the longest time and it wasn't because he left us. It was because he gets to live in silence, in peace. Most of all, he gets to die." Senid sighed, his black eyes expressing his sadness. "I'm tired. I'm tired of hating him, I'm tired of living. And I'm sick and tired of the goddess's whispers in my head. I'm going to let him kill me. That will be his first true step into darkness."

"Senid," she whimpered, tears falling down her cheeks.

"Shh. You'll regain him, of that I am sure." He bend his head down to her, touching his forehead to hers. "They will whisper to you Shira, and you will pick up where I leave off."

"Please brother, don't."

Senid kissed her forehead and hugged and hugged her tightly. "Forever sister." He left her standing there. That was the last time she saw him.

Shira opened her eyes and wiped away the tears that had fallen down her cheeks. She pulled out her brothers' blade from her boot and fingered it gently. The shadows flickered on the blade, recognizing her presence. "I miss you too Senid."

***

Negal watched Evida enter her room with a bow. "Haven't you heard of knocking?"

"Forgive me Negal, but I think there is something you should know."

"What?"

"Shira, she is helping Eris. He's—he's been having her kill those humans that are on the news. He's already searching for Jason and they have begun having an affair. I—I do not like this. Shira lives too long in the past. Eris does not know yet of Selene's friendship with him and I fear Shira may find a loophole in our pact. That mother will let her destroy every-thing. I fear she may be obsessed. I do not like this and I know Ettore and Vega are keeping an eye on Jason and I would like to request that I join Shira, watch her and Eris and report—"

"Done." Negal's long black nails dug into the arms of her chair. "Go, now. I want to know everything."

Evida bowed. "Of course Negal." Evida left the room,

seeping out the cracks of the door, and feeling pleased with herself. Shira was waiting for her in her room, staring at her with her coal black eyes.

"Well?"

"It worked. Now what?"

Shira smiled. "Now we go see Eris."

Twenty Six

Eris searched through the shadow realm for new prey. This would be his third victim. He knew it was daylight, which would make this attack a risky one. It would, however, catch his sister off guard. Thinking about his sister made him realize that something was off about her. He couldn't understand why she would fear him. He loved her. She was Selene, his little sister who had always looked up to him and would look after him. Those had been the last words she had ever spoken with their father. Her birth father, not his. His was dead.

Selene meant more to him than anything and he would tell her, he would explain everything to her once he found Jason and found out once and for all if he was born of Light or Shadows. She would understand, and she would go back to being the endearing little sister she always had been. Wouldn't she? The question ate away at him, giving him cause to worry.

If he found out that Jason was born of darkness, he would kill him and hide it from her. He would not let another pair eyes of lifeless teal eyes look up at her.

Eris hated those of the dark, now more than ever. Pietro wasn't suppose to exist, Eris had always known that since the moment he saw him, staring at Selene. The immediate attraction had felt wrong. Pietro had felt out of place and Eris had wanted him to stay out of their lives. Instead, he had pursued her and she had fallen madly in love. It hadn't truly been Pietro's fault, he knew that. Pietro was just a pawn used by those of the dark. A pawn used...but for what? He still didn't know. It was the not knowing that bothered him the most. What also bothered him was that Jason was alive. It felt wrong. No, wrong was not the right word. Jason's presence felt...different. Yes, that is it. Different. The distinction of the two did not ease his nerves. Were the gods further tormenting her or giving her one more chance? He hated the Gods. There were using Eris, Selene and possibly Jason as pawns against each other.

Eris started walking again and thought about Negal. As always he knew that she knew more than she was telling him. He knew that trusting her was a thing of the past. The look in her eye, long ago when he had first inquired about Jason confirmed that. She knew who Jason was, knew whether he was of light or dark. She knew and was not divulging anything. Why? Did he truly see him differently? Maybe he was different but he was doing what he thought was best for Selene. Selene was his priority. His sister who seemed so scared of him. Maybe he was being to rash when he talked to her and acted the way he did. He was just so damn worried and frightened for her. In the end, she had to understand, she just had to.

A scent caught his attention, he looked at the prey. A lovely girl was leaving the Darkling District. He licked his lips and looked down the alleyway through the shadows. No one was around. Eris seeped from the brick and stonewalls that lined the alleyway and wrapped one hand around her mouth while he wrapped the other around her waist. The girl kicked and fought, making him want to laugh. But what good would that possibly do. She was scared, and rightfully so. He pitied the poor girl, half wishing that he could only harm her and not kill her. But sadly, there was a need for collateral damage.

"Shh, don't worry, your death is for a deserving cause." He saw her green eyes will up with tears and she continued to struggle and whimper as his fangs sunk deeply into her neck. It took time, but her whimpering began to cease and the tears stopped falling down her cheeks as her eyes shut. Her head fell limp and her blond hair covered her face. Finally done, Eris laid her down on the cobblestone ground gently, licking his lips. She almost looked like she was sleeping.

Staring down at her, Eris's eyes were drawn to her big black purse. He looked back at the doorway to the Darkling District. For some reason, he didn't want anyone to know that she had been there. Grabbing her purse he pulled out the black candles, the syringes, and the Fairy Dust. He looked back at her saddened and pulled her blond hair out of her face, realizing what she had been about to do. If only Pietro had never been brought into the picture, none of this would be happening. Except Pietro was not the only problem, the dagger was too, Nuri's shadow. That dagger that had almost poisoned her. The dagger that had made her immune to the darkness and shadows. Her weapon of choice that was tightly bound to her leg like a garter. She knew what it did. Selene knew that if left to long in a body it stopped poisoning. Instead it took over the host.

Looking back at the girl, he stroked her face. She was beautiful. Damn you Pietro, he thought, it was his fault Eris was doing these extreme. The poor girl was now another body count, although looking at her bag, she would have been anyway. Now he only needed one more body and the Garrison would arrive.

"Hello Eris." Eris turned around, confused by the sight of Evida next to Shira. She eyed his respectfully, unnerving him with her almost empty eyes.

"Yes?"

"We're here to help."

"Her included?" He tilted his head towards Evida. She still creeped him out like she did thousands of years ago. He can still remember her flinging his sister into the darkness, still watch her red eyes glowing as she stepped from the dark hall.

"Yes."

"Good. Alert the Enforcers and media and I'll be at the cave." Eris looked at Evida once more. Something about her bothered him. He wondered if he could truly trust her.

"Don't dawdle," said Eris looking away from them both as he sunk back into the shadows. Once again he asked himself the same question he did everyday: was he doing to right thing?

Twenty Seven

Selene jolted awake when she heard the door slam. She quickly grabbed her dagger and lowered the volume on the ResoScreen; she could care less about the news right now. Selene tilted her head up, sniffing the air before taking a calming breath. When the bedroom door opened, she offered Jason a confused look. His face was constricted, strained, and flushed, as though he ran all the way back home.

"Jason? What's wrong?"

"Honestly, I don't have a freaking clue. You know, everything was fine, absolutely fine, until you came into my life. And that was one of the best things ever. I mean, I see things—people—differently. I open my eyes. Shadowlings and Vampyres, they aren't evil. I mean some are evil, but some are good and I—okay I'm getting off base but look, I don't know how I feel about you and I don't how you feel about me, so don't kill me for this." Selene's eyes widened when his lips met hers. It was different that she imagined it. Wait, when did I imagine this? Her eyes fluttered shut and she found her arms wrapping around his neck on their own accord. Kissing him felt more right than any kiss she had shared with Pietro. Jason felt more right. Even now she didn't know how she felt. What was she doing? Her emotions were taking over and she felt that surge of power. Her runes were burning. Selene jerked her eyes open and pulled herself away from him

"You—I." Selene suddenly felt very lightheaded. "I don't know." Her knees buckled and she fell forward, into Jason's arms. Selene didn't pass out this time and distantly heard his voice. She was too distracted with why she was glowing.

"Selene I—"

"No, don't say anything. Jason I'm not sure how I feel about you. I mean I wish I did but I still think of Pietro and you're with Miranda and I—I just don't know."

"I know. I'm sorry. Look, I don't know either, I just, I hoped it would...I don't know, clear things up but—"

"Shut up already," she said smiling. He smiled back at her, still holding her close. Selene stared up at him, staring at his face, her eyes lingering on his lips thinking of kissing him again. That was until she heard the broadcast.

"This just in. The body of a young girl was found at Number Three East Darkling District Entrance. There were bite marks on her neck and it has been determined that she was snatched, dragged into the alleyway and drained of blood. The Enforcers feel confident in saying that it is the same Vampyre responsible for recent attacks on the community and they ensure us that they are working with the Hunters to try and find the Vampyre responsible." Selene, still leaning on Jason, stared out the window at the bright and sunny day.

"I need to go."

"You can't, it's too bright out, you'll only be able to withstand the sun for maybe twenty minutes."

"Probably less, but I have to get to the crime scene while it's fresh." Selene gathered her strength and stepped away from him, giving him a reassuring smile. "I'll be quick, I promise." She kissed his cheek without thinking and grabbed her blue corset and black pants from her bag.

***

Selene went through the Darkling District. When she reached the Third East Exit she was glad to note that the rest of the Hunters were already at the crime scene. The Enforcers had put up a magical shade to protect them from the sun. They all offered her weak, frightful smiles. All except Jeanette who crossed her arms.

"There is no scent but somethings off. I can feel it in the air, and look at her, can you see it?"

Selene looked at the body and saw it instantly. Something was very wrong and very different. This girl had been handled with care. The girl had been laid onto the ground, not dropped down carelessly. Not even a strand of hair covered her face, which was odd considering how windy it was. The body was to fresh as well. Selene looked off to the side were a black purse lay, far away from the body.

"Was this bag here the entire time?" she asked going through the bag.

"Uh, yes," answered the Enforcer James.

"Thought as much. The bag has been messed with." Selene sniffed the bag. "I smell dark magic, fresh dark magic components."

"But there's none in there," said Blake taking the bag.

"Exactly. It seems our killer has a bit of a conscience. This wasn't an accident. He meant to kill her but look around, it looks like he felt bad about it, bad enough to rid the dark materials she would have been found with. Whoever this Vampyre is, they care about these people, to some degree." Selene placed her hands on her hip and looked around, analyzing the crime scene.

"Why the change," asked Eno stepping forward. "This type of emotion, it's not rational."

"Whatever the reasons, they are testing my patience. I've no desire for the Garrison to arrive. Contact the city council, talk to the City Guards and Enforcers. We need a Dimmer."

"Isn't that a little drastic," said Eno.

"I want this person found and I want them found now."

"Very well," relented Eno, "we'll contact the Council and get the spell up and running. How long should be keep it up?"

"Until we find the murderer or until the Garrison arrives, whichever comes first."

"Very well." Eno bid farewell and descended into the Darkling District.

"Jeanette, Blake can one of you report this to Eris, I have no desire to see him at the moment."

"Eris will be upset," said Dimitri leaning on the wall. He eyed her curiously, a look that made her smile.

"Then let him. My patience is running thin and I don't feel like being debased and yelled at by he who is a child."

"Why do you put up with it," asked Jeanette.

Turning her back to her comrades and looking up past the spell that shielded her from the sun, she muttered, "because someone needs to keep an eye on him and I promised our father I would." Selene called James over and handed him the bag. She didn't bother to mention the stink of Dark Magic. Whoever this Vampyre was, at least in one respect, they had the right intentions.

Twenty Eight

Jason sat in bed watching his ResoScreen. Classes had been postponed until the Dimmer was lifted. A Dimmer put everyone on high alert. It only happened when an entire Coven was called into the city which meant that there was a serious murderer on the loose. It also put businesses and people on a curfew. Five hours after the high moon rose, businesses were ordered to be closed and an hour after that, people were ordered to be home. By the time the first moon was at the skies horizon, only Military personnel were allowed on the streets.

"How can you not have any food," called a voice. Jason rolled his eyes and got out of bed in a feeble attempt to try and prevent Ettore from destroying his fridge.

"I forgot to go grocery shopping, besides, you're an Immortal Shadowling, you don't need food."

"Ah, how true, but I like to eat when I get bored."

"Selene said she would pick up some food and drop

by later, okay?"

"Not quick enough." Ettore closed the fridge door with a thud. "You realize her brother is on her tail thirty hours a day, nine days a week right? It's pretty hazardous for her.

"Well then, why can't either you or Vega pick up food?"

"We could but then who would keep an eye on you?"

"I think I'll be fine for half and hour."

"Hmm, maybe, but Eris has his own Shadowling friends. My sister being one of them. I still don't know how she tricked Negal, but go figure." Ettore shrugged, crossing his arms and leaning against the silver kitchen sink counter.

"Well the Oath binds them so I should be safe, right?"

"We're not taking that risk, which is why Vega is busying herself by watching your friends. Shira is a slippery one."

"Oh yay," he muttered sarcastically. He made his way back to his bedroom when knocking on his door stopped him. Jason exchanged a questionable look with Ettore when Vega appeared near the doorway smiling.

"It's your comrades. I would open the door."

"What?" Jason ran to his door, waving the lock open. Ettore and Vega stood together, their bodies already fading into the wall. "No, stay, I told them about you two."

"Oh dear," said Vega while Ettore laughed. Jason sighed and opened the door. Cecilia and Nicholas rushed in and just as quickly, Jason bolted the door shut.

"Hey Jason," said Cecilia a little out of breath.

"My man."

"How the heck did you guys even get here? We're under curfew!"

"Darkling District," said Cecilia matter-of-factly. "We snuck down there them came back up here. It was a pain but look," she exclaimed holding up his brown weather beaten bag. "We have your bag from the other day!"

Jason rolled his eyes, snatching his bag. "Really? My bag? Cecilia what's going on?"

"They've been out doing research," said Vega stepping into the hallway. Ettore joined her.

"Holy crap! A real Shadowling!" Nicholas laughed. "That Selene knows the coolest people. Nice to see you again man."

"Same here 'my man'." Ettore laughed. Cecilia chuckled along with him. Jason stared at them, annoyed.

"Cecilia," he said, his tone cold and firm. "What are you doing here?"

"Don't be mad, but we went through your bag and I found, and read, the letter your mom sent and so I did some research and I think I know how I can get you out of the whole proposal."

"Proposal?" questioned Ettore. The fear in his eyes made Jason's blood run cold.

"His mom is making him propose to Miranda," answered Nicholas.

"That is not good," muttered Vega, her black eyes wide.

"Tell me about it. Wouldn't want to be him right now."

"I'm right here Nicholas."

"Right, sorry my man."

Jason sighed and rubbed his temples, tired and annoyed. "Let's sit down." Jason headed to his living room. Vega took the seat next to Ettore. Cecilia sat next to him and pulled out a punch of papers, along with an old leather bound notebook.

"Okay, so I found out a lot. I did some research on Miranda's side of the family okay. Selene had every right to kill them, they were seriously unstable. Katherine's brother and nephew, they were already under investigation by the town's law enforcement. It's speculated that his wife was just another one of his victims, probably the first. He told officer that she left, but just like the many other women seen, they were only ever seen entering, never leaving. After Selene killed him, a royal Guard named Uriel did some investigating to prove her innocence. There were bodies of women under the house. All dead. He killed those woman with his son. That's what the official report says.

"How did you get that stuff?"

"My brother James is an Enforcer remember, I had him dig up these files and make a few calls." Cecilia swallowed and pulled out more files. "Anyway, my point is, that family, her family, was deranged and seriously unstable. Katherine's sister, she killed her husband, poisoned him. It was never proven though, but everyone knew it. All their marriages were arranged and it seemed that Christopher, Katherine's brother, well it seemed as though his wife knew, same goes for Katherine's sisters husband. It looked like she killed him over money because he left everything to his children and had it ordered that she could not have a cent. That woman abused her children. When Selene killed their mother, they personally asked to speak on her behalf at her hearing. They loved her. She was their savior. I mean, that woman did unspeakable things to them, her own children.

"Katherine was different though, she was only their half sister. Her father was a Reborn, she had the same gift Miranda does, and used it in the same way. She wasn't like her brother and sister, she had good in her, she cared about other people. Look, this is her diary." Cecilia held up the worn leather bound notebook. "She loved Pietro but he didn't love her and he constantly, painfully, made her aware of it. The only reason he had two children with her was because of his drunken stupors, that she welcomed because then he would actually want to touch her, actually welcome her into his bedchamber. Jealously made he kill him. Pietro broke her and used her. He was—"

"Intrusive, arrogant and obnoxious," finished Ettore. "Never understood why Selene loved him. He did treat her better than he did anyone else so that might explain it."

"In any case, he was quite cruel to her. It is awful, to murder him the way she did, but it was his own fault. It's his own fault why she stabbed his twenty-three times and slit his throat."

"Why are you telling me this?"

"Because you aren't Pietro, and you should not suffer his fate." Cecilia took his hands in hers. "Miranda loves you and despite her faults, she's a good person, you know this. If you love her, marry her but if you don't, if you have even the slightest feelings for Selene, you will end things with Miranda. You need to choose. You've only got a month—"

"Look," interrupted Jason. "I already kissed Selene to try and figure stuff out but it only complicated things."

"You kissed Selene?"

"Oh no," muttered Vega putting her hand to her mouth.

"Oh crap," said Ettore, who was now rubbing his temples.

"Jason, you only have until the Silmarine Solstice!"

"Thanks for the reminder," he snapped pulling his hands away from Cecilia.

"Don't break her heart or else she'll turn into Katherine and you'll suffer like Pietro and Selene will die because she cares about you and will get revenge. She has no more passes Jason."

"Yeah, I know," muttered Jason, he looked out the window at the steady rainfall tapping against his glass, obscuring the world outside.

One month.

Eris stood in the rain, on the clock tower ledge, and looked over his city. He had been born here, over two thousand years ago and had seen and watched, his little village flourish and bloom into the beautiful thriving city it was, equal to Nephilium and Seraphim. Even in darkness it was beautiful. Still, it made it hard for him to hunt for his prey. Now he was going to have to break into a house early. It made things a little tricky for him. But Eris needed the body to be found, and sooner rather than later. Crossing his arms over his soaking wet black t-shirt. A presence arrived at his side and he turned to look at Nivette. She regarded him differently that she used to.

"Yes."

"Gabrielle sent word."

He scrunched up his forehead making sure he heard her right. "The Kings' Garrison Gabrielle?"

"Yes. She wants to know how on top if this you are and who is leading the investigation." Her tone was cold, detached, mirroring the look in her azure eyes that seemed to glow with the growing red outline of her iris.

"Did you already reply."

"Yes. I said we had a Dimmer in place 30/9, and that you are in charge with Selene as your second."

"I am not in charge, Selene is leading the investigation.

Nivette let out a cold and harsh laugh. "You can't honestly believe that. Selene is following your orders. You haven't let her do anything the way she wants. Why do you think the other Hunters look at you with such disdain. Everyone tiptoes around you because they're scared darling." Eris winced at the revulsion that emanated from the tender word and stared, confused by the hatred in her now red eyes. Eris suddenly had the sinking feeling that she knew about Shira, about everything.

"Nivette I—"

"Save it. I'm not someone you need to apologize to."

"You are if you feel the same way."

"I feel many things, but fear is not one of them."

"Do you still love me?"

"That's a funny question coming from you," she said, eyebrows raised.

"Nivette, I love you."

Nivette chuckled. It was a bitter chuckle, masked with sadness and pain. "Sure." Eris could not handle it, he suddenly saw her standing outside a barrier, sad and angry. Erin lunged at her, cupped her face, pushing her black hair out of her face.

"Nivette, I do love you. Believe me."

Shaking her head, a sad smile on her pink lips, Nivette pulled away from him, eyes shifting back to their deep blue. "I wish I could believe that." Nivette stepped back on the clock tower edge, poised to jump off. "Don't expect me tonight, I'll be returning to my old bedchamber." Nivette stepped off and knowing her the way he did, she had landed with such feline grace. Eris clutched his fist tightly. They shook with such anger at himself.

"Eris?" Eris spun around and was faced with Evida. She had that same detached and empty look in her coal black eyes. Chills went down his spine.

"What is it?"

"Shira believes she has found one of the Roamers. She sent me to inform you that she will be keeping an eye on him."

"Good." Eris looked away from her, back towards the rain. Contemplating. He stared at the apartments across the way. "Come with me."

"Do you have a target?"

"We will in the morning. Right now, we are going to look for a woman who will be missed. Come." Eris slunk into the shadows alongside Evida, unaware of the laughter in the dark heavens that mocked her sisters' futility.

Eris watched a woman talk on her Con-Ex. A perfect prey, she was supposed to arrive to work early and have breakfast with her coworkers. Someone who appeared to always be on time and who worked at the corner market. It was almost too easy, too perfect. He could feel Evida's dark eyes burning holes into his back annoyingly. It was as though she was his watch dog. Unfortunately—or fortunately, he still couldn't decide which— had Selene for that.

His eyes watched for a moment, until the woman was at ease. She was watching her ResoScreen, keeping track on the ongoing news as she strapped on her watch. According to the news, flashing a picture of his beloved sister, the anchor reported that she was investigating. The woman pulled her eyes from the screen to walk quickly to the kitchen where she poured herself a glass of Rueberry wine. The dark and rich liquid sent his senses buzzing. He watched it slide down her throat with each gulp she touch, further enticed. The liquid always made the blood that much sweeter.

Eris watched the woman in her loose white blouse finish off her wine, leaving the glass on the kitchen counter before returning to her auburn shaded sofa, her eyes attached to the screen. A strand of hair fell over her face and, almost absent-mindedly, she tucked it behind her ear, sparing a brief glance at her watch.

Stepping from the shadows, he continued to watched her. On the far side of the room, in the corner of the blue painted living room there was a mirror, capturing his ever fading existence. The more the Blood Hunger rose, the less reflective image one had. A perk of hunting and also a warning to the Vampyre. It meant there was a risk of succumbing to the Hunger.

His tongue ran over his lips as he tasted the air and dug his fangs into her meaty flesh. She tried to fight him off, tried to scream, her arms flaying trying to push him off, her legs kicking the air, knocking back her coffee table sending candles and incense flying. All her efforts were in vain.

The red liquid that ran down her neck and his chin was tangy and sweet. The Rueberry aftertaste in it warmed his own blood. Eris loved it.

Staring at her body Eris served himself a glass of Rueberry and drank it down. Back across the room, he saw his reflection.

It was whole again and captured the blood on his chin and limp pale hand that hung over the sofa.

S elene stood over the body of the fourth victim, livid. She wanted to shake the victim, take out her anger on her, but she knew that would be wrong. The thought itself was unforgivable. Selene tried to calm her breathing, to relax and calm down, but she couldn't. Nivette had already sent word to the Kings' Garrison and they readily replied. They would be here in two days time and Gabrielle had personally asked to see Selene when she arrived. Selene wondered if her failure here had caused her luck to run out. Hopefully not. Selene had no desire to meet the King and Queen and face death; she wasn't ready to die now. Not like she had before.

"No sign of forced entry," said Blake.

"Looks like she invited them here and shared some wine with them," said Jeanette picking up the bottle on the counter. "Oh my. This is Rueberry Wine, dated 562 A.B.F. Over a thousand years ago. This must have cost her."

"Check her financial records, see if anything, and I mean anything, seems wrong. The same goes for the first three victims. See if there is any connection or if they're just random. Next, I want everyone in the building interviewed." Selene slumped down into a nearby seat and held her head in her hands. She was one of the best Hunters in centuries, one of the best fighters and magic users imaginable. No one has ever evaded her for this long, no one had ever beat her. Those were reasons why the Kings' Garrison wanted her dead. As well as the rune on her right wrist. She was dangerous, a capable killer and too tied to Darkness. She could kill them all. Every one of them. What frightened her was how much she wanted to.

Selene looked down at the strength rune etched onto her right wrist, darkness forever writhing beneath her skin. She usually hid it under her black steel wrist bands, but today she had been in too much of a hurry to properly cover herself up. Now two of her eight runes revealed themselves. It was something all the Enforcers looked down upon.

"Um, excuse me Selene," came a voice. Selene looked up at James, one of her more favorable Enforcers and smiled.

"Yes James?"

"I overheard that the Kings' Garrison will be arriving. I know about your past. We're required to know who the Hunters are and, I, well I hope that they don't judge you harshly. I hope that they let you do your job. You're good at it."

Selene smiled. "Thank you James, that means a lot, but they will be harsh to me. Their job is to catch murderers. Too them, I am a murder. Even if those I killed deserved their fate."

"You're a good person, they should be able to see that."

At this, Selene couldn't help but laugh. "I doubt they will, but a girl can hope." He looked up at him, finally taking in his features. There was something familiar about him, something about his eyes and cheekbones that stuck out. "James, do you have any siblings?"

"Yeah, a sister. Her name is Cecilia. Why?"

"Just curious." Selene looked out the window on the far side of the room. "I'll be going for a little walk. If you see my brother, tell him that."

"Of course. Oh and one more thing," he said, stopping her in her tracks. "I'm an older brother and I see the way he's been acting and forgive me if I overstep my bounds, but he has no right, even if he's being protective. It's not right and it looks to me that everyone agrees."

"They do." Selene waved goodbye and ran off. She only had one place in mind to go.

Selene flitted through family portraits waiting as she leaned back and forth on her wooden chair. There were so many photographs of a happy family, so many bright smiles, silly faces and scowls. All the happy faces made her envious. She heard a waking sigh and shut the book. She heard the mumblings of a waking person, heard the footsteps echo down the hall to the kitchen where she sat, surrounded by shades of lilac on the walls. Selene took a sit of the drink she had served herself and smiled as the door opened.

"Holy mother of light! How did you get in here?"

"Sit down Cecilia, we need to talk."

"Does Jason know you're here?"

"No, and I won't be able to see him for a little while longer. The Kings' Garrison is arriving."

"I see." Selene watched Cecilia take a seat next to her. "You could have at least made breakfast, would have been kind for breaking and entering."

"I didn't have the time." She smiled at her. "How long have you known about me?"

"Well I saw your portrait, then the dinner and eight runes? It's like you handed me your identity."

"What about Nicholas and Miranda?"

"Nicholas may have a think head but he pays close attention to girls. I'm actually shocked he didn't catch it first. Miranda, on the other hand, never looked at the portrait. She was blinded by fury. And she didn't get a chance to read your history, I was holding those papers. She heard your name then shut. She wants you dead."

Selene almost wanted to laugh at the familiarity of the statement. It left her with an ominous feeling that writhed in her stomach and reached her chest. "She's too much like Katherine."

"Katherine wasn't all bad, Pietro had a hand in his own demise."

"I know," she muttered. Pietro had been too cruel and cold. "I know full well."

"Why didn't you talk to him?"

"Don't you think I did? But that arrogant ass wouldn't listen. Besides, she had a choice, she could have left. He would have let her."

"Society—"

"Damn society!" Selene slammed her hand on the table, breaking off a piece of wood. "Forgive me." Selene waved her hand over the wood, making it whole again with a charm. "I've met your brother, good guy. I used to be lucky like that." Selene swallowed back the tears and anguish that threatened to overwhelm her. "Tell Jason I said I'll see him soon." Selene left, heading out the kitchen with the wood door singing closed behind her. She along the wood floor that was padded with blue and gray rugs. A cat crossed her path. A little boy with a short and stubby tail and a little pudgy belly. Selene bent down and stroked his little head. His blue gray fur was like silver in the light, and there was a hint of brown all the way down at the roots, giving him a steel gray look. He reminded her of her familiar Ultima, and wondered is she had been reincarnated into this life.

"His name is Little One," echoed Cecilia's voice from the kitchen. Selene smiled and scratched his little chin.

"Take care of her Little One." With that, she left, leaving the house more heart broken than when she had entered.

Thirty One

Eris stood at the edge of the forest on the west side. Selene was at his side, a sour expression on her face as she twirled Nuri's Shadow in her hand. Her eyes were blood red, reflecting her rage. She was not happy that they were coming, nor was she happy that they had asked for her. Eris had not anticipated that. Reaching out, he clasped her hand tightly, looking at her, giving her a reassuring smile. He watched her stare at his hand confused before finally smiling up at him. She looked like her old confident self. The one who was always serious, but always smiling. There was light in her eyes that hadn't been there for quite some time. He tightened his grip and she returned the gesture with her own hand.

"Remember when we were kids?"

"Which instance?"

"When you took a knife and cut your hair."

Selene laughed. "I was trying to look more like you. Mother

got so furious. She yelled at you first until I, as always, spoke up and got you out of trouble."

"Ever the caretaker."

"Well, someone needs to watch over you and keep you in line. You don't listen to anyone else. It's a fault dear brother."

"I disagree little sister darling."

"Disagree all you want, it's the truth." She laughed and smiled, her laughing lines brightening up her face, until a twig broke in the darkness. Her face went still, her eyes wide and red, and much like a cat, her ears twitched, searching for sound.

Eris looked into the darkness of the forest, through the fog left behind by the days' rain. Gabrielle emerged, her bright green eyes lit up by the red, while her shoulder length auburn hair made her pale face glow in the dim moonlight. They were Touched Born Vampyres, almost as old as the King, his most valiant soldiers, those who had never succumbed to the Blood Hunger. Gabrielle stopped in her tracks and stared at him coldly, her hands on her hips, highlighting how thin she was. An amused smile betrayed her indifference.

"My, my, if it isn't the Great Coven Master Eris Sintas and his murderous sister, Selene Sintas."

"It's nice to see you too Gabrielle," mocked Selene.

Gabrielle's green eyes flashed red. "I should have killed you the instant I saw you. Would have saved my King from making the mistake of keeping you alive."

"A pity I never got to actually meet his majesty, or his Queen. I hear she fancies me."

"Don't be cocky Selene, I still need a private word with you."

"Not that private if the entire Garrison is going to be there

Gabrielle."

"Okay enough," said Eris. "You came to find a killer, to assist where we have failed. Selene is in charge, you are not. Do not trifle with us."

"You should watch what you say Eris," said Gabrielle. "We are Touched Born's as well and older, even with magic you two could not kill us."

Eris almost lost it when he saw Selene lunge and grip Gabrielle's throat, she had her dagger poised to near Gabrielle's hear. Most shocking of all, were her runes, all lit with a dark light.

"Selene!"

"I have something to say. I have studied you, all of you, I know your abilities, and I know how to handle you, so trust me when I say I can kill all of you. I do not need Eris' help for that."

Eris pulled his sister back, Nivette took her by the shoulder and held her close. "Gabrielle, I would say forgive her but we all know you wouldn't. But if you're going to interrogate her, you can leave."

"Even if I wanted to, I can't and trust me I don't want to be here. Four murders have been committed; therefore, we are here to assist with our skills." He watched as Gabrielle glared at his sister and was glad when Selene returned it with an obnoxious smirk.

"I'll show you to your chambers," began Nivette, letting Selene go from her motherly embrace.

"No need, we should begin now, gather the Hunters."

"They're already gathered," said Selene turning away. "You should follow me, if you're in such a hurry." She walked off, twirling her dagger in her hand. Eris shared a smile with Nivette as the Garrison walked on past them. He would feel their anger with every step they took and their heads held high arrogantly. Hunters always formed a bond with one another and an even stronger bond to their leader, regardless of the Coven Master. He knew that the Hunters Chamber would turn into a war zone if Selene and Gabrielle did not keep their anger in check.

"Well, this should be interesting," said Nivette walking after them. Eris agreed and stared after his sister, wondering when she had learned how to tap into the Darkness. He wondered if it was good or bad.

She is the Light Eris, whispered a gentle voice in the wind. *Don't let her lose it. She is the one who will save the souls touched by Darkness. She is the light, she can touch the dark and not be tainted. Watch over her. She can save you.* The voice vanished and the wind stopped, leaving him alone with his thoughts. He knew I was the Goddess. Selene was the Light.

Thirty Two

Selene's seat at the end of the table was tall and set on a black marble pedestal. It had belonged to the former Blood Hunter, the title given to the head Hunter. She could have done without the title, reminded her too much of Blood Hunger. But it was what it was. Of course, she didn't care for the high chair either The back went two feet over her head, cutting off her vision if she were to ever be attacked from behind, which might just happen with the Garrison here. It was unnecessarily large, with jewels all around the top and sides. Selene had made changes though, tirelessly renovating it. There were short knives, dagger and other sharp weapons hidden within the chair. Only she knew where, and she intended on keeping it that way.

Looking over at Jeanette, she nodded. "Begin."

Returning the gesture, Jeanette stood from her seat and began passing around copies of her report to the Garrison.

"The first victim was a woman, she was walking home from work and was attacked right outside her house. There was no evidence, no scent and no magic."

"There was nothing?" asked Penelope. Her short blonde hair was tucked behind her ears and her blue eyes studied Jeanette who could easily pass as her sister. Selene knew her. She was the last Touched Born to join the Garrison and the youngest, that is if you counted sixty-eight thousand four hundred and fifty two young. Still, she was powerful though, and a threat to Selene with her ability to manipulate others magic.

"None," continued Jeanette. "We did a thorough check with help from the cities Enforcers. We found nothing."

"And the second," asked Hetiro. His hair was wavy and went down to his shoulders, when not tied to the back. He had blue eyes that appeared brightened by the red Those same blue eyes stared at her fixated, reflecting what he was trying to do. Thought readers knew no bounds. Selene was, thankfully, strong enough to keep him out. His eyes left her, leaving her with a headache that faded with each breath she took while her anger grew at the invasion.

"A male," said Eno. Selene felt herself calm down slowly. "Middle-aged, fifty two years old. He had been on his way to meet his sister for dinner. It appeared as though he had been lured deep into the alley. It was a dead end, so there was no reason for him to go down there.

"His body went through a thorough examination, not a drop of blood of left. There did, however, appear to be a struggle. Unfortunately we found no fibers and no DNA, nothing to lead us to the killer. And, once again, no scent."

"How is that even possible," asked Artesia, Hetiro's twin sister. She twirled a finger in the air, conjuring a flaming sharp knife in her hand. Any weapon she wanted, any weapon she thought of, she could conjure. She twirled the little fiery knife and eyed Selene menacingly. Selene greeted her with a smile, activating her fire rune. Artesia's frown deepened and she looked away, crossing her arms, making her knife vanish in the process.

"At first we thought it was magic," began Blake, "but we performed a web tracer and found that there was no magic involved during the time of death. So we came to the conclusion that it is a Vampire using Fairy Dust."

"Use of that is prohibited," snarled Gabrielle

"But not even the King enforces that law." Selene looked around the room, watched her comrades eye each other warily and watched her cautiously as she spoke. "There is still much we don't know about the use of Fairy Dust which is why it's not enforced. Fairy Dust has only begun to be abused these past few centuries, but for the most part it has been justifiably used. Hence the term Roamers correct? All Roamers are to be questioned, correct, not killed? When it comes to simple Binding, the most we know is that it hides scent."

Gabrielle flipped her hair over her shoulder, leaning back on her chair with flippant disregard towards Selene's leadership. "Well then we should get started—"

"We already have a list of all the Vampyres who buy Fairy Dust," interrupted Jeanette, sharing a gratified smile with Selene causing her to almost laugh.

"Roamers?"

"Four," answered Selene standing up. "After the third murder we put up the Dimmer. Obviously we'll take them down now."

"Then we should go, before they leave the city." Gabrielle

stood up from the other end of the table, dragging her nails along the granite table, sending sharp shrill noises into the air. Pure vehemence seeped from her pores and dove into her eyes, turning them a bright blood red. "Lead the way Selene."

Thirty Three

Darkness hovered over them in the Shadowling Realm. Eris sat with Evida is Shira's dark room. Black tapestries lay about the room doing nothing to calm him as he sat unnerved by Evida. She was looking at him, but it felt as though she was looking through him, taking apart everything that made him whole. No wonder she was destined to be with Void, he had that same look as well, only with him, it was one of detachment. Eris felt pity for him, something he did not feel for her. She already looked dead, like something was taken from her, leaving her with nothing.

Eris's mind wandered, he was standing by a tree, watching Evida play with a duck in a nearby pond.

"Nuri! Come over here! The water is so calming!"

"I'm fine Evida," he said making his way to her.

"You're thinking of her again aren't you? The winged one?" Evida picked up the duck and placed it on her lap, stoking it's feathered back. The thick branches blocked out most of the sun, turning it's brown feathers black. "She is pretty and her smile is nice. But you know, the Dark Ones, they say you can't."

"I know. But," he paused, at a loss for words as he stared into the horizon. "I should stop thinking about her shouldn't I?"

Evida shrugged her small nimble shoulders. "You don't have to. Negal seems to like her. Shira is the one who is threatened. Her and Senid."

"I know exactly how Senid feels. He won't talk to me."

"You know why right?"

"He feels betrayed right now. He's still my best friend Evida, he's like my brother. He shouldn't feel betrayed."

Evida shrugged. "Well that's how he feels. Void thinks you should just leave her alone and talk to Senid. Ettore agrees."

"Void is too lonely." Eris smiled expectantly.

"Not true! He enjoys my company." Eris saw himself laugh when she blushed.

"You're too bright sometimes."

"Is that bad?"

"No. In fact, don't ever change." She smiled and let the duck walk off her lap back into the crystal blue pond, fracturing its surface.

Eris eyes adjusted to the dim lighting of the room as his memories caught up with him and he stared at Evida, disheartened. There was no similarity between her now, and then.

"What happened to you?"

"My comrade left and the Dark One's came to me and asked for my help. I agreed. The result was taking a part of my soul. She said she would need it. I still don't know why."

"So you weren't always like this?"

"No. My comrade...my friend, he called me bright. Do I look bright?"

"You look dead."

"Same difference. Darkness is the opposite of light. Death is the absence of life."

"Why do it? Why give away half of yourself?"

"I missed my friend, is that so hard to believe?"

"Sounds like you had a soul."

"All beings do, some are just darker than others. Mine is only darkness. Even Senid had light in his. He was torn over his friend, his brother by spirit if not by blood."

"Surprisingly, I don't find that hard to believe." She continued to stare at him. "Do you even feel alive."

"I'm half of a whole, I feel...some things, but I am only half of myself. Sometimes I feel nothing and other days I feel...alive."

"Seems hard."

Evida's lips slipped into a small and delicate smile. "It is. But one day, I'll get my other half back. Of that I am sure."

"Are you?" Evida never got a chance to answer when Shira appeared. He saw the urgency in her eyes.

"If you want to see him, now would be the time."

"It could wait—"

"The Garrison is closing in him. They already found the other two Roamers and an opportunity like this won't happen again."

"Why is that?'

"A girl is in his home. Evida go block the exit, I'll grab the Roamer and keep him quiet." Eris looked out the window of Shira's bedroom then back at Evida.

"Let's go, I don't know how much longer Selene can continue playing nice." Shira smiled then blew off into darkness, leaving her little doorway open. Evida followed through but stopped briefly.

"She had a beautiful smile, your Azelia. You should look for her." Without another word, Evida walked off into the darkness. Bewildered, Eris stared ahead before following them into the void.

He didn't look back.

Dim light filled the room of the lightly furnished apartment. Before him were two people, beaten down to the ground. The man tried to get up, but Shira kicked the man back down, her foot pressed against his chest effortlessly. His head hit the ground with a loud thump, a small head wound formed and only a little blood escaped before the wound healed. The sun glinted into the room from a far away window.

It was pathetic, the whole scene and as much as he was disgusted with himself, all he wanted to do was laugh while he picked up the limp Witch from the ground. She already had bite marks on her neck. There was already blood on the Vampyres lips, smelling more of human than Vampyre. He groaned and tried to look around. When his green eyes fell on Eris.

"Let her go."

"If only it were that simple, but see, you're going to be joining her soon, my sister will see to that." Eris dug his fangs into the girls neck. He heard the Vampyres scream become muffled but Shira. The girl, already knocked out from Shira, did not struggle, and when the last drop slipped down his throat, she looked as though she was sleeping. Looking back at the Vampire, he carelessly, let the girl slip from his arms.

"What's his name?"

"Axel," answered Shira.

"Okay." Eris knelt down and eyed the Vampyre Axel sadly. "When I leave, you should run. You're scent is all over this place and you are in possession of Fairy Dust. Not to mention now you have dead girl here. I am the Coven Master, so I'm telling you, the only way you're going to survive is if you run." Axel tried to say something but Shira placed her hand on his mouth, hoisting him to his feet. "Let go Shira, he's broken enough." Shira dropped him to the ground carelessly and stepped back. The smile on her face as she stared at the body of the dead girl was unmistakable. Eris, trying to ignore her, helped Axel sit up.

"Why?"

"I need to keep my sister preoccupied. There's someone out there I would rather she not meet, nor see. It's a complex story."

Axel's eyes narrowed, understandingly. "It was you. You killed all those people, you killed my—"

"Yes, indeed I did, but see you need to understand, it's a complex story."

Axel's eyes stared back at him defiantly. "Not if your sister is Selene Sintas. We all know her story." Rage enveloped Eris and his kindness vanished. His hand gripped Axel's throat tightly.

"Run."

Thirty Four

Selene sat in the room, staring down at the body. Just hours, they had been late by a mere three hours. Only one good thing had come from this disaster: they finally had a scent. Surveying the room, she stared into the darkness, the shadows on the walls, high and low, some even looked misplaced at one second, then fine the next. A trick of the mind perhaps, but there was still something wrong with the room other than the unusual darkness. All the evidence was here, laid out for her. There was even a dead body. It all felt wrong. Selene felt something moving in her mind and looked up at Hetiro as he continued to try to worm his way into her psyche. With blinding fury, she shoved him out of her mind with such force, gratified by his wince.

Bristled, Selene returned her attention back to the body. Closing her eyes, she breathed in the room. The stench of Darkness was everywhere. Selene made her way to the body and knelt down to examine the wound. Gabrielle knelt down beside and stared at her uncertain.

"What are you looking for?"

Selene's eyes slanted in confusion. "Don't you smell it? The Darkness?"

"No. What Darkness?" Selene watched as Gabrielle's jaw tightened making her quickly regret her choice of words. She couldn't give Gabrielle more ammunition to think her crazy. Doing that would quickly make her life forfeit. Biting the inside of her mouth, she shook her head.

"Forget it. It's nothing." Selene stepped up and moved away from the body in order to allow the Enforcers to bag the body and move it onto a stretcher.

"The other Roamers said they saw Axel around the Darkling District. They said he seemed lonely."

Selene shook her head. "That girl lived here and I'm willing to bet that the reason he killed those people was so he wouldn't kill her. He loved her."

"You're making assumptions," growled Gabrielle.

"No, I'm taking in the facts."

There was a brief moment of silence, until Eno coughed, gathering everyone's attention. "Well now he's on the run and we still need to stop him."

"What would you do Selene?" asked Penelope.

Selene smiled at the exchanged of fearful glances between her comrades. The comment, however sly, had been unintentional, lacking the malice any of the others would have used. It seemed that she was genuinely curious. Selene violet eyes flitted past Penelope's shoulder towards the window where the sun was setting. "I'd head for the forest."

"Then let's go." Gabrielle walked off. Her comrades followed after, all but Hetiro. Selene caught the glimpses from her friends as Hetiro made his way to her. She made a slight nod of her head, urging them to follow Gabrielle.

Crossing her arms, she had to admit, she wanted a moment alone with him. "Shouldn't you be going?"

"Shouldn't you?"

"Gabrielle can handle things, can't she? She is the oldest after all."

"True, but even we admit, you are the best hunter there ever was. That's why Gabrielle can't understand how you let there be five victims."

Brushing her fangs with her tongue, her arms tightened around her. "True enough, I've been off my game. Go figure. Happens doesn't it?"

"You know I can read your soul."

"Oh yay, a mind and soul reader. Anything else?"

"I know about Jason. Even a sly little glimpse into your thoughts let me decipher the secrets of your soul."

"Stay out of my head," she hissed growing rigid.

"Eris is looking for him." Selene's heart stopped and she stared at Hetiro frightened.

"What?"

"Eris is looking for Jason, he knows he exists. I can't read more of his thoughts, they seem locked away, hidden. Selene your soul is light, pure and pained. His—his is darkness."

"Eris is good." She said trying to convince herself more than she was him.

"Is he? Look, as a friend, I am telling you to be careful."

"Friend?" Trying to imagine any of these Vampyres as a friend was a hard feat, but the look in Hetiro's eyes was sincere.

"Yes, friend. It's why I haven't told Gabrielle you buy Fairy Dust nor that you are involved with a Witch who has an uncanny resemblance to Pietro. So yes, a friend. I see what they don't, even after you killed the Levine siblings. You seem to be nothing but light."

Selene almost laughed. "Glad to be seen I guess." He smiled at her and she returned it, hesitantly, but grateful. "Let's get going."

Selene stood at the edge of the forest and the city. She made the wind blow towards her and closed her eyes for focus. Except she couldn't focus. Hetiro's words rang though her mind. Eris know Jason existed, but how? What was going on? Did he know about her relationship with him? Selene shook the thought away. If he did knew, she would be in serious trouble. She bit down on her lip and pushed her hair over her shoulder to braid.

Somewhere in the distance, a twig broke, jerking Selene to her feet. She ran in the direction, and in the corner of her eye, running ahead of her, was the Vampyre Axel. Selene surged forward, her arms pumping at her sides, her feet, in thick heeled boots, drummed against the ground, breaking branches and leaves in their wake. Looking on ahead at the back of Axel's head. His feet pounded against the ground, harder and faster as he tried, in vain, to escape her.

But she needed to stop him, and she needed this chase to be done with. Urgently, she looked ahead of her for something to slow him down. There was a log, right in her path, ready for her. She increased her speed and slid on, kicking up the log with such force, hopeful that it would hits its mark.

One, two, three...

The log slammed into his, sending him crashing into another tree, dazing him as he fell to the ground. Selene made her way to him, dusting off the dirt from her red and black corset. Finally, the Vampyre who had complicated her life, had killed so many, and had brought the Garrison down on her was at her mercy. He looked up at her, catching her off guard. The fear in his eyes was not a look she had expected to see in someone who was supposed to be insane.

"You're making a mistake," he said as he tried to crawl away from her, blood dripping down his face from the gash on his forehead.

"You aren't the first person to say that."

"I am not the killer. I'm innocent."

Cocking her head to the side, she gave him her most sardonic smile. "So you're saying you don't know how that girl came to be dead in your apartment."

"Oh, I know how Selene Sintas. I'm being set up."

"By whom huh? Why would anyone set you up, hmm?"

"Your brother."

Selene's anger flared. "You're lying."

"You're blind. Eris is behind this. All of this."

"You filthy lying killer!"

"I'm innocent!"

"No you're not." Selene lunged at him but he fought back. He punched her, hitting her in the jaw, kicked her, tried to push her off him, trying to escape. But she would not budge. Her nails tore at his shirt, pulled at his hair. He screamed when she bit into his arm and kneed him, with all her might, in the stomach. Finally she was on top of him, her black hair disheveled, her hands around his throat, her nails dug in deep to hold him still. She could barely recognize herself as she stared at her reflection in his eyes. His eyes now filled with pity more than they were fear.

"Sh-shadowlings." Selene's fear took control and her love for her brother joined it. Without realizing it, she snapped his neck, ripping open his neck in the process. Scrambling away from his limp body and lifeless eyes, hands covered in blood and for the first time ever, truly felt herself break.

Thirty Five

Selene sat there, huddled against the tree, knees close to her chin, blood covering her hands, eyes tired from staring at the lifeless and broken body of Axel. Much like he looked, she felt, broken and bloody, sad and pitiful.

Eris.

Shadowlings.

Jason.

What was going on? Had she just killed an innocent man? Her fathers' words rang through her mind. She had promised her father that she would watch over Eris, but did that include covering up his mess? His murders, if that was truly the case. No, even her father would have wanted him to pay for his crimes. He was Eris, her brother, she knew him, he was not a murder. At least he hadn't been until they were turned into killers.

Sitting alone in the dark forest, she agonized over the possibility of what might be true and what might be false. It was killing her, slowly chipping away at her already broken heart. She had believed that his worst side was his careless attitude towards women. But even that had amused her because she had never cared for any of the girls, including Jeanette. Nevertheless, things had changed, and Eris, despite her hope, had not.

She recognized the signs instantly and already knew about his affair, all the while wondering who had replaced Nivette. Selene had always though and believed that was as dark as he got, as horrible as he could ever be.

Maybe she was wrong.

Sitting there, Selene felt more broken than she ever had. Selene pulled her knees close to her chest, holding them tightly and did something she had not done in centuries. Selene cried.

***

Blake ran through the forest, searching for either Selene or Jeanette. He had lost the scent of Axel.

Stopping the edge of the nearby creek, he sniffed catching a whiff of Selene and death combined. Worry and fear overtook him, forcing him to follow her scent. Finally seeing her, he stopped in his tracks.

Blake couldn't remember the last time he had seen Selene cry. Even when they had been together, she had only ever cried once and was mainly due to her injuring herself upon falling out of a tree. Eris had been there for her though, had carried her back home and banned Blake from seeing her for days. That had been the first of two times. The second had been when she heard of Pietro's death.

"Selene—" Blake didn't finish his sentence. He saw a body lying not too far away from her. Blake circled around carefully, watching Selene cry. "Selene, is that Axel?"

"Yes." She lifted her head, wiping away her tears with the back of her hands. Her eyes were still puffy and red. "That is Axel and he is dead."

"Why are you crying?"

"Because he may have been innocent."

"What are you saying?" Blake ran to her side and cupped her face urgently. "Selene look at me. He was not innocent—"

"He might have been! Blake, he said it was Eris and Shadowlings. He said it was Eris!" Her voice rose but her sobs quickly bubbled over it.

"Then why kill him? We could have had Hetiro read his thoughts."

"I know."

"Then why did you kill him?"

"Because I don't want to know! I mean he isn't capable of murder, right? He can't be. Eris, he's many things but he could not have killed those people."Blake saw the pleading look in her violet red-rimmed eyes. He knelt there frozen, looking at her, wishing he could hold her and say Eris would never kill an innocent soul. Centuries ago that would have held true. No matter how much he disliked his friend, he would never have believed he would kill someone, would never had any doubt about it. Now all he had were doubts.

"I don't know Selene."

***

Selene stood while Gabrielle examined both her and the body. She yanked Selene's arms and looked her in the eyes. Selene knew that she was thinking of killing her.

"It was self-defense," lied Hetiro. He looked at her sadly as she held her thoughts open for him. "And he was guilty."

"Please Gabrielle," began his sister Artesia, "let it be. Her actions were quite justified."

"So why don't I believe that," she growled, taking a tight hold of Selene's chin. Selene wanted to spit into her face and laugh at the pure hatred coming from her, on any other day she would have, but right now was not the time and her thoughts were preoccupied elsewhere. "Damien, look back."

"I can't," muttered Damien in a low and defeated voice. "The gods forbd it. I see him running, then nothing."

"Damn Those of the Dark."

"It isn't Those of the Dark!" exclaimed Jeanette. "It is the High Goddess of the Light. Do not taint Selene with your hatred."

Gabrielle sneered at Jeanette, offering her a scolding glare. "As if I could believe that, even if I were to—"

"You should," muttered Hetiro. "Her soul is a blinding white light, with no touch of darkness. An oddity considering what she is and what is on her right wrist."

Gabrielle's grip on her chin tightened, half-frightening. Selene that she would die, half hoping that her neck would snap. But no, death would not come so easily to her. Death would never be an easy escape for her.

"Gabrielle, perhaps there is truth in what Hetiro says," said Damien. His green eyes fell on her, no longer holding the malice they did a few days ago.

"Perhaps," said Feltor. He continued to stare at her with mistrust, rather than with hatred. "In any case, we have found the murderer, which was our assignment. Let us finish up and leave."

Selene watched Gabrielle's fury boil over, watched as her chest heave heavier and heavier, threatening to burst the green corset that was tightly wound over her torso. Selene looked at her, stared deep into her green eyes and waited for her to let go. When Gabrielle finally did, she did so, shoving her into a tree, cutting Selene's cheek with her long plain nails.

"Very well then." She turned her back to Selene who wiped

away the blood on her cheek as her wounds healed. "Someone pick up the body and bring it back to the cave, we have a Burning to prepare."

Thirty Six

Eris stood at the forefront of the Burning Ceremony. A magical burning was one of the ways to ensure a Vampyres death if their diet included blood. Those of the Dark had a sick sense of humor. Only three things could kill the for sure. A magical burning, decapitation and, of course, ripping out their hearts. Eris and Selene had learned that the hard way when they had killed the original Coven Master.

Behind him, to his left, he spied Selene, her head down, black hair falling in strands over her face, slowly slipping out of her lose ponytail, obscuring it. In it's current state, she looked disturbed and beaten. He watched her raise her head and look at him. Eris jerked his eyes away, returning his gaze towards the fire. He saw Hetiro looking at him while he talked to Gabrielle. He hoped that Hetiro had not been attempting to wriggle himself into his mind like a worm. He watched the pair of them more intensely now. Gabrielle opened her mouth to speak, but Hetiro spoke first, seemingly answering her thoughts. Eris grew uneasy watching them over the flickering flames of the fire that licked the air.

"Why must this ceremony take so long," he muttered to no one is particular.

"This cannot be rushed Eris," answered Nivette, stepping up to his side. "We can't risk that he has even one drop of human blood in his system that can breathe life back into him. At least this will ensure his way to the Farplane."

"I just want them gone."

"They will leave when all is done," muttered a different voice. Eris turned around and stared at Selene who continued to watch the fire. Eris wondered why she looked so sad. It was strange, but she almost looked, impossibly, older. No not older. She looked defeated. He looked up at Nivette who was already walking away.

"I know," began Eris, eyebrows pinched together by worry. "Selene are all right?"

"It doesn't matter right now Eris. We'll discuss it later."

"Can you look at me when you talk Selene," he said in a lighthearted tone, trying to lighten the mood.

"No." The curt answer took him by surprise. It was unlike her, cold and distant. Hurt took hold of him and made him wonder what he did to deserve this attitude. His heart skipped a beat and he looked back through the flames at Hetiro who was staring at him unwaveringly. Eris hoped Selene did not know of his recent activities. His stomach began to churn at the thought.

"Selene—"

"Shut up Eris and let the ceremony be. Right now is not the

place for me to ask what I need to ask."

The uneasy feeling in his stomach grew, knotting his insides. Turning back to the ceremony, he watched the fire burn.

***

Eris sat in his dark bedchamber with its bleak looking stone walls. He sat there, gripping the edge of his bed glad that the Garrison had left.

The door slammed, magic filled the air. He could feel the tendrils of energy in the air vibrate before settling against the walls. Eris looked up at the fuming and formidable looking Selene. Her fists were clenched to tight her, he could see the bone underneath.

"Tell me it's not true."

"I will once I know what I am denying. I'm not a mind reader like Pietro." He smiled at the flicker of her stable resolve shatter. Regret quickly followed when her hand flew across his face. The impact itself felt like needles were raining across his face. The nails, drawing blood, seemed to sooth it though.

"Now is not the time to be smug and arrogant, let alone a pompous spoiled brat!" She screamed the last part, causing his eardrums to throb. "Now tell me Axel was not innocent. Tell me that you did not kill any of those people! Tel me you were not working with Shadowlings to set him up!"

Eris maintained his calm, but the guilt squeezed his heart tightly. He watched her for a moment, watched her body shake with anger, watched her purple eyes turn bright blood red with fear rather than rage. Not once in his life had he ever really lied to her...

Until now.

"None of that is true Selene." He stood up and looked her in the eye, placing his hands on her shaking shoulders. "Where did you hear that?"

"From Axel. I thought I had killed and innocent man, to protect you."

"Have I changed that much that you would believe that? Do you really think me a cold blooded killer?"

Selene stared at him for a brief moment before looking away. "You've been acting strange lately. I didn't know what to think. And when he said something about Shadowlings, how could I not believe him? Not many know of your relations to them."

Eris pulled her into his arms, laying his head on the top of hers. It was comforting thought, knowing that she would kill for him, to protect him. Tightening his arms around her he spoke, "Selene, unlike you, I don't normally befriend and hang out with Shadowlings." Each lie he told broke his heart. This was his sister. "But if you believed it why did you kill him?"

"I promised dad I would take care of you." Her head shifted and he looked down at her tearful purple eyes. For a moment she looked more than human, she looked innocent. "I'll be in my room if you need me. See you later brother dear." She hugged him tightly, burrowing her head in his chest before giving him the softest kiss on the cheek. The touch was so faint like feathers brushing against his skin, it could have been imagined.

***

Selene sat in her room trying not to cry. Every time she blinked her eyes began to sting as the tears threatened to come. She had the sinking feeling her brother had just lied to her. What had become of him? Furiously, with the back of her hand she rubbed her eyes and wiped the tears away. Selene tried to compose herself as best she could, slipping off her shoes and ripping off her corset.

In the mirror, set in the dark corner of her room, she caught her reflection. But it was the light that drew her to stare. In the center of her bosom, attached to the center of her bra, was the marble of light, pulsing with its own life. Selene plucked it from its spot and threw it up it the air, holding it with a spell.

"You haven't forsaken me have you?" said Selene in a weak and heavy voice.

Never my dear. You have simply been put in the middle. I am trying to fight the destiny others have in mind.

"Did he?"

There was a pause, an echo of silence in the air, in her thoughts before she finally responded. By then, the silence had already answered her.

Yes. But don't fret, either way, you will save the souls of those you love and cleanse them of all darkness.

"Just a pawn in game," she muttered before snatching the marble from the air and placed it back near her heart.

Selene changed quickly into a black loose tank top and some purple shorts she usually slept in. She buckled her dagger back onto her thigh before grabbing her only black sweater that she rarely ever wore. Staring at the heavy oak door in front of her, she thought about what she was doing. But she had no other choice.

Taking a deep breath, she picked up her head, held it high and made her way to the Hunters Chamber.

It took a moment for her to enter, knowing that everyone was waiting for her. This was the only safe place. A place no shadow could enter. A place safe from her brother. Although, that had not been her original intent.

Closing the door as softly as she could, she made her way to her seat, ignoring the stares but answering them with the simple phrase, "he killed them."

"Are you sure," asked Eno.

"Yes," she answered sitting down. "I saw the look in his eyes. He killed them all." Saying it aloud, made the world feel heavy, made her want to collapse and die. Every fiber of her being felt like it was shattering, ripping apart her spirit. "He killed them, and I killed an innocent man, the only proof we had."

"Can't Hetiro read his mind," asked Jeanette.

"No. He said it's shrouded in darkness, keeping his thoughts locked away, hidden."

"Is Gabrielle holding you responsible," asked Blake.

"No. They all believe my life is in danger." She swallowed down the bile that rose up her throat and looked away. "Pietro was Reborn. His name is Jason and he's a Touched Born with the same gift. I have been—we're friends. Eris knows he exists." Selene scanned the room, noting the fear in their eyes. It was fear for her life.

"Does Eris know you're friends with him?"

"I don't think I'd be here right now if he did. I'd be locked up, maybe dead. Of course, Jason's death would be a certainty." The thought broke Selene. She collapsed in her grief, burying her head in her hands as she cried. "What happened to my brother?"

"Oh Selene." Selene felt Jeanette wrap her arms around her, and pat her head like the other sister she thought herself centuries ago. There was so much comfort in the embrace; Selene could no push her away.

"What now?" asked Dimitri.

Selene pulled away from Jeanette wiped away her tears before looking at her comrades. "Now we watch ourselves, we watch him and we act like we know nothing. I made a deal with Gabrielle, if we find evidence or suspect Eris has done anything else, we are to inform on him." Everyone nodded, understanding what this meant while she kept asking herself the same question repeatedly. What Darkness had taken over Eris?

Thirty Seven

J ason sat on his sofa watching the news. He had watched
it nonstop, following the coverage of the hunt. Something
compelled him to watch, and he knew exactly what: his
need to see what Selene was up against.

Cecilia and Nicholas came by often. He hadn't seen
much of Miranda, leaving him more grateful than lonely. Her
family had bought her a one way ticket back home until the
Vampyre situation was resolved. It had been weeks since the
Kings Garrison came and now, it was over.

Jason watched Selene give her speech, thanking the
Vampire King's Garrison and the city's Enforcers for their
help, reassuring the people of Telos of their returned safety.
As always, she looked too young to be in charge. However,
everything about her, the sorrow in her eyes, the way she held
herself, with a high head and straight posture, said she was
centuries old. Looking at her now, Jason noticed she wasn't

as self-assured as usual. She looked broken. No, that was the wrong word. She looked defeated. The normal sorrow in her eyes was gone, leaving her gaze vacant. The way she talked, her voice had little confidence, cracking as though her throat were sore every few words while her lips twitched in the corners with every pause. Something had happened to break her spirit leaving her to look like a version of her former self.

Jason watched her leave the podium, replaced by her brother. It still amazed Jason to look at the man who was Selene's brother. Selene had always spoken highly of him until recently. She always told him how much she loved him and how much he looked out for her. But something had changed between them, even now he could see it, the distance between them.

Thinking of his own life, he thought of how much he changed when Selene had entered his life alongside the Shadowlings. The thought made him laugh when he thought about how his uptight mother would react to that. Like most Witches, she didn't hate the creatures of Darkness, respecting the balance of darkness and light. That did not mean she liked them. She knew most were good and were their protectors from the rabid ones, but the fact that they lived off life and blood meant that sooner or later, the Blood Hunger would take over. She pitied them rather than hated them and he gave his mother credit for that.

Turning his attention back to the screen, he watched Selene. She stood, her head high, her hands folded behind her back, her eyes centered on her brother. The vacant stare was gone, replaced with something new, pain and regret telling him exactly what was wrong with her.

"Are you Jason?" Jason jumped from the seat, knocking over

his coffee table. What was it doing so close to the damn sofa anyway, he thought trying to ignore the pain in his knee. A girl with hazel eyes was looking at him. He fought the calming feeling warming him like a blanket.

"Oh my, you do look like Pietro."

"Who are you?" Jason studied her, unaware if she was friend or foe.

"Oh! I'm so sorry. I am Eno," she began with a small tilt of her head, "Selene sent me. I am one of her Hunters."

"Why you?"

"Because I'm a Calmer."

"What?"

The girl Eno touched the bridge of her nose with one finger, all the while smiling. "Oh dear, has Selene told you nothing? Before I was a Vampyre I was a Touched Born with the ability to sense emotion. When I as turned my powers were amplified. I can manipulate emotions. My kind are called Calmers as we are most used to calm tense situations."

"There are more of you?"

"Not many, but that doesn't matter. Problems have developed."

"Like what?" he asked leaning against the wall.

"Hold that thought. Ettore? Vega? Please come out, this involves you as well." Shadows stepped from the walls, one from next to him, causing him to jump further. Ettore grinned at him, patting him on the shoulder condescendingly.

"Yes?" asked Vega.

"Block off the Shadowrealm." Jason watched the Shadowling couple exchange worried glances, the smug arrogance vanishing from Ettore face. He watched both throw pairs of their daggers across the room. Dark light illuminated each weapon before vanishing, leaving the weapons embedded in his walls while tendrils of darkness leaked from them, spreading across the walls menacingly. Jason winced, thinking of his deposit, a stupid thought he admitted, knowing this was serious situation. Even the smug look on Ettore's face was gone.

"What's going on?" asked Jason.

"Eris knows of your existence and we have yet to establish how and what he will do should he find you. Thankfully he doesn't know of your friendship with Selene. Of course, the other bad news is that Eris is responsible for the recent tragedies—"

"Don't sugar coat it Eno," interrupted Ettore hotly. Jason stared at him, more frightened by the anger set alight in his pulsing red eyes, burning away his usual cool demeanor. "He killed all those people didn't he?"

Nodding, Eno said, "Yes, but that's not all. Before Selene killed the innocent Roamer Axel, whom Eris set up, he said something about Shadowlings."

"Shira!" Vega gasped, holding her hand over her mouth. Ettore took her hand and stared at Jason.

"I never thought she would stoop so low and become so desperate," growled Ettore.

"Can someone explain to me what is going on?" Ettore exchanged a few glances with Eno and Vega. Both girls nodded. Ettore smiled, his smug arrogance briefly returning.

"So unlike Pietro," began Eno. "You ask, you don't demand. And you're not an arrogant jerk." She offered him a gentle smile, washing him with another wave of soothing calmness. "Eris is the murderer and Selene, in her fear, killed the only proof of it. And now we know he wasn't alone. He was working with a Shadowling."

"And not just any Shadowling," began Ettore sighing. "Shira

is the sister of the not-so-late Senid, our former King."

"I thought Shadowlings couldn't die."

"Eris found a way," said Vega, her eyes on the ground, staring at the wood floorboards distantly.

"Is Selene's life in danger?"

"We don't know." All of them exchanged glances, with hope that someone would say no. Jason hoped one of them would say no. "Eris loves his sister," continued Eno, "but we don't know anymore how much he loves her, we don't know what he will do to keep her safe. You didn't see her after Pietro died, we did, Eris did. We have no idea to what he will do to keep her safe. Besides, Selene is more worried about you than herself."

"That sounds like her," said Jason, sliding down his wall, falling onto his floor. He looked back at the screen were Eris and Selene stood. Selene, broken, defeated...torn. "Now what?"

"Now we keep you safe," said Vega, indicating herself and Ettore.

"While we look after Selene and watch Eris," continued Eno. Jason nodded, biting down on his nail, watching Selene on the screen looking like the unassuming sister, the obedient soldier.

Thirty Eight

Selene sat on Jason's bed waiting for him to come home. Ettore sat next to her, popping fruit into his mouth carelessly while he watched a drama on the ResoScreen mounted on his wall.

"Why are you watching this?" she snorted.

"It's amusing."

"It's stupid actually. What do these people know of pain and anguish? Nothing!"

"Oh not true. The main actress, Celine Karver, she's going a real divorce with a cheating husband."

She only crossed her arms and stared at him unimpressed and unsympathetic. "It's hard to feel pity when that sounds like just another farce."

Ettore shrugged. "Maybe it's a publicity stunt, but it is happening, and it is really happening to her. Besides, watching this show is good for a laugh. I mean really, who goes into a catatonic state and wakes up with a new face? It may be stupid, but it is hilarious."

"Hilariously fake."

"And for your information, just because they don't know your type of anguish doesn't mean they don't suffer. Everyone has their own type of anguish Selene." Selene stared at him before looking at the screen for a moment. The scene on the screen, the diction they used, the farce presented, made her buckle over and laugh. Ettore stopped eating to stare at her, frightened by the release of laughter, a sound he no longer thought her capable of. His expression made her laugh even more and it took her a few moments to compose herself enough to hug him.

"What's this for," he asked, genuinely surprised. He couldn't remember the last time she had given him a hug. "You don't plan on killing me do you? Not like you could but still, a stab in the back would hurt."

"No, there will be no stabbing. This is for trying to make me forget. For making me laugh."

"I don't enjoy your company when you've become stoic and cynical. It's depressing. You've been so depressing since Pietro's untimely death. Just like Negal. You used to be so full of life."

"Was I?"

Ettore nodded, popping another purple fruit into his mouth. "Remember when we first met. You were so scared but ready to stand and fight. You were quite amusing."

"Amusing? Your sister had just flung me off a balcony. I did not find that amusing at all."

"That may be, but you were still full of life Selene, ready to fight, ready to live."

"Well," she began, looking away towards the cracks in the

floorboards, "stuff happens."

"I know. But hey, at least you're not like Negal. All she does is mope around or stay in bed. You could hardly call her a queen anymore."

Selene sat there, tracing her fingertips over her protection rune on the back of her left wrist, just above her vein. "She really loved him didn't she."

"Well yeah, they had been together since the beginning, literally. And—oh! Vega's knocking." Ettore pulled out his knife from the floor. Within seconds Vega rose from the ground, waving hello to Selene. Selene returned the gesture, a knife flying past her face and sticking into the wall on her right. Irritated, she shot Ettore a look, her lips pursed and eyes narrowed disapprovingly. All he did was grin back.

"Is Jason almost home?"

Vega nodded. "In the stairwell. He'll be unlocking the door any moment now." The moment the Vega finished her sentence, timing her wording perfectly, Selene heard the front door lock click open. Selene watched her throw a knife of her own against the hallway wall. Standing up and staring, Selene wished she understood how Shadowling magic worked.

Jason stood in his doorway, holding hid bag loosely in his hand. He stood there, still as a statue, in his wrinkled black shirt over a blue long sleeve shirt and jeans, stubble on his face darkening his features. It had been weeks since she last saw him, and after sending Eno to tell him everything, she still had not had the courage to see him. Selene had been worried, even secretly hoped, that he would look at her differently. He didn't.

"Long time," she said feigning a smile.

"You can say that again." Jason dropped his bag to

the ground and walked over to her slowly, cupping her face when he reached her. Selene tried to hide her disappointment when he pulled her into a hug.

"Are you sure you should be here." He warm breath fell down her neck sending chills over her body.

"I told my brother I would be out of the city. He was thrilled to hear it."

Jason pulled away, leaving his hands on her shoulders. "I'm leaving soon. It's about time for the Silmarine Solstice and, well, my mother expects me to come home for the holidays."

Selene nodded. "I understand." Selene a step back, slipping from his hands, watching them fall to his sides. "How have you been?"

"I could ask you the same thing."

"Are you going to?"

"Do you want me to?" The question almost made her want to laugh. It further made it easier to distinguish between Pietro and Jason.

"Go ahead. I know you want to."

Jason smiled, taking a step closer to her. Selene was suddenly very aware of how alone they were. No shadows watching, flickering, no Ettore making jokes. "How have you been?"

Shrugging, she came up with the only the thing she could. "Okay, all things considered."

"Should I believe that?" Jason stared at her sadly, the fingers on his right hand twitching, as though itching to touch something.

"I wish you would."

"All right then." Moving past her, he headed to the kitchen offering up hello's to both Ettore and Vega in his wake. Ettore materialized next to the wall.

"And here I was beginning to think he had forgotten about me."

"If only forgetting you were so easy," joked Selene making her way into the kitchen.

"Oh! That was not nice Selene!" exclaimed Ettore, following her.

"No, but it was amusing." She sat down at the table and watched Jason make himself a sandwich. Ettore stayed by the kitchen door, picking at his nails.

"You can stay here, if you want. I won't be here for the next two weeks, maybe less, depending on some circumstances." Jason bit down on his cuticles.

"Like what," asked Selene, impulsively worried.

Jason shrugged, sitting down. "It's nothing you need to worry about, just my own family drama." His mouth slid into a crooked smile.

"Okay." She looked up at Jason. She felt breathless as he sat there giving her a look of wanting. Her heart ached and her insides knotted when she saw the pain within then.

"I would like it if you stayed here. It would be nice, to see you when I get back." The smile on his face that made his eyes sparkle made her heart beat even faster. She couldn't help but feel there was something he wanted to tell her.

His slender hand moved through his smooth shiny sandy-blond locks. The hair fell back over his eyes, turning the teal into a dark sea green.

"I need to take a nap before I catch the train at Diamond Tower." He walked out of the room, leaving his sandwich untouched. Selene looked at Ettore.

"Do you know what's going on?" Ettore merely shrugged, shaking his head, looking as confused as she felt.

Thirty Nine

Jason boarded the train alongside Cecilia, hardly aware that he was even walking. He knew he legs were pushing him forward, but a part of him wondered if Cecilia had just spelled his legs to make him move. Even her voice sounded far away despite the fact that she was a mere foot from him.

Taking his seat on the train, he stared out the window. Jason used to love riding the train, used to love staring down at the beautiful cities beneath him, especially during the four Silmarine months, when everything was coated in a layer of snow. He loved how beautiful the snow looked when sunlight and moonlight bounced off it. But at that moment, he felt like he was falling.

Jason propped his feet on the chair facing soon, soon feeling a kick in his shin.

"What? Oh, sorry, were you talking?"

Cecilia gave him her most petulant gaze. "I asked if you had decided what you were going to do."

Jason shook his head. "While Selene was gone, I thought about Miranda and being with her, what our life would be like and I liked the idea. Now, Selene has returned and all I think about is her. When I first saw her again, all I wanted to do was kiss her and hold her, and restraining myself from doing so was so hard. I felt like I was tearing out my own heart. Miranda, she has become a distant memory. I can't marry her, I won't repeat Pietro's mistake."

"Are you admitting it then?" she asked, a sparkle in her eyes reflecting her grin.

Jason groaned. "Yes Cecilia, I love Selene."

"Well it's about damn time." The voice was chilling but held no malice. Jason watched as Ettore slipped from the shadows and materialized in the seat in front of Cecilia. She kicked him, her lips pursed in a frown.

"Can' you not do that, you know pop out like that! You scare me half to death every time you do."

"Oops, so sorry Cecilia," he said grinning.

"Oh you are so not sorry."

Ettore laughed briefly, his eyes falling deadly on Jason. "So that's why you were acting weird earlier. You made Selene worry."

"You can't tell her," pleaded Jason.

"I won't because I know you will...provided you don't screw up and ask Kath—oops, I mean Miranda, to marry you." Jason glared at Ettore, wishing he could punch that smug grin off his face. "I'll be going now." His body slithered in a hundred different direction, slinking back to rejoin the dark shadows among the train.

"So " began Cecilia clearing her throat, "you'll be riding

until the end?"

"Yeah, you?"

"I have to connect in the next city to catch the train at Wingsong Tower. Heading west remember?"

"Lucky you, I have to ride this one all the way there."

"Well, at least you'll have time to think about what you're going to tell Miranda and your mother."

"Yeah, lucky me." He sat there, leaning is head against the window, watching the city beneath him turn into a blue and meld with the sky at the horizon.

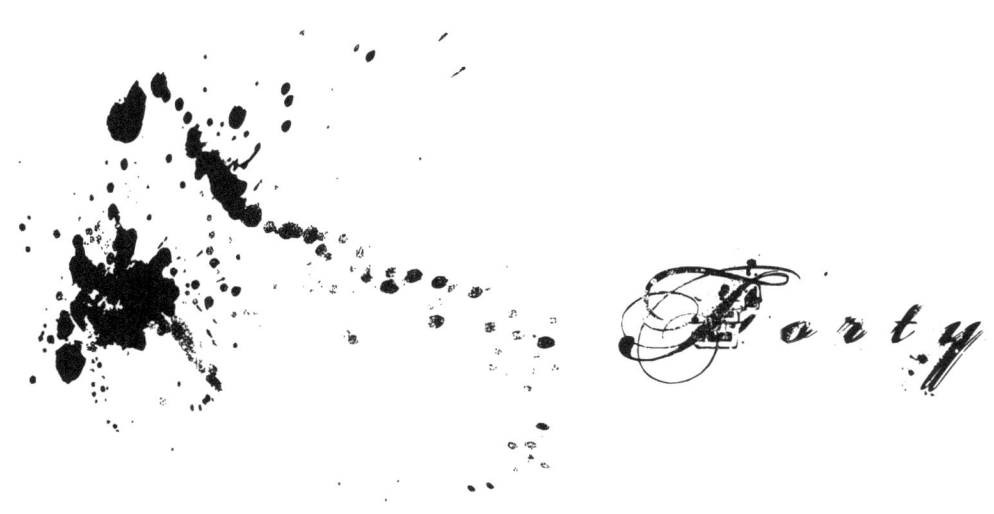

Forty

J ason heard the train whistle blow. Peaking out the window, he stared at the shinning brilliant city of Seraphim, his home. The final stop from Telos. Jason grabbed his bag from the metal bars above his seat and walked down the chrome aisle off the train. Waiting for him on the platform was his father. Jason greeted him with a warm hug.

"Have you talked to mom," he asked his father, leading the way out of the terminal. He looked back at his dad just a few steps behind him. His mouth was set in a grim frown, his bright blue wings folded.

"She wants to hear what you say. By the way, Miranda and her parents are at our home." Jason nearly fell down the stairs as he approached them

"How am I suppose to end things now?" he asked, his voice rising to a higher pitch.

"Son, I haven't the slightest idea. You should have ended

things the moment you started to have feelings for Selene. But, just so you know, Miranda's mother is against this. The moment she saw the picture of you she has been trying to talk to Miranda."

"She knew Pietro?"

"It just so happens Miranda's mother is one of my Lieutenants. She was a comrade of Selene, even wanted to speak at her hearing. Selene made many friends at the Royal Court, especially with the Royal Guards."

"How does she feel about Miranda looking like Katherine?"

His father bit his bit thoughtfully, looking for the right words to say. "Uneasy, but that does not diminish her love for her daughter. Besides, I love you and you're nothing like Pietro. Hopefully Miranda is nothing like Katherine."

"I wouldn't be too hopeful," he said hoisting his bag over his shoulder. "Cecilia did some research, they're more alike than I care to admit." Jason stared down at the shining tile floor, pressing the elevator button. "Does Miranda's mom know about Selene's existence?"

"I couldn't exactly keep it from her, it is important."

Jason entered the sphere shaped crystal elevator, followed closely by his father. "This should be fun."

***

"Jason!" exclaimed his mother, wrapping him in a warm, almost suffocating hug. Her voice while being high pitched, perfect for her singing career, was soothing. However, it had lost some of its touch at being the perfect voice to calm him to matter how terse his nerves got. "It's so good to have you home."

"Yeah mom, it is." Dropping his bag to hug her back, he looked over her shoulder, passed her golden brown hair and stared at Miranda who stared back. Miranda had on a turtleneck with jeans, looking very much like she belonged in his house. Staring at him, she smiled, one of those sweet smiles that used to make Jason want to kiss her. He watched her smile falter, watched her eyes widen and muscles in her tighten and twitch, making her drink swish every so slightly. It was obvious what she was doing. *Crap*, he thought, guiltily shifting his thoughts to Selene, her smile, the way she looked when she was sleeping, and he quickly calmed down, feeling warm all over. Looking back at her, he saw her relax and smile brightly again, even widening more so. Did he really love Selene that much? Oh what a mess his life had turned into.

When his mother finally let go of him, letting him breath, he made his way to Miranda. Behind her, stood her mother and father. Her father looked fine, but her mother looked as though she hadn't slept in days, her eyes marred by deep heavy circles beneath her eyes. Jason could tell that the smile on her face was fake.

"I've missed you!" exclaimed Miranda, throwing her arms around him, spilling some drink down his backside. Oh, this holiday was going to be a mess.

Hugging her back, even nuzzling her neck he answered, "I missed you too," not knowing if the dread he was feeling was due to the cold liquid falling down his back or to the situation.

Jason sat in his kitchen, staring at the white tile beneath him. The curtains on the kitchen window were still the same white linen with lavender flowers embroidered along the bottom. There had been a time when sitting here would warm him up and give him a sense of peace. Looking down at his tea that steadily got colder, he wished he had made some excuse to not come home. But there was nothing he could have said other than "mom, I am in love with a Vampyre, you know, the one my ancestor Pietro fell in love with." Dropping his head, he imagined all the disastrous ways that would go. Why had the Gods done this? It wasn't fair to Selene, Miranda or himself.

"I simply wanted to give Selene another chance at love."

Jason jumped back, knocking over his hair, leaving his tea further untouched. Jason quickly thought of some defensive and aggressive spells, but the longer he stared at the woman in white sitting at the table, the more he began to calm.

"Who are you?"

"She of the Light as most refer to me. I find it silly that I have yet to be given a name. I do have one you know."

"What are you doing here?"

"Answering your questions. If I were you I'd ask as much as you want before Laura wakes up."

"What?"

The Goddess rolled her eyes and let out a tired sigh. "Ask a question."

"Um," began Jason picking up his chair and sitting back down, "why was I Reborn?"

"To give Selene happiness."

"Miranda? Katherine? Why not give Selene happiness with Pietro?"

"Pietro was not my doing. My sister saw what I was doing, saw my plans for Selene and Eris and then began to unravel them. Pietro was the catalyst of darkness and while I tried to sway his destiny, I was not successful. I had not realized the extent of my sisters treachery, the calamity she turned him into.

"As for Katherine...she was a mistake my brother made that

my sister twisted. Miranda...she was my sisters doing. She seeks to repeat history for her own twisted desire and seeks to retrieve your soul."

"What was Selene's destiny?"

The Goddess laughed, a laughter that sounded like music in the air. "She was suppose to marry Uriel and bring peace with the Vampyres. The latter she achieved through sheer will and my strength. I would not let my sister have that satisfaction."

"What is her fate now?"

Sadness filled the room, strongly emanating from the Goddess. "I hope it is the one, I never want to happen."

"What do you mean?" he asked his heart racing. Selene deserved happiness, after everything the damnable Goddess of Darkness had done; Selene deserved a speck of light in her life.

"Although you are Reborn from Light, you are still her creation, which means should any type of darkness touch you, She will regain you. I am trying my best to not let that happen because there's always room for error. And should it happen, great sorrow will fill her life and to truly cleanse you, a heavy price must be paid."

The words carried a heavy weight with them as them hung in the air. Above his head he heard a door opened and looked at the Goddess. "Should I marry Miranda?"

"If you want to save Selene from sorrow, then yes. However, if you want to be with Selene, then no, don't marry her. I know I said sorrow will befall her, but in the end, her life will fill with great light." She twinkled out of existence. Leaving him alone for only a moment when a door opened. Miranda's mom walked in, flicking the kitchen light on as she did. Jason smiled at her as best he could as she stood in the doorway, her eyes wide.

"I couldn't sleep," he said.

"Ah, well, neither could I." She stared at him a moment longer, before stepping into the kitchen. He watched as she paused at the fridge door to look back at him, studying him with her light brown eyes. "I'm glad you're awake though, we didn't get a chance to talk earlier."

"Yeah, I think that was Miranda's intention." Jason took a sip form his tea. It was still warm, but he could feel it cooling down.

Laura poured herself a regular tall glass of water and closed the fridge. She leaned against the counter, fixing him with a steady stare. Jason felt that she was trying to keep her distance from him.

"Yes. she's far too much like her, I must grudgingly admit that."

"I'm sorry."

She waved away his apology with a delicate hand. "Don't be, you have nothing to be sorry for. You didn't ask to be reborn anymore than she did." She sighed. "I'm grateful that the only qualities you share with him are your looks and gift."

"I don't think that changes much." He paused, preparing what he had to say. "I love Selene but—"

"If you love Selene don't marry my daughter." Her voice was sharp, but her tone held a gentleness to it. "If you do marry her, please treat her fair."

"I haven't decided what I'm going to do. I...the Goddess, She of the Light, she was just here and...I'll bring nothing but sadness to Selene's life. Marrying Miranda could prevent that."

"So you would marry my daughter to prevent sadness onto an already darkened life? I can respect that, but I cannot condone it."

"I figured." He looked away from her and back at his tea, seeing his teal eyes and face, he wanted to curse himself. "I wish I knew what to do," he began more to himself than to her, "I wish I had ended things long ago."

"Why didn't you?"

"I still loved her then."

"Was Selene the reason you stopped?"

Jason shook his head. "No, she was just the...the cherry on top for lack of a better phrase. Miranda...she's always abusing her gift, never leaving people with their thoughts or secrets. She always so—"

"Selfish?" A thin smile pressed itself onto her delicate features. "Yes, I know. It's a trait of the blood."

"But—I don't understand. Selene saved her ancestors, you are her mother, why is she so intrusive, angry and selfish?"

"Oh, how I wished I knew. Even her father doesn't understand. I always chastised her on being the way she is. Her father and I both tried to teach her not to hate Vampyres. She was born with it, I think." Jason saw a tear roll down her cheek. "She is Katherine; my daughter is that wretched girl. Those of the Dark, they did this, that much I know. Witches are not to be reborn Jason, only one before you two have, and he was not even a Witch to begin with. You are fortunate She of the Light gave you life this second time."

"I don't feel very fortunate."

"Understandable." Laura finished off her water, placing the empty crystal cup in the sink. "Do whatever you feel is right Jason. Whatever the outcome, I will not blame you. Miranda is Katherine, I accept that." She walked away, her golden hair glowing even in the florescent lighting of the kitchen. Jason got up to flick off the light, taking up his seat in the dark where he drank is cold tea, watching the two moons fade behind the winter clouds.

Forty One

Jason stared at the little burgundy velvet box in his hand. He hadn't exactly gotten around to talking to his mother and he knew why: she was purposely keeping herself busy. Right about now, Jason was ready to scream at her in front of everyone, at least then he could say everything he needed to say to Miranda too. Taking a deep breath, grasping the little box, continued to lean against the white counter in the empty kitchen, waiting for his mother who would enter carrying yet another tray of food. She would need to come in eventually to grab the last tray of food. If she thought for a moment that serving as the party's own waiter would keep them apart, she was sorely mistaken.

The kitchen door swung open, letting in the party noises, the laughter and holiday music, a compilation of the harp and piano. Seeing the startled look on his mothers face, it took all of Jason's willpower not to greet her with a smug smile.

"Jason, what are you doing here," she asked, avoiding his gaze as she busied herself by reorganizing the already organized food on the platter.

"Mom, we need to talk."

"Jason it's the holiday—"

"I don't think I should marry Miranda." The words just flew out, taking with them the heavy weight that had been on his shoulders. Finally saying it aloud confirmed that it was the right decision.

"You father and Laura have been saying the same thing," she said wiping her hands down on her pink plaid apron. "Your father brought up ancient history and Laura said her daughter was Reborn, as if that was possible. What would you care to share?" She crossed her arms and stared at him, her mouth set in a straight line, her eyes wide with fury.

"Mom, there is so much you don't know about out family history." He stopped talking as she scoffed and rolled her eyes, returning her attention to the tray.

"What does that matter?"

"Pietro mom, Pietro matters. Haven't you noticed? I mean you can't be that blind! I am reborn except, I'm different. I have his face, his gift—"

"Stop it."

"No, I won't! You need to listen to me! I have his face. I have his gift and sometimes, I even have these dreams that I am him! Do you even know how he died? I can tell you. He was stabbed—"

"Enough!" she exclaimed, finally giving him her full attention. "Only Reborns are reborn, witches can't be and as for Pietro, yes, I know how he died. His wife—"

"Is Miranda. Miranda is Katherine, inside and out. Even her

mom thinks so."

"No. You are not him and she is not her."

"Oh come on mom, are you really that blind?" He tried to keep his voice level, tried not to yell, but he was losing his patience. Why couldn't his mother just understand? "I mean, you have to be to not see what we all see. Besides, I don't love her, I love someone else."

"Really?" The disbelief dripping off the word like dew on a rose. "Then why didn't you say anything? Does this person love you back? Why aren't you with them right now."

"It's complicated mom."

"Jason, there is a girl in the other room who loves you and wants to be with you. If you and this other girl can't be together, then move on." She picked up the tray of food she had reorganized twice and prepared to leave. "Besides, it might save everyone a lot of heartache." Jason watched her leave the room and looked at the box in his hand. A part of him wanted to throw the damn thing down the sink and walk out of his house. Then he thought about what the Goddess had said and maybe his mother was right. He had three choices when he thought about it: bring sorrow into Selene's life, risk death, or give Miranda his heart. He looked down at the little box.

Shoving his hand in his pocket and left the kitchen. Miranda kissed his cheek gently, obviously not snooping into his aura. He smiled down at her, happy to see that she was changing, even if it was such a tiny change. Picking up a sparkling glass filled with Dia Elixir, a gold shaded champagne that sparkled in the light, he looked down at Miranda and thought of what they could have. Even he had to admit to himself that it made him happy. His mind, however, returned to thoughts of Selene, about how much he loved, about her brilliant small smile and big purple eyes that spoke for her, that spoke volumes of love and happiness and sadness more than words ever could.

Jason cleared his throat and everyone looked at him expectantly.

"I, uh, would like to say that this has been a good holiday." *If only,* he thought. "I love being home and I love being around people with whom I love being with." He put his drink on the white stone shelf above his fireplace and got down on one knee. Time seemed to slow and his heart felt like it would burst from his chest. A part of him hoped it would.

"Miranda, will you marry me?"

"Oh Jason, of course!" She engulfed him in a kiss and Jason—once again—wished that he hadn't come home.

***

Jason sat on the edge of his bed. The walls were still a pale blue and his sheets were still a shade of royal blue, old and a little scratchy when he slept. Once upon a time he would have found them comforting, but those days were long gone. Now he felt like the walls were closing in on him. Jason couldn't breathe, he needed to get out.

All packed up, Jason ran from the room, skidding to a stop on the stairs as his father held a travel mug out.

"Tell Selene I said hello." His dad handed him the mug, hugging him, shoving a wad of cash into his coat. "There is a train due to leave the station in a few minutes, I'd run if I were you." Jason smiled at his father, running from the house and down the sidewalk.

"You don't have enough time." Jason skidded to a stop, nearly slipping on the icy ground. There was Vega, her hand held out. Jason didn't hesitate to grab it, letting her drag him into darkness. "Don't let go, I'll have you at Noir Tower in just a moment." Even in the darkness her voice was soothing.

Then the world opened up before him, and he stepped out. Looking back he saw Vega smiling at him, leaning on a dark doorway.

"Hurry up, you have a train to catch." The doorway closed up on her, and Jason, feeling free, ran to catch the train.

**

Selene slept in one of Jason's long sleeve shirts. It smelled just like him, musty, warm, like the woods after a rainy day. All she had was what she had run off in when she lied to her brother. Why pack? Eris had been too glad to see her run off and she didn't want to raise any suspicions.

Tossing and turning, thoughts of her brother kept her awake. What was he planning? How did he know? Why did he kill those people? She looked out the window at the moon high in the sky. A daunting feeling filled her stomach. She blamed it on the timing. The night of the Eclipse was coming, her anniversary of her second birth. It was a spectacular sight, when one moon went in front of the other, and they turned red. A sight only came once every three hundred and twenty-six years. It was a sight that always gave Selene a bad feeling. Tossing again, staring at the ceiling, she felt justified in feeling the way she did.

"You worry too much," came a sing-song voice, like a mockingbird. Selene sat up and looked towards the door. She of the Light stood there smiling innocently. "You should leave the worrying up to me."

"Why are you here?"

"To ask you a question."

"Then ask away, your brightness," she said rolling her eyes, only slightly annoyed.

"Testy aren't we. Oh well." She sighed and looked at Selene, her white eyes studying her, sending shivers down Selene's spine. "Selene, would you sacrifice love to suffer no sadness? Or would you welcome tragedy to have love in your life?"

Selene knew what was going on. This had to do with Jason and her brother. Selene swallowed down the lump that had grown in her throat.

"No. I would rather love and lose."

"So you would suffer to love?" Selene nodded. "Ah, so this is your destiny. What a great and beautiful creature you will be."

"What do you mean?"

"You will be the light in the dark Selene." Her light faded taking with it, her physical form. Selene pulled her legs up to her chest and held herself tightly, fighting the urge to cry. And then, she heard a lock click.

Selene walked carefully to the hallway, on the balls of her feet so as not to make a sound, grabbing her dagger as she made her way. She nearly dropped it when she saw Jason enter, kicking the door shut behind him.

"Jason? What are you doing back to early?"

"I made a mistake. I stupidly asked Miranda to marry me. I was trying not to be selfish but I can't, I can't marry her. So I rushed back here, making sure that what I am about to do and say are not mistakes."

"You're not making any sense."

"Yeah, I guess so." He laughed as he walked over to her in just three strides. "I was told marrying Miranda would save you, but I can't. Call me selfish but I can't marry someone I don't love."

"Jason," she began, only to be cut off by his lips pressing

against hers. This time Selene couldn't fight it, and she didn't want to. Dropping her dagger to the ground, she melted into the kiss wrapping her arms around his neck. His arms wrapped around her, pulling her closer to him.

Jason felt bad snooping in her head, but he had to know, had to make sure that she loved him not Pietro. Swimming through her thoughts, he saw. She loved him, not because of who he resembled but despite it. Pulling away briefly, he rested his forehead against hers, still holding her close.

"I love you Selene."

"I love you too." Jason touched her face gently, seeing the worry in her eyes. "We'll figure something out," he said before kissing her again.

***

Jason opened his eyes, loving of sight of Selene next to him. Last night had been beyond words, different from anything he had ever shared with Miranda. With Selene everything had felt perfect, had felt right. He closed his eyes, taking in the scent of her hair. She smelled like Gardenias.

"Are you awake?"

"I am a Vampyre, I don't require sleep."

Jason laughed. "Don't you like sleep?"

"I do." She looked up at him, her purple eyes rimmed in red. She was like a beautiful rose covered in thorns.

"You're beautiful, you know that."

"I hadn't been told." She laughed and laid her head back down on his chest.

"You look more beautiful when you smile. You're always so serious."

"It's easier to shut off rather than feel."

"I've noticed." He hugged her tightly and kissed the top of her head. "Selene, I have something—" Jason didn't get a chance to finish his sentence when a series on knocks echoed on his door. He watched Selene get up and dressed within a blink of an eye. She was wearing one of her black leather pants and a blue and black corset. She held her dagger tightly, when she grabbed it, he probably missed as he got dressed. Walking up to her, he thought her hand was turning blue.

"I'll get the door, just stand behind me," he said. Selene nodded reluctantly as he made his way to the door.

Forty Two

O w!" exclaimed Jason as Cecilia smacked him in the head while she stormed into his apartment. Nicholas laughed as he followed her in. Selene let herself smile from the back of the room, placing her icy cold dagger back in its sheath. She waved at Cecilia, causing her to smack Jason again.

"How much of an idiot are you? You must be your own special kind of stupid because I get a call in the middle of the night from none other than Miranda saying that you proposed! Granted it was her morning, but still, I was sleeping peacefully thinking you weren't going to marry her!"

"I made a mistake, I know okay. Wait, how did you know I'd be here?"

"Between sobs she mentioned you vanished. I knew you'd catch the first Red Eye to get out." She paused to smile at Selene. "Hello Selene, it's nice to see you," she said genuinely.

"Agreed."

"Man, you look different when you're not human. You're so pale." Nicholas looked at her up and down.

"Shut up Nicholas," said Jason.

"What? I'm just saying—"

"Shut up Nicholas," echoed Cecilia leaning against the living room wall. "Miranda is on her way, I hope you know. She went to catch another red eye. She left a few hours after you, not buying your fathers excuse."

"Well then I should probably leave," said Selene placing her hand on her dagger. Her fingers nearly froze from the touch and she had to activate her fire rune to warm her hand.

"Why leave now." The voice was chilling, cold and unmistakable, belonging to Miranda. To be here this fast, she must have caught a Red Eye. Red Eyes went through magical portals, connecting far places. A weeks journey, took two days, a day's journey only a few hours.

Jason stared at her, watched her slam the door shut behind her. Nicholas leaned against the wall, his beefy arms crossed, giving her a scathing look. Cecilia took a closer step to Jason, standing in front of him in a defending manner. Jason continued to stare at her as time slowed. He was sorry that he was the cause of the pain in her eyes. The anger though, that was ill-placed at Selene, who looked ready to kill with her hand on her dagger and fist clenched tightly, turning her knuckles bone white.

"I can't tell who you are," came Selene's somber voice beside him. He knew exactly what she meant. Cecilia looked at him confused, the understanding lingering in her peripherals. She would understand soon enough.

"I should kill you! *Infirage*!" Flames burst from her

fingertips causing all except Selene to drop to the ground. The fire circled around an unflinching Selene before blowing out leaving behind the smell of smoke. Jason heard Nicholas curse, calling Miranda something obscene.

"Fire rune, remember? Besides, verbal spells weaken spells." She snapped her fingers, flinging Miranda against the ground. "See what I mean?"

"I hate you," snarled Miranda as she got up. Selene simply shrugged.

"I don't care."

"You killed my bloodline!" Miranda's voice was shrill as she screamed, like the howling winds in a storm beating against the walls of a house.

"I took life away from those who did not deserve it. From murderers and abusers. Is that the bloodline you're so keen on protecting?"

"Selene, she's Katherine. She's been Reborn." Jason stood as he spoke, helping Cecilia, who was coughing, stand. "Her mother told me so.'

"Hmm, I thought as much but hoped I was wrong. How sad." He saw the pity on her eyes, it made her look older, more somber. She was no doubt remembering the past, the pain, the horror.

"Wait! Miranda," began Cecilia as she rushed to Miranda's side, coughing slightly, "don't be angry please. We care about you—"

"You lied to me!" Miranda shoved her against the wall. Nicholas ran to Cecilia's side, pulling her close to him.

"Damn right we lied, so what?" Nicolas glared at her, holding Cecilia close to his chest. "You think everyone and everything should surround you, what you think, what you want. All you care about is yourself. You make it hard for anyone to tell you what they're thinking. You don't even give them the chance!" Jason wondered how long he had been holding in all the fury, all the dislike.

"You're a bastard," she muttered. "And you," she screamed pointing at Jason, "you know what she is. You know what she's done!"

"Yeah, I know, but I also know who you are and your lineage." He paused, noticing all eyes were on him. Swallowing his nerves, he straightened his back he stared at Miranda. "I thought I loved you, thought I could love you, but you are a much darker person than I first realized. Everyone saw it, except me. Selene is good, she feels more than you ever will. She is full of light. You aren't." He glared at her. "Marrying you would've be a mistake, one I can't repeat."

Everyone stood there. Silence bounced off the walls, weighing down on their shoulders. Static electricity passed between everyone and despite herself, Selene felt pity for Miranda as she once had for Katherine. But the madness in Miranda's wide eyes, the wild and feral eyes in her wide and enlarged eyes stopped her from feeling.

"I will make you all pay." Miranda looked around the room, her wild eyes settling on Selene, sending and involuntary shiver down her spine. "Especially you." Miranda spun on her heel, throwing the door open, sending it against slamming against the wall of the hallway.

Running his hands through his hair and slumping against the wall, Jason spoke.

"Why the hell didn't either of you lock the door?"

***

Miranda made her way through the Darkling District. She

pat her chest pocket to double check that her letter was there. Wiping away her tears, she shoved her way through the throng of dark dealings. Miranda had sought information about Selene. Her brother was the Coven Master, firm and strict. He was the person she needed to talk to. Vampyres were forbidden to have relations' with Witches, that law was common knowledge. But Miranda was having problems getting into contact with him. Anyone who was loyal to Selene would probably kill her.

Her foot caught on a loose cobblestone that was the ground of the darkling district. Miranda was sure her head was going to hit the staircase she had been approaching. Instead she feel into someone's arms. Miranda looked up at the woman holding her. Her scream caught in her throat.

"I am Evida, Miranda, I believe you're looking for Eris?"

"You're a Shadowling."

"I am, as well as a friend to Eris. I believe you want to tell him about Jason and Selene."

"You know."

"And was forbidden to say a word."

"Take me to him!" Miranda grabbed Evida's arm urgently. She watched the Shadowling smile. Miranda almost pulled away. Something wasn't right about her. Looking at her eyes, Miranda noticed that they were empty. There seemed to be no life in them, no emotion.

"Very well then." Miranda almost screamed as she fell into darkness. But as soon as she entered she was in a world much like her own, only bleak and somber looking.

"What is this place?"

"Home of the Shadowlings. Outsiders call it the Shadowrealm, we call it home." Miranda looked at the structure before here, it palace of black stone that shimmered in the faintest of light. "Stay close and speak to no one." Evida opened the palace door and her flat boots squeaked against the black marble floor. Wind made her long black trench coat flap against her legs.

Miranda stayed close to her side, observing the walls around her. She was so distracted and barely aware of turning a corner, that she didn't notice when Evida stopped walking. In front of them there stood a male Shadowling, his hands tucked into his pockets, his eyes full of torment. His eyes slanted as they stared at Miranda.

"Evida, why is this Witch here?"

"It's none of your concern Void."

"I'm making it my concern." His eyes never left Miranda, studying her like she was a worm.

"Shira wants to speak to her, that's all. Besides, I thought you wanted to be kept out."

"Maybe I'm changing my mind." He walked past her, still keeping his eye on Miranda. "Be careful Evida," he muttered before vanishing into darkness.

"Who—"

"Hush." Miranda shut her mouth promptly and followed Evida down the hall and into a room. A beautiful yet deadly looking woman sat before her, with eyes as red as blood. She smiled when she saw Miranda.

"Oh my, Katherine?"

"My name is Miranda."

"She wants to talk to Eris Shira," said Evida crossing her arms, her muscles flexed her feet hip apart. Miranda wondered what she was guarding, or if she was preparing to fight, or kill her.

"Does she, why?"

"Our loophole."

Shira's eyes widened, her irises turning black instantly. "Oh yay, how I've waited for this." Shira stood up and in three paces, made her way to Miranda, gripping her arm. Miranda winced as her long nails dug into her skin. "Hold on," she said, her face close to hers, studying her. Then suddenly, the floor fell before her and was submerged into darkness. Just as quickly, she was back in her own world, facing a man with jade green eyes. Anger flared in his blood red eyes.

"You!"

"Darling this isn't her," said Shira letting go to step in front of her. Her voice was soothing, low, tender. "This is the descendant of Katherine's niece. Her name is Miranda and she has information pertaining to Jason."

"Jason?" Eris looked at her coolly, the red in his eyes slowly fading. "Who are you?"

Miranda swallowed hard and took a deep breath to calm her heart. It didn't work. "My name is Miranda and I was involved with Jason until a few nights ago. H-he left me to be with your sister—"

"What?" Miranda flinched, taking a fearful step away from him. Shira smiled.

"Let her talk Eris, you're frightening the poor thing." Looking over at Miranda, her smile widened. "Continue dear."

No longer trusting these things Miranda wanted to turn and leave. Looking at Evida who had the same stance she had before, she knew there was no turning back.

Swallowing again, she continued, "He has been seeing Selene behind my back and my friends knew. A Shadowling also knew. I thought I was seeing things at first, when I read his aura but I know now I was right, it matches theirs."

"How long?"

"Um, I don't know, a few months now would be my best guest."

Eris took a step toward her, touching her chin so gently, reminding her of how fragile she was compared to him. It made her flinch. "Why are you telling me this?"

"Because I want you to do something," she exclaimed her anger replacing her fear. "Jason is mine! He should be mine, not a Vampyres! She has broken the law and I came here to tell you I want her to suffer for it."

"Hmm, for a moment there," he began smiling, "I almost thought you weren't Katherine." His hand latched onto her throat, tightening, preventing her from breathing. Miranda tried to pull them off but he was too strong. "Turns out," he continued, "you're exactly like her and, quite frankly, I hated her for what she did. The pain she caused You're no different." Eris let go of her, allowing her to inhale once before backhanding her with such force her neck snapped. For Miranda, everything went black and there was not chance for her to think. She was dead before she hit the ground.

"Oh my."

"Shut up Shira," he said walking off.

Forty Three

Eris sat in bed fuming. Most of his furniture lay in pieces around his room, he didn't really care. Every time he thought about Selene and the secret she had kept, his anger flared without subsidence. He just wanted to scream at her. All those people he killed, he had done it to try and buy him time to figure out the Jason/Pietro situation. But no, it had all been for nothing. Eris dug his fingernails into the palms of his hand. He didn't bother to look behind him at the sudden appearance of Shira.

"Did you know?"

"I was forbidden from telling you. Negal made the whole council swear an oath. It's unbreakable. Mother thought about breaking it but instead she gave us our loophole, now its broken, all on it's own." Her grin was simple, closed, stretching from ear to ear.

"So Negal knew."

"Yes and Ettore and Vega have been watching over Jason for quite sometime now."

"Can you kill him?"

"No, both Those of the Dark and Those of the Light have forbidden it. He's off limits my dear."

"So who created him!" he yelled. "I will not have Selene suffer again!"

"That I don't know Eris. You need him for that."

"Then tell me where he is!"

"Forbidden Eris."

"Then how do I find him?"

"Well, I wasn't forbidden from following his friends."

***

Selene lay in bed with Jason, curled up tightly to him. Every moment with him was a precious one, every moment she loved and cherished. She listened to him stir and open his eyes.

"Do you ever sleep?"

"I haven't lately."

"Yeah, I've noticed." Music filled the air and Selene fixed herself on the bed as Jason reached over for him ConEx and answered.

"Hello?"

"Turn on your ResoScreen right now." Jason bolted up in bed at the urgency in Cecilia's voice. Jason fumbled around for the remote when it suddenly turned on.

"Magic," muttered Selene leaning forward.

"Cecilia what's—" he broke off when he saw Miranda's smiling face appear on the screen. He waved his hand, raising the volume.

"Miranda Leina, a Senior at the Silver Sintas University was found dead early this morning. Her neck was snapped, and preliminary reports say that the blow she took was instantaneous. There are no suspects at the moment but reports say Miranda was adamantly against Vampyres and stressors may have forced her to hunt a Vampyre and attack.

"Miranda was a Touched Born and is survived by her parents, one of which is Second in Command of the Royal Armada, Reborn Laura Leina. She will be arriving later today to claim the remains."

"She was in the Shadowrealm." Jason jumped, early falling out of bed. Sitting on his nightstand, next to Selene, was a dark and bleak looking man with unwavering broody eyes.

"Selene?"

"He's a friend...I think. I haven't seen him in roughly two thousand nine hundred and sixty-two years."

"Sixty-three," corrected Void. "I was staying out of it, but she," he said pointing at the screen, "disturbed me. There are some things I do not approve of my Goddess doing. Katherine is one."

"Why was she in the Shadowrealm?"

"She was with Evida and Evida is working for Shira who—"

"Who is working for Eris." Selene swore

"I already alerted Ettore and Vega. They removed their protection to allow me in and to alert you. Although I don't know much of what's going on."

"Do Shadowlings ever knock," said Jason fumbling as he put his jeans on. Both Selene and Void answered "no".

"Should I ask why I haven't heard from you?"

"Do you truly want to know?"

"Hello? Jason? Selene?!"

"*Futuo.*" Jason snatched up his phone from the bed. "Cecilia I'll call you back. Just call me when Laura—"

"She already called me. How did she have my   umber?" Cecilia's voice rang out through his ConEx.

"I don't know—"

"She wants you and Selene to meet her at the morgue. She's bringing your dad."

"Okay. I'll talk to you later then." Jason hung up, tossed the phone on his bed and resting his hands on the bed looked up at Void. "What's going on?"

"I don't know yet."

***

Jeanette jumped when she bumped into Eris. His eyes were darker, more threatening. She stopped being scared of him a long time ago, but now, staring at him, with his darkened eyes and firm mouth, made her feel more frightened than she ever had been.

"Where's Selene?"

"I–I don't know," she lied. "She went off, didn't tell me a thing."

"Look for her. I want her back here."

"Very well then. I'll gather the Hunters and we'll go fetch her."

"You do that." Jeanette watched him disperse into shadows, looking more like a Shadowling than a Vampire. A chill went down her spine. When she was sure he was gone, it at the very least, not watching, Jeanette ran to Blake's room, slamming the door behind her.

"*Furuo* Jeanette!" picking up the book he had drop. "Ever heard of knocking?"

"Eris wants us to get Selene. Now."

"What a coincidence," came a voice. Jeanette and Black jumped at the sight of Void. "Selene sent me to get you. I think it's a bit urgent you meet her at the city morgue. Room B. You should hurry, and there's no need to be discreet, the Witches there are expecting you." He turned to leave but Jeanette stopped him, placing a cold hand on his even colder shoulder.

"Can't you take us?" He stared at her hand, causing her to remove it, promptly. Blake stepped up, close to her side. Void looked over his shoulder at her, his black irises, emotionless.

"I suppose it would be safer that way. Stay close to me." A space in the wall turned into a swirl of darkness. Jeanette uneasily made her way through, Blake close at her heels.

Jeanette stood close to Blake holding his hand. The place was, even for a Vampyre. Most things didn't feel cold or hot, she was dead, technically speaking. Nevertheless, this word made her bones cold.

"Welcome to the Shadowrealm." Void walked off ahead of them, leaving Jeanette and Blake to follow. The realm was deathly quiet compared to her world there was no life, only a faint wind that blew through the air like a soft whistle. The sky was darkened by clouds, shrouding the world in a dim light. It was bleak and gray, and not even a bird nor cricket made a sound. Beneath her feet, the grass looked like fine silver.

Seeing this world, Jeanette could understand their hatred for the Reborns. If she had to live here, hearing a song that never stopped, she would go insane. It was a curse to live for eternity in a world such as this.

"All right, we're here." He waved his hand and through another black portal. Jeanette hurried after him, eager to escape his world, gripping Blake's hand tighter.

Jeanette entered a room where two reborn stood along with Ettore, Vega, Selene, Jason, James the enforcer and two other Witches she didn't know. Selene was staring hard, unwavering, her hands gripping the table, creating slight dents, at a body on the table. Jeanette, moving over to Selene's side and letting of Blake, nearly gasped at the face of the dead girl.

"This is Miranda, Jason's ex-fiancée. Her neck was broken, instantaneously. Laura, her mother, said it was Eris and after reading it, I agree."

"What does the letter say?" asked Blake.

Selene almost smiled. "Dead mom. If you're reading this, then I'm dead. Murdered or suicide. I have recently found out that Jason us involved with the Hunter leader, Selene Sintas, the woman who killed my ancestor. I know this family has always been thankful to her and, in a way, a part of me was. I think that small part of me, and you, are the only things that have made me different from Katherine." Selene paused, reading ahead quickly.

"But I'm her, I know I am. I know that in some twisted way I have been Reborn. Those of the Dark did this to me, but She of the Light, she came to me once. I never told you because I was sure it was a dream, but she told me that in a way, I would help her chosen Light Bringer save two souls. It was so long ago, I barely remember. I can't forgive myself though. I know that I should be happy for Jason and Selene, and I am. I am which is why I don't understand why I'm about to do what I do. Maybe it's a twist of fate. I hope you can figure it out someday. I think it may be Katherine.

"I'm going to find Eris. I'm going to tell him about Selene and Jason. I know they're keeping it a secret from him. I've done my research. I know he won't be pleased. Something or someone tells me he won't.

"I'm sure he's going to kill me and I accept my death. It's

what I deserve for being her. For being an abomination. I shouldn't have been reborn.

"Mom, tell Jason I'm sorry and that I, Miranda, am happy for him and Selene. Please tell Selene how sorry I am. I wish I could stop myself but I can't. Please forgive me. All my love, Miranda Selivra."

Jeanette wondered how many times she had read the letter. She wanted to hug her, but her muscles tensed up. She did not want to be touched.

"That was not my daughter's name," muttered the Reborn across the table.

"No," muttered Selene, "Selivra was Katherine's maiden name."

"She was losing herself," said the female Witch with the chestnut hair, eyes brimmed in tears.

"Selene?" Jason gently touching her shoulder. Jeanette shot him a pitied glance.

"He knows then doesn't he." It wasn't a question, it was a statement. Selene's back straightened and she let go of the table to clench her hands. Her violet eyes never left Miranda's face.

"Now what?" asked the tall bulking male Witch.

"We hide you, all of you."

Forty Four

"Why do we have to hide," asked Cecilia shoving clothes into a light blue duffel bag. Selene sighed, she knew that look, it was the look of "why me", a look her mirror had made her very familiar with.

"I'm sorry, I really am but they—"

"They found Miranda which means they were probably watching her which means that they are watching us. Yeah, I know." Cecilia shoved the last of her clothing into the back and zipped it shut. Shoving her bangs out of her face, she leaned against her bed frame. "I just wished this wasn't happening. No one deserves this."

"I understand."

"Has anyone informed Jason's mother yet?"

"No, not yet," she said peeking over her shoulder at Jason on the balcony, his head hung low. "Jason's trying to figure out how to tell her and Laura, well, she just wants to be left out.

She somewhat knew that this was going to happen. I don't blame her for wanting to be left alone. I actually wished she hated me just a little. It would be fair, but she's to understanding."

"I still can't believe Miranda would do what she did."

"She wasn't herself, not anymore and I can't hate her for that. . She knew she was going to die. Her letter is proof of that. She was more of her own person for a little while there, so I can't hate her. Katherine I can, Katherine I can always hate."

"Even I hate Katherine. She murdered Pietro—"

"Horrifyingly, yes." Selene sighed. "He should have treated her better though. I was the only person he wasn't an obnoxious ass too. That's probably the reason I love Jason. Pietro is more of a fond memory now."

There was a moment of silence between them before Cecilia cleared her throat. Selene looked at her abashed. How had she gotten so off topic?

"So where are we going? If they notice we're gone they'll obviously start looking."

"Don't take this the wrong way but I'm counting on them watching. This place, Nicholas's place and Jason's are all going to be decoys. If they think this place is spellbound they'll assume you're here under house arrest. I'll have Void and Vega and Ettore make daily trips to your places. They'll be watching them too." The glass door behind them opened, letting in the cold air behind Jason.

"Hmm, well I don't think his mother will be happy with the impromptu visit."

"I don't care." Selene looked over at Jason standing a t the glass doors, his gaze still fixed at the starry night. "Are you ready?"

Cecilia stared at Jason, her frustration fading away. "Uh

yeah. Are we really going to catch the train?"

"Nope." Selene walked over to Cecilia's large oval shaped mirror. "Cecilia, how fond are you of this mirror?"

"Um, not that fond, I bought it a thrift store."

"Good." Selene picked it up and made her way to the Calling Circle. Back in the day, it was just called the Rune circle, but times changed and even Selene had to admit, Calling Circle seemed more appropriate. The Runes were set to call on magic and the Gods. There were two sets of circles forming it, each one made of Runes with no duplicated. The diameter of the Circle equaled to roughly three feet. The circle was a necessity to Witching life. You couldn't enter a house without seeing at least one.

Selene had Void hold the mirror while she grabbed a Sapphire from her bag that lay just outside the circle. It was uncut, unpolished, making it appear foggy. Next she grabbed a Water Gem, a clear gem with Water swirling inside. The gems were unnecessary really, just sered as magic enhancers. If only she had them so many years ago.

Shaking her head, centering herself, she closed her eyes, she pushed the old thoughts aside and tapped into the power that was inside of her. She felt her body warm up and could feel the dagger sheathed on her thigh grow colder, as though it were in pain. Ignoring it, she clasped the gems, on in each hand, before slamming them together, crushing them.

"*Sancti dea, audire me. Aperire ostium.*" She said rubbing her palms together, crushing what was left in her hands in a fine powder. She blew the powder out of her hands, and watching the dust swirl to the appropriate runes as the liquid from the water gem pooled at her feet. Stepping out of the circle, she hesitantly grabbed the mirror. The last time she had performed this particular spell had been the night of the Eclipse. The right she died. Pushing those feelings aside, she swore this would be different and smashed the mirror into the circle. The mirror broke, and as it shattered, it turned into a liquid pool of silver. Calling Jason over and spoke.

"Focus on your house." Jason nodded, taking her hand while he closed his eyes. Selene watched the pool shimmer and settle, showing a calm sitting from where there was a fireplace and three beige sitting chairs.

"Whoa," exclaimed Nicholas. "Even Cecilia could never get this spell right. Why do you think she buys her mirrors at the Thrift Store." He laughed while Cecilia scowled, crossing her arms.

"It's not that hard," said Selene, trying not to laugh at the face that Cecilia was making. "It just takes a little willpower and concentration. Having a purpose helps and the gems work as a little cheat." She leaned against the sofa on her left, not letting go of Jason's hand. "You all go. Blake, Void, stay behind for a second." They nodded, and then suddenly, lips were pressing against hers. The kiss had a sense of urgency in it, the way his lips pressed and moved, making hers sore. It made her feel as though her heart was breaking.

"Be quick," he whispered, before falling through the liquid glass, his hand slipping from hers. Everyone else quickly followed, leaving her alone with Blake and Void.

"What do you need?" asked Blake stepping to her side.

"I need you to go fetch Zoë and tell her to bring her stash of Fairy Dust."

He scrunched up his eyes, confused. "The Witchling? Why?"

"Because she's powerful Blake, besides," she continued on smiling, "I've noticed you've been spending a lot of time with her. Why?"

Blake smiled at her, "She reminds me of someone we used to know." Heading for the dark void that Void opened. Turning back, looking suddenly very serious he said, "You know Selene, you don't have to be so strong." She gave him a weak smile, watching him walk into the darkness before him.

As Selene waited she thought about what he had said. She didn't have to be strong, that was true, but she needed to be. Selene knew that the moment she let her emotions take control, let the walls she built fall all would be lost. She would lose her focus. She would break down and cry. Sorrow...when would it all end?"

"Oh this is just the beginning Selene Sintas."

Selene spun around, finding herself face to face with a woman who looked a lot like She of the Light. Except, her eyes and hair were pitch black, making her dull skin look like hard porcelain. It was her horror, her nightmare, staring straight at her with a vicious little smile.

"You're the dark one."

"Very good. You know, your creation was a mistake. You threw off everything. I blame my brother, he always needs to interfere in this war between my sister and I. She made good use of you, but so did I. You are very fun to play with." She laughed. It was a cold laughter, mocking, cruel, making her blood both boil and freeze at the same time.

"What do you want?"

"I want what is mine. What I breathed life into." Here black eyes widened, making her look insane. "I'm so close to getting it back Selene. It's pathetic how much my adores you." She bit down on the side of her lip, smiling, letting a dark chuckle escape her black lips. "It makes my life so much fun though."

"What was yours?"

"Nuri!" she screamed, frightening Selene. "He was mine. His shadow is mine. I want him back. He's more than just that shadow trapped in that blade. I want my Shadowling back, I want my first born back. I lost Senid, a pity but a brilliant sacrifice I won't let be in vain."

"Just take me."

Eying her, she let out a shrill laugh, tracing a cold finger down Selene's face. "Oh how cute. You really are clever. But no, I can't taint you. I tried once, tried to take the little darling of light. You should have died. It would have sent him into oblivion. But that didn't happen. No, I won't take you, instead I'll give you a choice: Eris or Jason?"

Selene shook her head frantically. "I won't choose."

"You will have to choose, especially if things take a turn for the worst."

"I can't."

"You will have to. The pieces aren't set yet, the choices, not made. Save one and damn the other." Her laughter continued, bouncing off the walls, making Selene's ears bleed. "Oh, I hope Eris leaves Jason alive! Tick tock, tick tock. Start deciding little human." She vanished in a swirl of shadows that licked at the air like flames. Selene barely had a moment to regain herself when Blake and Void returned with Zoë.

"Hey Selene, is everything okay?"

"I need your help." She looked at her, still in shock, hoping it didn't show, hoping no one could see the fear and anguish in her eyes.

"Let me guess, Shadowlings and uninvited Vampyres?"

"It's like you can read my mind.

Zoë winked. "Maybe I'm just a little more insightful than

that." She offered her a smile. But it was forced, Selene could tell that much by the sadness I her drooping eyes. Her golden eyes were contracted like the cat she was inside, angled sharp irises and her had no warmth, drooped at the side while it rose on the other. She vanished in the pool of silver at her feet followed by Blake and Void. Selene stood there, staring down, needing a moment to herself. Closing her eyes, she closed of her emotions, building her walls higher, before taking a step, letting the liquid envelop her skin. It felt like the ocean before a storm, smooth and tranquil.

Her feet touched the ground as she landed agilely, knees bent, torso bent forward, helping her keep her balance. Through the vibrations in the air, she felt something thrown her way. Selene, standing, muttered a dispersal spell, snapping her fingers for a theatrical effect.

"I am not one to trifle with right now," she growled, uncaring if this woman was Jason's mother.

"Mom, this is Selene."

"I know who she is!" screamed Jason's mother. "She is the reason Pietro died! I will not—"

"It's a little late for that considering my brother killed Miranda." The room fell silent. Worried glances exchanged between the people in the room, and Jason's mother promptly shut her mouth, her rage clearly replaced by fear.

"What?" her voice was soft, barely above a whisper.

"My brother killed Miranda. She went looking for him, she wanted to talk to him about Jason and now she is dead and Jason is next."

"Why? Why would he want to kill my son?"

"That's something I don't understand either," spoke Cecilia. "He knows you loved Pietro, why wouldn't he just give you another chance."

"Because, I killed Katherine not just for revenge. I was hoping that the Vampyre King would kill me. Eris swore to me that he would not let me get that close to death again."

"He's always been a pompous ass," added Blake in a low voice.

"In any case, I need to spell this place quickly. There is a rune, one of my own creation. It keeps out Shadowlings. That catch is you need to use a Shadowling Blade or else it won't work."

"What about Vampyres," asked Nicholas.

"I doubt Eris will issue an order to send Vampyres. No one will cross Selene," stated Blake. "Besides, all us Hunters are loyal to Selene first and Eris second. If there is an order, we would catch wind of it and scare the coven back into it's proper place."

"Or tear it into pieces," added Jeanette looking dangerous with her arms crossed and muscles flexed.

"I'll do the first rune. Zoë please hand everyone some Fairy Dust." Pulling out her dagger, Selene approached the fireplace, digging her blade into the stone, ignoring the dust that floated downward. This was her rune, her creation, and it was a damn good one.

Taking a step back when she was done, she examined her handy work, a tri-moon design with criss crossing infinity lines:

Blowing Fairy Dust onto it, she muttered a binding spell. Vega, Ettore and Void let out moans of anguish and receded into the hallway.

"A little warning would have been nice," groaned Ettore.

"You know what I was doing," she said simply, sheathing her dagger. "Ettore if you don't mind handing out some daggers."

"Only if everyone promises to give me some forewarning."

Void surprisingly smacked him behind the head. "They promise Ettore." Ettore gave his brother-in-law a glowering stare before handing out some daggers to the Witches and Vampyres in the room.

"Why are we spelling this place?" asked Jason.

"This will make is harder for Shira and Evida to locate you," began Ettore.

"And if they ever locate this spell, not even Eris would tear it apart," continued Selene. "There are too many people working the spell." Selene grabbed a vial of Fairy Dust. "That's why your places will be decoys. If one of you Shadowlings wouldn't mind." Vega was the first to open a portal.

"See you all very soon."

***

The house was secure, as were the apartments. Selene was happy for that. But still, nothing was really safe. She adjusted her sunglasses. She knew it was silly for her to be wearing sunglasses indoors in the middle of the night but it was better than spooking the Real Estate Agent with her red-rimmed eyes. She looked at Jason who was leaning against the glass doors that lead onto the twenty-fourth floor balcony overlooking Nephilium.

"As you can see it is fully furnished, the electricity and water connection spells are already set up and are holding strong. The calling circle is clean and freshly polished and is in perfect working order. Both circles and runes are smooth and perfect."

"How much is the rent?"

"It's. .well if you don't mind me asking, are you even old enough to be renting this place?"

"Believe me, I'm much older than I look."

"Oh, okay. Well the rent is 3.6 Felucians a month. I hope that's okay. You see, you've picked one of the more expensive of apartments."

Selene fished through her bag and pulled out an uncut diamond the size of her fist and a ruby that was a bit smaller. "This should cover it right?"

"Uh, oh my yes." The Real Estate Agent stared at her awestruck.

"I'm an alchemist," she shrugged.

"Oh! Well, excellent. You must be very powerful to conjure these."

"I guess." Selene looked around. "How much for the year?"

The Agent licked her forefinger and looked through the pages. "That would be 48.6 Duo-Felucians."

Selene nodded and dumped the contents of her purse onto the living room table. "Do me a favor and try to keep this to yourself."

"Of course!" She beamed, pulling out a pen from her front breast pocket of her navy blue suit. Handing over the pen she held out the open folder. "I do still need your signature for my records."

Understanding, Selene signed her name on the dotted line.

After that, she watched her leave, locking the door behind her. Jason still didn't budge.

"I'm sorry."

"Don't be. I had a choice. I have faith in you and I believe Eris will do what you want. It just looks like he cares about you a lot."

Selene nodded. "He does." Looking wary she pulled out her dagger from her purse. "I should spell the place while the moons are still high." Jason nodded, turning back to face the city lights. Selene hoped Jason was right about her brother.

Forty Five

Eris watched Selene enter the Grand Chamber. She walked in as always, casually with vacant eyes. She almost looked unsuspecting. But now he didn't know whether or not to trust that face. Eris couldn't trust her at all, not now.

"Welcome back little sister, how was your trip?"

Selene shrugged. "It was refreshing. All that business with the Roamer had me unnerved. I needed a break."

Eris leaned against his makeshift throne. It wasn't grand like her Hunter's chair but it had a sort of charm he could admire in the simplicity. "That's understandable considering the Garrison made matters worse for you."

"Not that much worse. They simply added to my annoyance of putting me under a microscope."

"Well, just as long as you're okay, I'm okay." Eris smiled at her, pulling her close in a warm embrace. Her body was slightly stiff, he could barely feel her hug him back.

"How are things here? The way Jeanette tells it you needed me quite urgently."

Eris looked at Jeanette who stared at him vehemently with blood red eyes. She stood behind Selene, sideways with her arms crossed with her blond hair draped over her shoulder in a loose braid. The hatred in her eyes had ever subsided, he didn't expect it to now.

Next to her stood Blake, his body facing Eris, his arms crossed as well. The look in his eyes was unmistakable, but they remained their honey like color.

"Oh no, what have I done now to insight such hateful looks?" He grinned, mocking them both.

"You—argh!" Jeanette stormed off leaving Blake to follow after. The pair of them were beginning to bore him.

"How was your trip," asked Nivette getting up from her seat to embrace Selene.

"Relaxing. I didn't have a care in the world. I forgot what that felt like."

"I'm glad, I was beginning to see the stress of things on your face. It must have been a long journey back, you should get some sleep."

"Oh no—"

"I insist Selene." Eris watched Selene shut her mouth confused, sparing a single glance at him before she nodded and walked off. The moment the door closed behind her, Nivette, in her skinny and sharp high heels, stepped in front of him. Her shoes clicked against the marble and granite flooring.

"Yes dear?"

"Oh shut it, what are you up to?"

"What are you talking about?"

"Don't play stupid. You've been acting different and I don't like it. Selene looks at you with fear. She's your sister!"

"Nivette, enough. Selene has no reason to fear me. I love and I will do everything and anything I can to protect her." Eris made his way around her, sick of her chastising.

"Is that why you killed all those people? To protect her?" Eris stopped in his tracks, his blood running cold. Slowly he turned around to see, facing her. He couldn't move, not as she took a step toward him, her heels scraping against the floor, her lip curled on the left. On her face she carried a look of triumph and despair. There was no light in her eyes, only sadness.

"How?"

Nivette scoffed, rolling her eyes. "I'm older than you and I'm your consort, I know when you're acting off and when you're up to something. I've been watching you and your Shadowling whore."

Her words stung like no others did. He saw her eyes water, but she did not falter, her breathing remained constant, her body still. Eris felt guiltier about hurting her than he did for killing those people.

"Nivette—"

"Save it. I've I stopped caring about what you do and who do a long time ago. I do however care about how it affects her. If what you're doing hurts her, believe me, she will find out and she will hate you for eternity." Nivette shoved passed him, making him stumble. What she added, in a tone barely above a whisper, made his breathing stop. "And eternity is a very long time Eris." The door slammed shut behind her and he fought the urge to stand tall and not crumble to his knees.

"Are you having second thoughts?" came Shira's sultry voice. Her hand wrapped around him and her head lay on his back.

"Go away Shira."

"Why should I?"

"I said go away!" He spun around, shoving her back with such force that she landed on the ground, making a crack in the flooring.

"You care about that Vampyre—"

"Shut up. Don't speak of her, never speak of her. Everything you say is vile."

"Then why do you care about me?" she asked standing straight hands on her hips, defiant. Her voice carried a mocking tone.

"How should I know! I just do." He turned to walk off, but Shira stopped him, materializing in front of him. Eris wished he wasn't drawn to her, wished that some part of him, the darker part of his soul, wasn't strangely in love with her. He wished it sickened him, but it didn't.

"What do you want?"

"Oh! That's right! I have an update, that is, of course if you want to know about dear Jason."

"Just tell me."

"I can't enter his house, something is blocking my entry. At first I thought that it was either Ettore or Vega blocking me, but I don't feel any Shadowling tricks."

"She knows," he muttered, rubbing the bridge of his nose stressfully. *Of course she would figure it out you idiot*, he scolded himself. *Selene has always been too damn brilliant.*

"Who she? Selene?"

"Yes. But—"

"Futuo," she cursed

Eris eyed her angrily and anxiously. "What? What do you know?"

"Miranda. Evida brought her to me through the Shadow realm. Void saw her—"

"And you thought to say nothing!" Eris allowed himself to relish in the fear in her eyes. But Shira was one of the originals and first of the Shadowlings. It took her several moments but she recovered her regal arrogance quickly.

"He said he would stay out of it. It appears as though he favors Selene more than Evida."

"Evida is different than she once was."

Smiling, she said, "And how would you know that?"

"I just do." Gathering his nerves, shoving his anger and fear back into the far pits of his mind, he pinched the bridge of his nose, nonetheless frustrated. "Take me to his apartment."

"His apartment is not the only one like that. His friends places are like that as well, as is his home." She stopped talking, taken back by Eris's sudden burst of laughter. All she could do was stare at him confused.

"Decoys! Selene is brilliant! She set up decoys to keep us at bay. Any one of those places could be where he is! And you'll never find out. Oh my I sometimes forget how brilliant my dear darling little sister is." Eris took a moment to calm himself from his insanity.

"Are you done yet?"

"For now," he said wiping a stray tear away, a tear brought forth by his sisters brilliance and deceit. "Tell me, how many Shadowlings are loyal to you?"

"How many do I need?"

Eris made a quick count. "Seven, including Evida. I want you to have one monitoring all the locations then I want Ettore, Vega and Void followed. I want you to stay idle, but try to keep them on you. I want to know where Jason is. Now."

***

Eris sat on the edge of Telos, alone. He loved how his homeland had flourished. He wondered if Selene and himself had been the reason for it. Either way, he loved it. He loved how the stars twinkled and lit up the sky. He loved how the light from the two moons made the buildings of stone and glass shimmer. His home was beautiful. Even the Darkling District wasn't displeasing to look at. It lacked the hums of light making it a more a kin to his Telos. It was nostalgic. His home was beautiful above and below ground. It was this that made him almost regret wanting to tear it to pieces in search for Jason. Almost

Eris shut his eyes. Deep within himself he found himself thinking of Azelia. He remembered her smile and honey gold wings. He remembered her big wide eyes. He wished that she were here now; he wished he could have saved her.

Clutching his fist tightly at the memory, his nails dug into the flesh of his palms, letting cold blood slip away from him. Senid. He wished the death of the Shadowling made him feel better but it only made him feel worse. Senid's death had not brought Azelia back. Her soul would be Reborn, he had known that even then. The question was when and how would he know. Evida had told him to look for him. Evida, who was only a fraction of herself. He opened his eyes and stared back into the night sky.

Over the centuries, he had woken up in tears. Nivette would hug him despite his rages at her, the blame he put on her for not letting him die. He cared for Nivette, could claim he loved her and mean it. Except, he also loved Shira, despite her dark soul. Despite his feelings for both though, his heart belonged to Azelia, the one person who wasn't with him.

"Eris, I have news." Eris tilted his head to his side and stared at Shira as she approached.

"Then talk."

"I think I found the true location of Jason but the magic surrounding it is more powerful and I cannot perform magic."

Eris wanted to curse Selene's brilliance. "Take me to it."

Shira bowed her head and opened a dark portal. "Step through and watch your step." Eris walked to roll his eyes, but he knew to listen to her. Eris knew here well enough to know that didn't waste words.

Eris stepped onto a downward slanted roof. Below him was a house with thick magic humming around it.

"What am I looking at?"

"The home of Jason's parents. Some of my colleagues have seen Jason's friends here. But they also see them leave their homes. We believe they are spelled together, to try and deter us. Your sister is quite the clever minx."

"Get on with it."

"The blocking spell is more powerful here."

Eris chuckled. "Oh the irony."

"What?"

"I need to do a Sensory Web. Selene, just so happens, to excel at those. It tells us how many spells are going on in one place. It also says if there is more than one person working the spell. Selene can narrow it down to a particular type of spell or area. I've never been that good."

"Well you need to be."

"Maybe not." Eris pondered for a moment. "I need you to get someone for me."

"Who?"

"Her name is Lilith. Find her and bring her here. Oh, and

be discreet."

"Of course." She fell into darkness leaving him alone to stare into the house. He watched the people through the window, tried to force his sight into the shadows within to see inside. But, as expected, he was unable to. Selene had even blocked the fireplace. She never ceased to amaze him. A glittering blue wing caught his sight and he soon found himself watching Uriel set a table. It was obvious that he was Jason's father.

"Well, that's just swell," he muttered to himself. "So you knew too huh? Didn't even think to give me warning years ago. Damn you Uriel."

"Eris?" Eris turned around, almost losing his footing. Behind him stood Shira alongside Lilith. Eris remembered the first time he had met her. She had been dying from the poison rune on her neck. When he had bit her, he had had to spit out her blood. Turning her had been difficult, and the after effects her rune had inflicted on her, unnerving. The white in her eyes was a sickly yellow, highlighted by her unnatural green eyes. She could not feed on humans, after the first time it was discovered that the thin coat on her fangs was pure poison rather than the normal Vampyre trait, now dubbed "virus" from the scientific community. Her nails were a pale red, as though stained by blood. She had joined with the rune that had been killing her and was deadly, almost as deadly as Selene, almost as powerful. Selene never did like her, for one reason alone: she was a Dark Witch.

"Thank you for coming Lilith."

Lilith bowed her head slightly. "You sent for me so I came."

"Obedient isn't she," muttered Shira, eyebrows arched.

"Enough Shira. Lilith, I need you to do a Sensor Web on this house."

"Why not ask Selene?"

Eris clenched his fist. "Selene was involved in the spells casting."

He watched Lilith's eyes widen, lips curve ever so slightly into a sinister smile. "Very well. I need some Diamond Dust."

"I'll be right back," muttered Shira rolling her eyes. She scattered into the shadows, letting Lilith approach him, cautiously.

"Eris, not to be out of place, but why are you trying to find out how many people cast the spell?"

Eris eyed her carefully her short curly blond hair looked pale white in the moonlight. "Can I trust you?"

"Of course. I owe you my life."

"Selene is hiding someone from me. It's possible that he is in this house. I need to get him."

"Very well then," she said nodding.

Eying her again, he chose his words carefully. "Lilith, how many Vampyres are loyal to you?"

"Versus what? Selene?"

"Yes."

A little sparkle went off in her eye. "There are ten people, all of whom are Dark Witches. You know how much she dislikes Darklings."

"I'm not quite fond of you guys either. No offense."

She shrugged. "None taken, you're still gracious enough to us."

"Someone has to be." *Besides, I'm not that innocent anymore*, he said to himself looking away from her.

"That's very generous of you," she said. She remained silent, still like a statue staring off.

Looking into the house, wondering what was taking Shira

so long, he wondered who was looking after this place. With every thought of who was betraying him, his fists clenched tighter and tighter, his heart constricted, his nostrils flared. Everyone he knew had lied to him, had hidden the truth. Did they all really believe him that far gone into darkness?

"Eris?" Eris jerked his head to the sound of Shira's voice. "Is something the matter?" It was strange, looking at her at that moment. She looked almost human. There was something genuine in the concern in her voice. For that, he wanted to be cruel to her.

"I'm fine," he said hotly, looking away.

"Very well." Shira tossed a bottle of Diamond Dust to Lilith who caught it daintily. Eris could feel Shira's attention on him. "Evida found something."

"What?"

"An apartment, sealed like this one only the spells around it are more powerful than even this place."

"Who does the apartment belong too?"

"No one it seems."

"Another decoy."

"That place?"

"No, this place. I know my sisters head, I know how she thinks. She thinks, since everyone else is here, that I will assume he's here. But I know her, I know how she thinks." Eris smiled, his lips curling upward in a menacing grin that showed off his fangs. "She can be so predictable."

"So now what?" she asked, picking at her black nails.

"Let's wait and see how many people worked this spell first then take us to that apartment so that Lilith can spell it. I want to know what she did."

"Of course." There was no more talk of it. They all remained silent, allowing Lilith to concentrate on the Webbing spell, watching it unfold. He watched a white line start at one point and connect to three other points. Then he saw various other lines, of various colors connect to other points. Soon a web formed. He counted the colors but Lilith answered anyway.

"Eight. The white line is the most powerful, probably Selene." Lilith waved her hand, making the spell crackle and vanish in the wind. Eris watched the Diamond Dust blow through the wind. It looked like a small rainbow in the moonlight. "It's a powerful spell, connecting to every room in the house. No one Vampyre can undo it."

Destroy...came a gently voice in the back of Eris's head. He shoved it away, making his head hurt. "You have loyalties correct?"

"Yes?"

"Good. I need all of your loyalties to undo this spell when I say so. Understood?"

Her red lips circled into a small smile that could have passed for innocence if not for the malevolence in her reddening eyes. "Of course."

"Good. Shira, take us to the apartment."

Forty Six

Selene sat with her brother in the dining area. She watched him as he mindlessly picked at his food, his thoughts elsewhere. Looking at his glass of the rich liquid they thrived on, she noticed that the red liquid was untouched. She could smell it sweeten in the air. Blood was always better when it was warmer...to a degree.

Looking back at Eris, a sick feeling grew in the pit of her stomach. She tried not to let it reflect on her visage.

"Eris, is everything all right?"

"Depends on your definition."

"You haven't touched your food...or your drink."

"Don't have an appetite."

"We're Vampyres we always have an appetite."

"I just have some stuff on my mind Selene."

"Anything you want to talk about?"

His lip lifted, curling into a smile as he looked at her sadly, his back hunched. "Don't worry about it Selene," he said standing, kissing her on the forehead. Selene smiled at the gentle touch. "Just think about what's in two days."

Her smile faltered. "The eclipse."

"Yup. Our birthday. Maybe we should plan a party."

Selene laughed despite herself. "Jeanette might kill you, besides, there's nothing to celebrate. Too many lives lost that day."

"Yeah, I guess it's not a celebrating day." He looked away thoughtfully. A familiar spark filled his eyes. "Then let's go, just you and me, to Seraphim or Nephilium. We should visit Naavah and the others. We should visit our friends. Let's go!" He gripped her hands looking at her with a wild look in his wide green eyes.

"Eris I—I don't know."

"They're our friends, we should see how they're doing. You haven't spoken to them for centuries."

"I'm well aware," she said shifting in her seat uncomfortable, she didn't want to talk about this.

"Why not?"

No, not this conversation, not again. "You know why."

"Oh yeah," he said, in a harsh tone, "as I recall you sought out death and they loved you."

"Eris—"

"No Selene," he said taking a step away from her, shaking his head and letting her hands slip away from him. "I'm still angry for you making that choice, and I have a feeling you would make it again."

"Eris—"

"Would you?" he asked, cutting her off, his eyes fixated on the ground, darkening.

"Would I what?" she asked all the while thinking: *don't think it, don't ask it, don't ask it and I will run off with you wherever Eris. Don't destroy us.*

"Would you make that choice again if Pietro were alive? Would you seek out death?"

Selene knew he testing her and she swore within herself, wishing she had the ability to lie to him.

She looked at him steadily, tears burning the back of her eye. "Yes."

"So you would abandon me? Your own brother?" His eyes were still cast down, but there was no mistaking the anger in his voice. His body shook with rage, his veins on his wrists throbbed.

"Eris, please."

"No. I've heard enough. I have things to do." With that he stomped off, his arms tight on his sides, his body stiff with rage and fists clenched. He didn't look back at her once as he left. Watching his leave she noticed a girl with short blond curls approach his side. Lilith. The girl gave her one of her poisonous looks as she walked in step with Eris. Selene never liked the Darkling.

Walking to her room alone, Selene thought about the Dark Goddess. She had told her to choose, Jason or her brother, a choice she had not made. A choice she didn't think she could make. But her indecision was costing her. Both were at peril and she knew of no way to save them. In her heart, she knew one would fall into darkness. It was a fact, one she bitterly acknowledged. Once again, she made a wish she had often made in the past: that she ever been turned. She wished the blood of a Vampyre had never fallen onto her lips. She wished she had stayed dead and not woken. Collapsing against the wall, she realized that the eclipse was just a horrible reminder.

"You're thinking dismal things. Keep it up and you may begin to look your age." Selene looked behind herself at the familiar voice.

"Hello Blake." She said turning so that her back leaned against the cold stone wall smoothed down by work and magic.

"Are you all right?"

"No. Eris asked me if I would repeat the past if Pietro were alive."

"I take it he didn't like the answer."

"Nope."

"That's unfortunate."

"And he walked off with Lilith."

"Lilith Siponi?"

"Yup.'

"Things just keep getting better and better." He leaned against the wall next to her. "Selene I want you to know that no matter what, I will always be on your side. I will always be here for you no matter what."

"I know."

"I'm just telling you in case things go—"

"Don't. If you think things go wrong than they will."

"Still superstitious?"

"Always." Selene placed her head on his shoulder while reaching for his hand for comfort. They stood there together, silent in the hallway until the clicking of heels caught them off guard. Pulling away from each other, they stared at Jeanette as she ran toward them, her long golden locks flowing behind her like a wave, a haggard expression on her face.

"I've been looking everywhere for you."

"Why? What happened? Is Jason—"

"Jason is fine. This doesn't concern him. Do you remember the Roamers?"

"Yes."

"Well one is dead and two are missing. I got a call from that Enforcer, James, after everything that happened I had a gut feeling and told him to keep an eye on them."

Resisting every urge in her body to punch the stone wall, Selene took a deep breath. "I'll go look for them. I want you and the others to keep an eye on Eris. This has his name written all over it." Both nodded in understand, letting Selene bite her lower lip with her fang. "Don't let him out of your sight." She ran off without another word. Had she waiting a moment she would have seen the shadows flicker where they shouldn't.

***

Eris sat on the edge of his bed, back bent forward, fingers laced forward with Lilith and Shira on either side of him. "She's leaving correct?"

"Yes," said Shira, picking at some dirt under her nails.

"The Hunters?"

"Ordered to stay and keep an eye on you."

"Good. Will she be gone until the eclipse?"

"I'm sure of it, I hid the bodies quite well."

"Good. Lilith, your friends?"

She nodded. "In place and ready."

"Good. Then in two days we attack." He stared at the fire burning brightly in the fireplace carved from stone. He knew Selene would hate him but it would be worth it to keep her safe from herself.

Forty Seven

Cecilia sat in the guest room, her temporary room, although lately, she was beginning to wonder just how temporary it was. She sat by the window, staring out into the stormy sky where rain pelted the glass, cascading down the glass, turning the outside world into a blur.

Despite the rain though, she could still see the moons high in the sky, one in front of the other, both turning red. She scratched her hip where her rune was, where it was glowing and itching. At school there would be a special ceremony for this occasion. A moment in time where magic was the strongest and Witches were most powerful. Laying her head on her knees she wished that she could step out of the house and feel safe.

A knock came at the door. Nicholas entered, offering her a warm smile.

"Dinner's ready." His voice was husky, low. Even now it made her heart race.

"Oh okay." She stood up, fully aware of how intently he was looking at her. Being alone together was starting to affect him.

"You all right?" he asked, standing next to her, hands hanging idly behind his side.

"Just tired."

"Maybe you should skip dinner and get some sleep."

"No, that wouldn't help. I should eat."

"If you're sure." He held the door open for her to pass and shut it behind her.

"Nicholas, do you have a bad feeling?"

"For a while now."

"Well yeah, but I mean, oh never mind, I'm probably just paranoid."

"Let's hope that's just it." Nicholas held her hand and pulled her along, lacing his fingers with her. Cecilia still had her bad feeling and it began to gnaw at her stomach.

***

Lilith watched them get settled for dinner. The Shadowling Evida stepped up to her side,

"We are ready," her tone empty, chilling.

"Good."

"Remember Lilith, Eris said not to kill."

"I know," she sighed. "Such a pity." Lilith flicker her fingers and sent a little flare up into the sky. Her comrades slunk from the shadows encircling the house. They had spelled the area around the house with dark magic, a skill they all excelled at. She heard them mutter the spell she had taught them, the spell she would soon be joining them in, as she silently made her way to the top of the house, to the center of the dark circle.

From her pocket she pulled out a smooth black stone. It was a rare stone, one that could only be purchased in the Darkling district or special orders through the Witch society. But why go through all that red tape, she was using it for dark magic anyway.

In the palm of her hand she crushed the stone while she focused on Selene's power, on her magic. The rain made it stick to her hand but with fire she burned it, sending a puff of smoke into the air where it circled around her, unnaturally.

"She of darkness, break this spell, sever the hold. Shatter the bind, split the protection. Let the darkness in, let it swarm and seep into the folds of light. Destroy the spell! Shatter her rule!" Her rune on the back of her neck was burning, throbbing against her skin, but it was worth it to help Eris break Selene.

She watched the thick cloud that enveloped her fall over the house. She could see it seep into the cracks, she the dark circle light up with an eerie green light. The air filled with shattering glass and screams.

Cecilia ducked under the table screaming. All around her glass shattered, filling the air with sharp shards. Peeking out she saw the place on the wall where the rune had been had exploded, leaving a hollow piece in the wall. Her bad feeling had been right. She felt Nicholas pull her close and lift her up from under the table. The Witchlings Zoë looked frightened with her irises dilated to see in the dark. Jason's father, Uriel grabbed a sword that hung on the wall. His wife huddled close to him. Soon a shadows appeared, forming into Vega and Void. Both held swords.

"Get down!" Cecilia fell to the ground, cutting herself on the glass. Looked at the others, she knew she wasn't the only one. A swarm of Shadowlings appeared and Cecilia caught sight of something she thought unimaginable. A Reborn fighting alongside two Shadowlings. The sounds of fighting made her flinch.

"We need to get out," said Nicholas in her ear, still holding her tightly. She nodded and looked at Uriel who was lifting up his wife. Zoë stood up quickly, reaching for her. In the time they had spent together, Cecilia had grown fond of her. Together they made their way through the darkness that had come, through the house that was falling down. Cecilia thought the house was going to collapse on her, and when she saw what was outside, she wished it had.

Before her stood almost a dozen Vampyres, none of which looked friendly. The blond at the forefront looked especially frightening.

"All this trouble for three little witches, a Reborn and a Witchling." Her eyes lit up. "This is so much fun." As if on cue the Vampyres charged. Cecilia cringed, thinking this the end but none other than Ettore, was at their aid. He snapped ones neck and fought off the others who quickly charged on him. Watching them fight Cecilia noticed a pattern. They were not trying to kill him, they were only trying to slow him down, keep him busy. But why?

Her thoughts were distracted by a running Zoë. She charged at the blond moving almost as fast as a Vampyre, catching the blond off guard. Cecilia ran to her aid, pulling away from Nicholas, knowing she couldn't handle the Vampyre on her own.

"Cecilia!" Cecilia spun around at the sound of her name. She caught sight of one Vampyre attacking Nicholas. She ran to his help, using a fire spell to get the Vampyre off. Clutching Nicholas and spelling a fire circle around them, she ripped off a piece of her shirt and placed it on his neck to stop the bleeding.

"Are you okay?" He didn't answer her, only stared ahead of her. Looking around she saw all the Shadowlings, her friends. That was where the attention was, not at the mortals. The realization dawned on her. She was about to shout out her answer when she saw what Nicholas was staring at. Zoë, screaming, a hand around her throat, fangs on her arm. The Vampyre met her gaze, her eyes a poisonous green. Cecilia watched her friend fall to the ground.

Zoë fell to the ground, convulsing. Her blood was hot, burning from within and her body felt cold. She knew she was dying, from inside out. Clutching her arms she stared up at the Vampyre who was licking her lips.

"Now look what you made me do. I was under orders not to harm you guys, just distract the Shadowlings." Her green eyes surveyed the area with a vast amount of glee. "It's going brilliantly if I do say so myself. It's a pity you're going to die. I'm like a snake you see, my fangs, my nails, even my blood, are all laced with poison."

Zoë wanted to scream in agony, but bit down on her tongue hard, tasting blood. She would not give this bitch the satisfaction.

"S-Selene will k-kill you."

"I doubt it. I was under Eris' orders."

"Sh-she will s-still k-kill you. A-and believe m-me, when sh-she's done w-with you, y-you will w-wish we-were already d-dead."

"And how would you know that?"

"Because, Lilith," she said happily sparking a bit of rage the green eyes, "y-you said s-so yours-self. You're a snake, j-just like h-him. And she d-did a-away w-with him d-delighf-fully."

Lilith's eyes flared, and Zoë could see something in her eyes break. "Just die already."

"Sh-she'll kill you, j-just like him." Zoë relished in the anger in the eyes as her heart began to slow. Shutting her eyes, she thought of Blake, muttering his name with her last breath.

***

Jeanette and Blake sat together in the library. Eris hadn't left the Coven once. Jeanette didn't know if that was a good thing or a bad thing. The door suddenly swung open and Eris strolled in, a serious yet charming smile on his face that made her skin crawl.

"I need the both of you to get to the Hunters Chambers. I have the rest of the Hunters gathered there already. There's something I need to talk to you people about quite urgently."

"About what?" asked Blake unmoving.

"Selene. Perfect timing since she's off investigating that Roamer situation."

Jeanette exchanged a worrisome glance with Blake. "We'll be there in a second."

"Why not come now? Come on, we'll walk together." Eris winked at her as he turned toward the door, holding it open for them. Jeanette didn't like this and continued to dislike it as a sickening feeling grew in the pit of her stomach. He looked like he used to, like the boy with no care in the world who thought the world revolved around him. And yet, there was something beneath the smile, something menacing, something threatening that she did not trust.

As they walked, Jeanette hoped that the matter of urgency was Jason. She hoped he wanted to confide in them, that way they could ease his troubles. Hoped that he wanted to repair what he was slowly chopping away at.

Jeanette spared a glance at Blake whose jaw was clenched tightly. He didn't trust Eris, but to be fair, he never really had. However, up until recently, even Blake would trust Eris when things concerned Selene. Those days were long gone. Jeanette could hardly blame him, their friend Eris seemed to be gone.

Jeanette and Blake continued to follow Eris down the curvy hallways. In the distance Jeanette could see the Hunters door approaching. The bad feeling she had earlier was growing in the ice cold hallway. When had the temperature dropped? Why had it dropped? These were questions she asked herself as she futility rubbed her arms for warmth. She was a Vampyre, undead.

"After you," said Eris opening the door. Jeanette walked in cautiously with Blake close at her heels. Eris shut the door, stepping in.

"What's so urgent?" asked Jeanette.

All familiarity vanished as he sneered at her. "Well first I would like to applaud you all in helping Selene keep Jason a secret. Bravo. Second, I just thought you should all know that I know where Jason is and I'm going to get him. You can all stay here." Eris turned to leave, but Jeanette and Blake lunged at him. Eris easily kicked Blake across the face, knocked him back against the wall and gripped his hand around Jeanette's throat. She thrashed about like a fish out of water only to find his fingers clench down tighter.

"All of you sit down or I will crush her throat. It may not kill her but the healing will be excruciating, I'll make sure of that. So sit down." Jeanette looked over at Blake. His eyes were blood red, fixated hatefully on Eris. He looked like a feral cat as he reluctantly sat down.

"The Shadowlings—," began Blake, quickly interrupted by Eris.

"Are all busy keeping Jason's home safe from a bunch of Vampyres and Shadowlings. They just attacked. Not to mention Selene is very far away from Nephilium. Believe me. Now, just sit tight,' he said slamming Jeanette into the floor, leaving the room in a flash, shutting the door tightly him. Jeanette lunged at the door, trying to open it despite its glowing edges.

"Jeanette, stop," muttered Damien. "We need to dispel the door first."

"We won't be able to," said Eno. "Eris has the Eclipsing rune and it's the night of the Eclipse."

"None of us are powerful enough to undo that spell or Selene's magic. There is no way for us to reach out to anyone. We'd need to dissect this one then the ones around the house, and by the time we're done, if we manage it, it'll be too late," said Blake, hanging his head in his hands. "There is only one other person we know just as talented and that's Lilith. If they attacked then that means the one and only person who could have possibly, maybe, saved us is on the other side."

"And it's the eclipse," repeated Eno. Jeanette flinched as Blake punched the table, swearing as loud as he could.

"We failed her," she mumbled slumped against the door. She could sense him on the other side of the door, could feel him there, listening. "She'll hate you."

"I know," came is voice.

Eris pulled away from the door and stared at it for a brief moment before walking away, his hands tucked into his denim pockets. Shira was waiting for him near the end of the curved hallway.

"She's almost near the Roamers. Should I wait for her?"

"Yes." Eris submerged himself in shadows, vanishing into Nephilium.

***

The rain was slowing Selene down. Weighing down on her head, soaking her hair and clothes. The ground was muddy, making it hard to keep her footing. The rain was messing with her sense of smell, heightening the smell of the earth around her. The mud swallowed up her foot, dragging her down, but she easily caught herself on her hands. Her runes itched and burned like they did every eclipse. Looking back at her foot, she yanked it out, hitting her knee on a rock, hidden by moss and mud. Groaning she stood up, allowing the rain to wash the mud off her as she continued on her way. Sniffing at the air, she caught a whiff of the Roamers scent and ran off. Her breath caught at the sight she discovered. Both Roamers lay next to one another, neatly placed, dead.

Selene made her way to the bodies, examining both. Their necks had been snapped, their hearts were gone.

"About damn time. Here I was beginning to think I may have hid the bodies a little too well." Selene spun around, facing a black eyed Shira. The Shadowling had her arms crossed and was leaning casually against a tree. The rain didn't seem to touch her.

"You did this."

"Yup. All me. But I was acting under orders."

"Whose?"

Her insidious grin widened. "I think you know."

"Why?"

"So that he could get Jason. Your brother finds you predictable. He knows Jason was in Nephilium and he's on his way to kill him."

"He wouldn't," said Selene trying to convince herself than contradict Shira.

"Oh but he would." She waved her hand and a dark portal appeared. Selene stared into the darkness. "If you're fast enough you just might be able to stop him." Selene stood there unmoving her breathing erratic. Shira's laugh echoed through the silent forest. "Tick tock Selene." Her laughter rang in Selene's ears as she ran through the portal...

Eris' boots squeaked against the tile floor. He was walking up the stair silently, leaving watery tracks behind...

Selene's feet pounded down the sidewalk. Her arms pumped at her sides and she willed herself to go faster and faster. Turning a corner she saw the apartment in sight. She ran faster through the rain, storming through the entrance.

"Please don't let me be to late," she muttered over and over again.

Eris walked down the hallway, tracing a finger across the wall and door approaching apartment 2306. He could feel the magic around the apartment, could smell it in the air. Eris never was great at magic but right now, he didn't need to be. Placing a silencing spell on the hallway, he studied the door, gently placing his hand on it before blowing it in, shattering all the spells Selene had up.

Eris stepped inside examining the plain apartment. The walls were plain with not a single decoration in the wall. It didn't look like anyone lived here, but he knew he was here, Eris could smell him. He smelled different than Pietro.

The living room was the only room really furnished with a

small coffee table and a ResoScreen. Eris leaning against the white wall and stared at him. He looked like Pietro except...

"You're Eris aren't you."

Nodding, Eris answered. "Yup. I think you know why I'm here."

"I'll fight you."

His statement made Eris laugh and grin. He knew his fangs were showing. "Go ahead."

Selene's feet pounded the floor beneath her. She slipped, and her body slammed against the cold and hard tile floor. Selene scolded herself as she tried to keep the tears at bay. Stumbling back onto her feet and ran, calling out her brothers name.

"Eris—!" her voice cracked when she saw the door in pieces. She tried to move, but her feet stayed pinned to the threshold. "J-Jason? Eris? Ettore!" The tears were spilling down her cheeks. She gripped the busted and bent doorway and pulled herself in, forcing herself to move. Every step she took felt like she was carrying weights on them. Her feet were heavy as they dragged her into the apartment. It was a disaster. The few tables and chairs were thrown apart, glass and drywall littered the ground, crunching beneath every step she took. The lights were all busted, humming and flickering above her head. Selene sniffed the air and smelled only Jason and...

She ran to the living room, where the ResoScreen was barely holding together, where the sofa and table were in pieces. Her breath caught and her knees finally caved in, slamming against the ground, when she saw the pool of blood on the floor, bits of it splattered over the wall and furniture.

Her body shook with rage and her body grew warm. She willed the power within her to stay hidden, if only for a moment.

"Shira," she said knowing full well that the girl was watching.

"Yes,' she said peeking her torso out from the shadows.

"Take me home." Selene stood, her fists clenched her head held high. The sparkle in Shira's eyes added to her anger. *How dare she play with me*, thought Selene making her way to her.

"Very well."

Selene approached the cave, her anger flaring more and more. She hated her brother, shoved away all the good memories, all the times they had played and laughed together; all the times they had sat together on the roof and by the lake. All the times he took care of her from when she was sick to when she was injured. That boy who used to be her brother was dead. The thing that had replaced him, it was a monster.

Selene passed the Hunters Chamber wishing she could break his magic. It was a sad fact that she could not she admitted making her way to the Grand Chamber. Using her magic she blew the doors open, as though they were on fragile hinges. He sat on his stupid macabre thrown with its ghastly ornate decorations' in expectation of her. Her heart raced as she made her way to him, clenching and unclenching her fists.

"I was beginning to—ugh!" Selene punched him in the face and then punched him in the gut. Stepping back she threw a kick at him, a kick he caught with his hand.

"Selene, let's not fight," he said using his other hand to wipe the blood from his lip.

"Burn brother." She used his weight against him, launching her other foot into the air, kicking him across the face. A surge of fire trailed it, causing him to scream and let her go. Twisting her body in the air, she landed on all fours, drawing out her long dagger. The cold stung her hand, sending needles of pain up her arm.

"Dammit Selene, what are you trying to do? Kill me?"

"Yes," she said then lunged. Eris stared at her angrily, sidestepping her attack in a crouch to sadly catch her and throw her against the ground. Ignoring the pain, she stabbed her dagger into his leg, tripping him while he tried to make his way from her. She pounced on him, yanking her dagger from him, holding it to his heart. The blade barely scrapped against his skin when he caught it, holding her at bay.

"Selene," he began through gritted teeth, holding her back, "anger is an unflattering look on you."

"I hate you!"

"It was for your own good."

"I loved him!" She felt the blade pierce his skin.

"And what of me! I'm your brother!"

"No, not anymore." Staring down at him, her anger subsided, replaced by grief. Staring down into his jade green eyes, she felt her own violet ones fill with grief. *Look after your brother...*

Selene jumped off him as the voice of her father echoed through her skull.

"Selene?"

"I hate you. I will live the rest of my life hating you." Sheathing her dagger she stared at him. "I will let you live, but I'm leaving. I'm leaving you and the Coven. But if you come after me I *will* kill you. If you send anyone after me, I *will* kill them. I'm letting you live because I promised dad I would look after you, but you are dead to me. If I see you again, I will kill you. Goodbye Eris," she finished wiping a tear away from her cheek. Running out of the cave, into the rain and night, she did not look back.

Epilogue

Selene was hungry, so hungry. Anger had fueled her as she ran, day after day, never fading. It had brought her close to Seraphim, so close. Just a few more miles, she told herself, keeping the anger close to her heart. Just a few more. Then, and only then, would be among friends.

She remembered making a journey similar to this. Anger had driven her then too, leading her to the treacherous Kyra and Larkin. This journey felt exactly the same.

The bright lights of city lit up the horizon, but she was so weak, so tired and dawn was coming dawn would come. She could do it, lay in the street as the sun rose, but she didn't want to die, didn't know what was keeping her alive. So she crawled up into the thick thicket of branches and leaves and hid there.

In the darkness her thoughts drifted toward Jason. He was gone, dead and gone. Her heart ached, more than betrayal than from loss. Try as she might she could not understand her brother. No, she reminded herself, he was no longer her brother. Nonetheless, it broke her heart to know that he would do this to her. In the darkness she drifted towards sleep where unpleasant dreams greeted her.

At nightfall she entered the city of Seraphim, the Felucian capital. The wind carried with it a familiar scent as she made her way down the empty street. Pulling out her dagger she made her way to it. The azure eyes almost glowed in the darkness.

"Nivette."

Her comrade cocked her head to her side, letting her hair fall over her shoulder. Ever so slightly, ever so sadly, her lip curled up on th on the side. "Hello Selene. Eris sent me to come and get you. He says it's time for you to return."

Selene's anger flared at the sound of his name. "Eris can burn. Leave Nivette."

"I'm not allowed to return empty handed. Forgive me."

"I won't go back."

"Then you leave me no choice."

"Don't, I don't want to kill you."

"Then come." Nivette held out a hand towards her, her eyes pleading. Still Selene shook her head.

"No."

Sighing, Nivette's outstretched hand fell limp. "So be it." Nivette ran towards her and Selene prepared herself.

So be it...

Acknowledgments

First and foremost I would like to thank my mother. There will not be a novel that i write that I will not extend my gratitude to because if it wasn't for her I wouldn't be the person that I am and this novel would not exits. Thank you mommy (yes, I still call her mommy) for reading Harry Potter to me and encouraging me to be a writer.

Next I would love to thank my amazing fiancée who, like my mother, continues to give me the encouragement that I need even when I doubt myself. Thank you for believing that I might follow in J. K. Rowling's footsteps even when I don't think I will. Seriously, that woman created a legacy and I can only hope to achieve that.

Love like the love they both offer me is what gives me strength and confidence.

And of course I want to thank all of you readers who made the first book possible as well as this one. I am thankful for every far that I hopefully created and each of you are amazing. I only hope that I keep you all hooked.

Finaly I would like to thank the people at Nook Press who worked so hard on the cover design of the novel. They executed my concept perfectly and captured the essence of my novel I think and without them, I don't know what I would have even been able to publish the book. So thank you all.

About the Author

Nia Dragin currently resides in Boston where she attends Emerson College as she continues to achieve her dream in becoming a well known author and starting her own publishing company. In the meantime she spends her days writing and reading and playing with her adorable narcissistic kittens whenever they take over her desk and notebooks.

EXPLORE THE WORLD OF

Nia Dragin

SEE WHERE IT ALL STARTED...

FOR EVERY SHADOW THERE IS LIGHT...

www.NiaDraginBooks.com

Lightning Source UK Ltd.
Milton Keynes UK
UKHW040624270519
343383UK00002B/575/P